ELIZABETH

THE NATIVE HEATH

ELIZABETH MARY FAIR was born in 1908 and brought up in Haigh, a small village in Lancashire, England. There her father was the land agent for Haigh Hall, then occupied by the Earl of Crawford and Balcorres, and there she and her sister were educated by a governess. After her father's death, in 1934, Miss Fair and her mother and sister removed to a small house with a large garden in the New Forest in Hampshire. From 1939 to 1944, she was an ambulance driver in the Civil Defence Corps, serving at Southampton, England; in 1944 she joined the British Red Cross and went overseas as a Welfare Officer, during which time she served in Belgium, India, and Ceylon.

Miss Fair's first novel, *Bramton Wick*, was published in 1952 and received with enthusiastic acclaim as 'perfect light reading with a dash of lemon in it ...' by *Time and Tide*. Between the years 1953 and 1960, five further novels followed: *Landscape in Sunlight, The Native Heath, Seaview House, A Winter Away*, and *The Mingham Air*. All are characterized by their English countryside settings and their shrewd and witty study of human nature.

Elizabeth Fair died in 1997.

By Elizabeth Fair

ELIZABETH FAIR

THE NATIVE HEATH

With an introduction
by Elizabeth Crawford

DEAN STREET PRESS

A Furrowed Middlebrow Book
FM16

Published by Dean Street Press 2017

First published in 1954 by Hutchinson

Cover by DSP
Cover illustration by Shirley Hughes

ISBN 978 1 911579 37 3

www.deanstreetpress.co.uk

INTRODUCTION

'DELICIOUS' WAS John Betjeman's verdict in the *Daily Telegraph* on *Bramton Wick* (1952), the first of Elizabeth Fair's six novels of 'polite provincial society', all of which are now republished as Furrowed Middlebrow books. In her witty *Daily Express* book column (17 April 1952), Nancy Spain characterised *Bramton Wick* as 'by Trollope out of Thirkell' and in *John O'London's Weekly* Stevie Smith was another who invoked the creator of the Chronicles of Barsetshire, praising the author's 'truly Trollopian air of benign maturity', while Compton Mackenzie pleased Elizabeth Fair greatly by describing it as 'humorous in the best tradition of English Humour, and by that I mean Jane Austen's humour'. The author herself was more prosaic, writing in her diary that *Bramton Wick* 'was pretty certain of a sale to lending libraries and devotees of light novels'. She was right; but who was this novelist who, over a brief publishing life, 1952-1960, enjoyed comparison with such eminent predecessors?

Elizabeth Mary Fair (1908-1997) was born at Haigh, a village on the outskirts of Wigan, Lancashire. Although the village as she described it was 'totally unpicturesque', Elizabeth was brought up in distinctly more pleasing surroundings. For the substantial stone-built house in which she was born and in which she lived for her first twenty-six years was 'Haighlands', set within the estate of Haigh Hall, one of the several seats of Scotland's premier earl, the Earl of Crawford and Balcarres. Haigh Hall dates from the 1830s/40s and it is likely that 'Haighlands' was built during that time specifically to house the Earl's estate manager, who, from the first years of the twentieth century until his rather premature death in 1934, was Elizabeth's father, Arthur Fair. The Fair family was generally prosperous; Arthur Fair's father had been a successful stockbroker and his mother was the daughter of Edward Rigby, a silk merchant who for a time in the 1850s had lived with his family in Swinton Park, an ancient house much augmented in the 19th century with towers and battlements, set in extensive parkland in the Yorkshire Dales. Portraits of Edward Rigby, his wife, and sister-in law were inherited by Elizabeth Fair, and, having graced her

Hampshire bungalow in the 1990s, were singled out for specific mention in her will, evidence of their importance to her. While hanging on the walls of 'Haighlands' they surely stimulated an interest in the stories of past generations that helped shape the future novelist's mental landscape.

On her mother's side, Elizabeth Fair was the grand-daughter of Thomas Ratcliffe Ellis, one of Wigan's leading citizens, a solicitor, and secretary from 1892 until 1921 to the Coalowners' Association. Wigan was a coal town, the Earl of Crawford owning numerous collieries in the area, and Ratcliffe Ellis, knighted in the 1911 Coronation Honours, played an important part nationally in dealing with the disputes between coal owners and miners that were such a feature of the early 20th century. Although the Ellises were politically Conservative, they were sufficiently liberal-minded as to encourage one daughter, Beth, in her desire to study at Lady Margaret Hall, Oxford. There she took first-class honours in English Literature and went on to write *First Impressions of Burmah* (1899), dedicated to her father and described by a modern authority as 'as one of the funniest travel books ever written'. She followed this with seven rollicking tales of 17th/18th-century derring-do. One, *Madam, Will You Walk?*, was staged by Gerald du Maurier at Wyndham's Theatre in 1911 and in 1923 a silent film was based on another. Although she died in childbirth when her niece and namesake was only five years old, her presence must surely have lingered not only on the 'Haighlands' bookshelves but in family stories told by her sister, Madge Fair. Another much-discussed Ellis connection was Madge's cousin, (Elizabeth) Lily Brayton, who was one of the early- 20th century's star actresses, playing the lead role in over 2000 performances of *Chu Chin Chow*, the musical comedy written by her husband that was such a hit of the London stage during the First World War. Young Elizabeth could hardly help but be interested in the achievements of such intriguing female relations.

Beth Ellis had, in the late-nineteenth century, been a boarding pupil at a school at New Southgate on the outskirts of London, but both Elizabeth Fair and her sister Helen (1910-1989) were educated by a governess at a time when, after the end of the First World War, it was far less usual than it had been previously to educate daughters at home. Although, in a later short biographical piece, Elizabeth mentioned that she 'had abandoned her ambition to become an architect', this may only have been a daydream as there is no evidence that she embarked on any post-schoolroom training. In her novels, however, she certainly demonstrates her interest in architecture, lovingly portraying the cottages, houses, villas, rectories, manors, and mansions that not only shelter her characters from the elements but do so much to delineate their status *vis à vis* each other. This was an interest of which Nancy Spain had perceptively remarked in her review of *Bramton Wick*, writing 'Miss Fair is refreshingly more interested in English landscape and architecture and its subsequent richening effect on English character than she is in social difference of rank, politics, and intellect'. In *The Mingham Air* (1960) we feel the author shudder with Mrs Hutton at the sight of Mingham Priory, enlarged and restored, 'All purple and yellow brick, and Victorian plate-glass windows, and a conservatory stuck at one side. A truly vulgar conservatory with a pinnacle.' Hester, her heroine, had recently been engaged to an architect and, before the engagement was broken, 'had lovingly submitted to his frequent corrections of her own remarks when they looked at buildings together'. One suspects that Elizabeth Fair was perhaps as a young woman not unfamiliar with being similarly patronised.

While in *The Mingham Air* Hester's ex-fiancé plays an off-stage role, in *Seaview House* (1955) another architect, Edward Wray, is very much to the fore. It is while he is planning 'a "select" little seaside place for the well-to-do' at Caweston on the bracing East Anglian coast that he encounters the inhabitants of 'Seaview House'. We soon feel quite at home in this draughty 'private hotel', its ambience so redolent of the 1950s, where the owners, two middle-aged sisters, Miss Edith Newby and widowed Mrs Rose Barlow, might be found on an off-season evening darning guest towels underneath the gaze of the late Canon Newby, whose portrait 'looked down at his daughters with a slight sneer'. By way of contrast, life in nearby 'Crow's Orchard', the home of Edward's godfather, Walter Heritage, whose butler and cook attend to his every needs and where even the hall was 'thickly curtained, softly lighted and deliciously warm', could not have been more comfortable.

Mr Heritage is one of Elizabeth Fair's specialities, the cosseted bachelor or widower, enjoying a life not dissimilar to that of her two unmarried Ellis uncles who, after the death of their parents, continued to live, tended by numerous servants, at 'The Hollies', the imposing Wigan family home. However, not all bachelors are as confirmed as Walter Heritage, for in *The Native Heath* (1954) another, Francis Heswald, proves himself, despite an inauspicious start, to be of definitely marriageable material. He has let Heswald Hall to the County Education Authority (in 1947 Haigh Hall had been bought by Wigan Corporation) and has moved from the ancestral home into what had been his bailiff's house. This was territory very familiar to the author and the geography of this novel, the only one set in the north of England, is clearly modelled on that in which the author grew up, with Goatstock, 'the native heath' to which the heroine has returned, being a village close to a manufacturing town that is 'a by- word for ugliness, dirt and progress'. In fact *Seaview House* and *The Native Heath* are the only Elizabeth Fair novels not set in southern England, the region in which she spent the greater part of her life. For after the death of Arthur Fair his widow and daughters moved to Hampshire, closer to Madge's sister, Dolly, living first in the village of Boldre and then in Brockenhurst. *Bramton Wick*, *Landscape in Sunlight* (1953), *A Winter Away* (1957), and *The Mingham Air* (1960) are all set in villages in indeterminate southern counties, the topographies of which hint variously at amalgams of Hampshire, Dorset, and Devon.

Elizabeth Fair's major break from village life came in 1939 when she joined what was to become the Civil Defence Service, drove ambulances in Southampton through the Blitz, and then in March 1945 went overseas with the Red Cross, working in Belgium, Ceylon, and India. An intermittently-kept diary reveals that by now she was a keen observer of character, describing in detail the background, as she perceived it, of a fellow Red Cross worker who had lived in 'such a narrow circle, the village, the fringes of the county, nice people but all of a pattern, all thinking on the same lines, reacting in the same way to given stimuli (the evacuees, the petty discomforts of war). So there she was, inexperienced but obstinate, self-confident but stupid, unadaptable, and yet nice. A nice girl, as perhaps I was six years ago, ignorant, arrogant and capable of condescension to inferiors. Such a lot to learn, and I hope she will learn it.' Clearly Elizabeth Fair felt that her war work had opened her own mind and broadened her horizons and it is hardly surprising that when this came to an end and she returned to village life in Hampshire she felt the need of greater stimulation. It was now that she embarked on novel writing and was successful in being added to the list of Innes Rose, one of London's leading literary agents, who placed *Bramton Wick* with Hutchinson & Co. However, as Elizabeth wrote in her diary around the time of publication, 'it still rankles a little that [the Hutchinson editor] bought *Bramton Wick* outright though I think it was worth it – to me – since I needed so badly to get started.'

However, although Hutchinson may have been careful with the money they paid the author, Elizabeth Fair's diary reveals that they were generous in the amount that was spent on *Bramton Wick*'s publicity, advertising liberally and commissioning the author's portrait from Angus McBean, one of the period's most successful photographers. Witty, elegant, and slightly quizzical, the resulting photograph appeared above a short biographical piece on the dust wrappers of her Hutchinson novels. The designs for these are all charming, that of *The Native Heath* being the work of a young Shirley Hughes, now the doyenne of children's book illustrators, with Hutchinson even going to the extra expense of decorating the front cloth boards of that novel and of *Landscape in Sunlight* with an evocative vignette. Elizabeth Fair did receive royalties on her second and third Hutchinson novels and then on the three she published with Macmillan, and was thrilled when an American publisher acquired the rights to *Landscape in Sunlight* after she had 'sent Innes Rose the masterful letter urging to try [the book] in America'. She considered the result 'the sort of fact one apprehends in a dream' and relished the new opportunities that now arose for visits to London, confiding in her diary that 'All these social interludes [are] extremely entertaining, since their talk mirrors a completely new life, new characters, new outlook. How terribly in a rut one gets.' There is something of an irony in the fact that by writing her novels of 'country life, lightly done, but delicately observed' (*The Times Literary Supplement*, 1 November 1957) Elizabeth Fair was for a time able to enjoy a glimpse of London literary life. But in 1960, after the publication of *The Mingham Air*, this interlude as an author came to an end. In her diary, which included sketches for scenes never used in the novel-in-hand, Elizabeth Fair had also, most intriguingly, noted ideas for future tales but, if it was ever written, no trace survives of a seventh novel. As it was, she continued to live a quiet Hampshire life for close on another forty years, doubtless still observing and being amused by the foibles of her neighbours.

Elizabeth Crawford

CHAPTER I

THE SUNLIGHT filtered through net curtains and filled the room with anaemic brightness. The furniture and pictures, which belonged to the flat and not to Julia, had looked better in mid-winter, on dark, rainy days when their shapes and colours were obscured and the room had been merely a warm and comfortable background. Sunshine, even the pale London sunshine of early spring, was too revealing; it showed Julia, at one glance, a number of objects she could hardly bear to live with. It showed them in all their horrid good taste and restrained opulence; there was nothing inharmonious or shabby or cheap, because it was a furnished flat in a modern block and a professional decorator had seen to it that good taste should prevail.

"Guaranteed not to offend," Julia said aloud. She admitted that the interior decorator had done his work well; it was the impersonality of the room—and of the flat—that annoyed her. It was a place designed to please *anyone*. It was not, and could never be, a home.

She stood on a chair and removed two pictures from the wall, leaving a blank space which was at least her own, and stacked them in the darkest corner. She dragged the round table into the window bay, and considered moving the sofa. Then she remembered that in another month she would be leaving the furnished flat for ever, and that a home of her own, a home which offered everything her present habitation lacked, was now receiving its final coats of paint in preparation for her coming. At least, she hoped it was. She left the sofa in its place and sat down at her desk—no, *the* desk—to write to Mr. Duffy, the local builder and decorator at Goatstock. He was a nice man, quite reliable and helpful, but it would do no harm to give him a prod.

If William had been alive, she thought, he would have gone to Goatstock and stood over Mr. Duffy and seen that he did the work properly. For a moment she felt lonely, helpless and neglected: a widow indeed. But these feelings, which might have intensified if she hadn't written 'Goatstock' on the blotting paper, dwindled away at the sight of it. She added 'Belmont House' above Goatstock, and above that her own name.

'Mrs. Dunstan
Belmont House
Goatstock.'

She looked at it, and as a finishing touch wrote *'nr. Reddrod'* at the bottom. The postal authorities insisted that Goatstock was near Reddrod, though in Julia's eyes the two places had nothing in common. Reddrod was an ugly industrial town. Goatstock was the village that contained Belmont House, and the church where the Heswalds were buried, and a number of charming, though as yet unknown, residents, who would provide her with a circle of friends.

A widow, at an age when birthdays are best forgotten, with no children to occupy her mind, can be very lonely. Julia Dunstan knew she was more fortunate than most widows, not merely because she was prosperous—as widows go—but because she had always taken an interest in other people. She believed in kind actions and good thoughts, and these, she found, helped to fill the gaps with which widowhood seemed to be associated.

Of course, the gaps were there; it was her own ability to fill them that saved her from isolation, loneliness, and discontent.

She disliked thinking of herself as a widow, because the word conjured up a picture of elderly, or at best middle-aged, resignation, of someone who had suffered a sad loss and perhaps come down in the world—widows somehow never went up—and wore drab clothes and talked about her grandchildren. Someone totally unlike herself.

The innocuous clock chimed four, in a subdued silvery tone which suggested a B.B.C. female announcer rather than Father Time. Julia frowned at it, and thought of Uncle James's massive grandfather clock in Belmont House, with a strike like doom, and scythe and hour-glass prominent among the emblems on its painted dial. Nevertheless, it was four o'clock; and Dora would be here in fifteen minutes. Her cousin Dora, whom she hadn't seen for so long, and who was now to step out of the past and become part of the future.

She crossed the narrow hall and opened the kitchen door. The kitchen was small, and so full of built-in cupboards and streamlined equipment that there was barely room for a human being. Her old nurse was sitting by the window on a high stool with a red leather seat, perched there sulkily between the sink and the enamel-topped table, darning Julia's stockings.

"Oh, Nanny, isn't this exciting?" Julia said.

"I don't know about exciting, Miss Julia. Seems to me *you've* no call to be excited, whatever that Miss Duckworth may think when she hears what you've got to say to her."

'That Miss Duckworth' was Dora. If Nanny had been word-perfect in her role she would have said 'Miss Dora'; but her willingness to be an old nurse was tempered by her fierce jealousy of anyone who might come between herself and Julia. It made things rather difficult.

"I'm simply longing to see her again," Julia said. "I expect she will have changed—she's had such a hard life—but I can't forget what friends we were when we were girls. At Belmont House, you know. We used to stay there for weeks at a time, with Uncle James. When I think of Belmont House I think of Dora as part of it."

"I can't put a face to her," Nanny said coldly. "But then I never really knew her. It isn't as if she stayed with you much in your own home, and you never had me with you when you went to General Heswald's."

"Of course I was nine or ten when he retired and they went to live there. I was able to manage without you—or they thought I was," Julia explained. Nanny's feelings were easily hurt; so there had to be an explanation of why she had not been there at Belmont House with Uncle James and Aunt Mary and Dora and the other sunlit figures of those happy days.

But this explanation conflicted with Nanny's memories, which were sometimes tactlessly different from Julia's. She laid the stocking down and gave her employer what she called 'a straight look'. This preliminary, and the little grunt that accompanied it, warned Julia that they were about to begin an argument; and although she did not doubt that she would triumph (Nanny was so old and her memory was not what it had been) she did not wish to be in the middle of an argument when Dora arrived. Arguments took time, and also a lot of tact and sympathy and loving remarks so that she and Nanny should finish up good friends. It wasn't—it simply could not be—the right moment for starting one.

"Listen! That's the gate of the lift," she said quickly. Nanny cocked her head; the flat was supposed to be sound-proof, but the kitchen wall was next to the lift-shaft and the architect had not worried about the effect of noise on the ears of cooks or daily obligers. To Julia's surprise she heard a faint, steady humming. "It isn't the gate," Nanny corrected her. "It's the lift coming up. Not that that means it's someone for us—we're not the only pebbles on *this* beach, Miss Julia."

Julia did not need to be reminded of it; though she likened herself to an ant in an ant-heap rather than a pebble on the beach. But the lift stopped at their floor, and the clock said four-fifteen. It must be Dora.

"I'll go to the door," Julia cried. "No—you go, Nanny dear. I'll be in the sitting-room." She had not quite made up her mind how to greet her cousin Dora—were they to kiss, or shake hands?—and she felt that the sudden opening of the front door, the face-to-face encounter on the threshold, wouldn't give her time to decide. She hurried back to the sitting-room as the doorbell rang.

Nanny was maddeningly slow. If she had been the garrulous and friendly old nurse of fiction one would have thought she was patting Dora's arm and pouring out sentimental greetings; but Julia knew she was doing nothing of the kind. Probably she was putting away the darning, tidying her hair, and deliberately keeping Dora waiting. In the midst of her impatience Julia found time to wish that Nanny would wear a cap and apron instead of a beige dress; but she couldn't *tell* her; and after all she could, and did, explain to everyone that Nanny was her old nurse.

The sitting-room door opened. Nanny said, "Miss Duckworth," in a disapproving voice. Julia, who was standing as far away from the door as possible, looked across the intervening space and saw, large and unmistakeable, the beloved Dora of the dear old days. That she was grey-haired, and much taller and plumper than one remembered her, was rather a shock; but Julia had been prepared for shocks. She knew Dora had had a hard life, and that hard lives were very ageing.

"Dora—at last!" she cried, hurrying forward. Dora hurried too, and they met, almost like two trains colliding, in the middle of the room. Since it was impossible, unless she stood on tiptoe, to fling her arms round Dora's neck and kiss her Julia decided on the loving handshake, using both hands and a variety of excited exclamations, to show her extreme delight in this reunion.

"So wonderful to see you again! . . . It's been such ages . . . so heavenly to hear you were in London! . . ."

"Yes, it's quite a while, isn't it?"

Dora stood like a rock while the waves of Julia's enthusiasm surged round her. But there was no doubt that she too was pleased and, in her own way, excited. Julia implored her to sit down, and sat down beside her. It was easier, once they were seated, to gaze at her face and assure her that she hadn't changed a bit.

"Rubbish," Dora said, smiling. "We all change—you've changed yourself. But not much," she added kindly. "I'd have known you anywhere."

"And I you," Julia insisted. In her heart she knew she was much more like her girlish self than Dora was like Dora's. But then her hair wasn't grey, and she had taken care of her complexion.

"And you know—you've heard my news?" she asked. She ought to have asked after Dora's health, and after the healths of other relatives; but the sight of Dora had so vividly recalled the past that she could think of nothing but Belmont House.

Dora hesitated, her smile faded; she looked kinder than ever, but embarrassed. "Of course," she said. "It—it must have been a great shock to you."

"Oh, it was. I'd never dreamt of it."

Dora looked at her rather oddly, and Julia wondered what was wrong. Then she realized that Dora—poor, hard-up Dora— might well be envious of her own good fortune. After all, they had both stayed at Belmont House, both been teased and petted by Uncle James; he was Dora's uncle as well as hers.

But he had left Belmont House to his niece Julia, not to his niece Dora.

"It came as a *complete* surprise," she went on quickly. "I simply could not believe it, when I first heard."

"Oh—were you away? How terrible for you."

Dora paused. "The shock, I mean," she added; for Julia did not look in the least bereaved and the way she spoke suggested that her husband's death was hardly a tragedy. Still, one must say something.

But this, apparently, was not the *right* thing. Julia looked bewildered—or perhaps it was grief. Dora, thinking she had mistaken fortitude for indifference, prepared to offer more sympathy. She said it must have made it even worse, happening in a foreign country.

"Oh—but you're speaking of my poor William?" Julia hurriedly assumed a suitable widowed expression. "It was hardly a foreign country to us, you know—we'd lived out there for years. William's business was there—at least, the head office. And there's quite a large British colony."

She was a little annoyed with Dora for making this mistake—after all, it was eighteen months since poor William's death, so naturally it was no longer the first thing one thought about—and for diverting the conversation from Belmont House. But in a moment she had mastered her annoyance; good thoughts came obediently to the surface and bad ones sank into dungeon depths. It wasn't Dora's fault that she was rather stupid and unobservant; and she obviously meant well. She was the same dear old Dora of the past, blundering but good-hearted, and in a way her silly mistake, which recalled other mistakes, simply made her more lovable.

Unobservant though she might be, Dora decided that no further reference need be made to William's death. No doubt the members of the large British colony had said all the right things at the time; and no doubt being a rich widow was less distressing than being a poor one.

"When did you come home?" she asked.

While Julia was telling her, Nanny appeared with the tea. She ought to have brought it as soon as Dora arrived, but considering her attitude to Dora the delay was understandable. Julia waited till Nanny had withdrawn before re-introducing the subject of Belmont House, because she did not want her joining in; it was regrettable that Nanny, though not yet word-perfect in her rôle, was quickly learning that old nurses are privileged to speak their minds in public.

"You see I've got Nanny back," she said casually, as the door slammed behind the retreating treasure. "My old nurse, you know. Poor old thing, she's rather past work, but I'd always kept up with her and when I came home she practically *insisted* on coming to look after me. It's rather touching."

"I don't remember her."

"No, of course you wouldn't—she never came to Belmont House. And isn't it odd, Dora, that you and I so seldom stayed with each other? It was only at Belmont House that we met. I used to look forward to it so tremendously—but then I was a very lonely child, at home."

At this stage of their reunion it did indeed seem odd; their girlhood friendship seemed to postulate a constant exchange of visits, an absolute dependence on each other's company. But it hadn't been odd at the time, Dora reflected; for surely they hadn't been such close, bosom friends as Julia seemed to think? The thought came and went. She looked at Julia, so pretty, elegant, and affectionate, and wondered if it was her own memory at fault.

"I somehow can't think of you as a widow," she remarked.

Julia brushed her widowhood aside. "Dora—you know about Belmont House? When Uncle James died, last year, he—he left it to me."

She watched her cousin anxiously; for, if Dora did not know, she might turn pale, gnash her teeth, or betray in less obvious ways the envy she must surely be feeling. But Dora laughed.

"Yes, of course I know. What a surprise for you." She spoke with complete tolerance; but then she had had time to get used to the idea.

"It was extraordinary," Julia said solemnly. "I hadn't seen him for years—only once since my marriage, when he was in London, just before Aunt Mary died. Before the war."

"Poor old boy, he must have been very lonely, living there by himself. I thought I ought to go to his funeral, but I couldn't get away."

"I was in Italy," Julia lamented. "I was dreadfully run down and the doctor said I must do a rest cure so I went for six weeks."

Dora wondered how she had managed about the currency.

"But if I'd *known*—!"

"You could hardly have got back in time for the funeral," Dora pointed out.

Julia said she could have flown. Dora said she couldn't have flown to Goatstock and the train journey north took more than four hours. Julia said she wished so dreadfully she had visited Goatstock once more in Uncle James's lifetime.

"If only I had gone when I first came back to England!"

"You would have been very uncomfortable. He lived like a hermit, and I suppose the house was in a terrible state, falling to bits. Did you manage to sell it?"

"Sell it!" Julia exclaimed. "But I am going to live there."

"Oh," said Dora. The furnished flat, which she thought of as luxurious, seemed exactly the right setting for Julia's elegance. She simply could not imagine her in Goatstock. "Do you mean you will settle down there for good?" she asked.

"Of course. It's obviously the right place. I've never had a real—a permanent—home. And then Goatstock is so close to Heswald, and you and I are Heswalds—"

"Well, I'm only a Heswald on my mother's side."

"It's the same thing," Julia said impatiently.

"The Heswalds of Heswald . . . I haven't thought about being a Heswald for years," Dora observed. "And we used to be so proud of it when we stayed at Goatstock. Do you remember that very fancy tomb in the church? I always envied Francis because it was in a way his property. I used to imagine he'd be buried there."

"He isn't dead yet," Julia pointed out.

"Well, of course not. He's not much older than us," said Dora, who rightly assumed that there were still a good many years ahead of her. "I never imagined him as *dead*—only as being buried in the tomb. Because he was the heir to Heswald and everything. The most important of our cousins."

"Yes." Julia thought of her cousin Francis, who had once been her devoted admirer but whom she had not seen for longer than she cared to remember. "Of course, he *is* important," she said firmly. "He's the head of the family."

"I hear he's turning into a recluse, like Uncle James."

Though the years had dimmed his memory, Julia disliked the idea of Francis turning into a recluse.

"Who told you?" she asked.

Dora had learned it from another cousin whom she'd met at a cocktail party, and she admitted that the story was mere hearsay, conveyed to the other cousin by an aunt who corresponded with someone who lived about thirty miles from Heswald.

"Probably it only means he isn't very sociable," she said.

Put like that, it sounded better; though Julia hoped Francis would not prove excessively unsociable, since she was looking forward to seeing him again.

"I'm longing for the day when I move in," she said. "Dear Goatstock! It's our native heath."

"It isn't exactly a heath," said the literal Dora. "It's just a little village."

But Julia was too enthralled to mind.

"I've always been happy there," she cried. "In the old days, with Uncle James and Aunt Mary, it was like heaven. I used to wish it was my home—"

"They were very fond of children. We must have been thoroughly spoiled—"

"And now it *will* be my home. I believe it's the hand of Fate!"

"You mean Uncle James dying just at the right moment?"

Julia looked wan. In a sense she did mean that, but Dora's words sounded harsh and unkind.

"I mean, that he should have been conscious of a bond, and left me the house," she said.

If it wasn't the hand of Fate it was certainly a remarkable coincidence, Dora thought. Julia had lived abroad for years, and during her brief visits to England she had never been back to Goatstock or shown much interest in her Heswald relatives. No one would have guessed that she was Fate's nominee for Belmont House.

It seemed quite natural, however, that she should wish to settle down; for in Dora's opinion she and Julia were at an age when future happiness began to present itself in terms of an adequate income, freedom from ill-health, and a roof over one's head. Lucky Julia, who need not worry about the roof or the income, and who looked astonishingly young and not at all as though she had spent years in the East.

"And, Dora, I've had the most wonderful idea," Julia said. "At least, I hope you'll think it's wonderful. I thought of it weeks ago, but I waited till Belmont House was ready, because—oh well, because it seemed more exciting that way!"

She leant forward and laid her hand on Dora's arm.

"I wondered if you would come and live with me. When I think of Belmont House I think of you—you're part of it, you see. And I don't like living alone—I think one isn't meant to. And Robert doesn't really count, and anyway he won't be there for long."

Dora was almost too surprised to speak.

"Who is Robert?" she asked, seizing on this unknown figure because he sounded solid and real.

Robert was William's nephew. He was an orphan, and William had paid for his education; and of course Julia had gone on paying for it after William's death. But he had recently qualified as an engineer and soon he would get a job. Probably he would go abroad.

"You and I were always such friends," Julia said. "And you would be such a help to me. I'm dreadfully stupid and helpless."

"Do you mean—share expenses and that sort of thing?" Dora said slowly.

Julia realized that her generous suggestion had been misunderstood, and she hastened to clarify it. She didn't expect Dora to go shares, no, of course not, she wanted her at Belmont House as—well, as a companion. She hated being alone. And perhaps to help a little in the house, if she didn't mind; all the little jobs like—like accounts, and perhaps shopping—and—She was really so helpless about housekeeping, because she had never had to do it in England.

"But mostly, to be *there*," she said. "Someone to talk to."

Dora was being offered a home, a roof over her head, a comfortable life. Julia didn't mention these advantages, but they were evident to her; and she hoped they would also be evident to Dora.

"As it happens, I'm out of a job at present," Dora said. "I've just heard of another, but . . ."

She looked at Julia. Julia's fond belief that blood was thicker than water, and that they had been bosom friends, was contagious. The talk of the past, too, had had its effect; Belmont House, seen across the years, made a pleasing contrast to the cheap residential hotel that was her present home. She would not be entirely dependent on Julia's bounty, for she had a small income of her own; not enough to live on, but enough if one wasn't paying for food and rent. And Julia—the present-day Julia—looked easy to live with.

"I don't see why we shouldn't try it," she said.

Julia had expected a warmer response—even a more grateful one. But the next instant Dora added that it was very good of her; and it was easy to imagine that she found it difficult to express her feelings. For someone who had had such a hard life the offer of a home and companionship must seem an almost unbelievable piece of good fortune. She could hardly, at first, take it in.

When Dora had gone Julia remembered that she hadn't asked for, or been told, any details of the hard life. How had Dora existed—by what exhausting efforts had she supported herself and, in earlier years, her widowed mother? Probably the poor dear was pining to talk about it, and to be given sympathy.

But there would be time for that, Julia thought happily, in the future.

CHAPTER II

"HAVE YOU HEARD?" asked Miss Pope. "Oh yes, my dear, it's quite *settled*. We're to be a New Town!"

"How dreadful," was Mrs. Prentice's first rejoinder; but it was said almost without thinking, in response rather to the tone of Miss Pope's voice than to the news itself. Mrs. Prentice had not had time to consider the implications of being a New Town; her mind worked slowly, taking things in rotation, and was at present fully occupied with thoughts of her daughter Marian's homecoming.

"We shall be swallowed up," said Miss Pope.

Mrs. Prentice looked at the vicarage, outside whose gates they were standing. She saw it engulfed, the solid stone walls and Gothic porch caving in as it disappeared into a huge crevasse, which slowly closed over its finialed gables. She had seen a house disappear like that in a film about San Francisco. But then she perceived that Miss Pope was speaking metaphorically.

"You mean, they'll pull down Goatstock to build a town?" she asked.

"No, no, but we shall be *in* it. Part of it. Streets, lamp posts, bricks and mortar. . . . Another bit of rural England gone."

"We could do with a few street lamps," said Mrs. Prentice, who was town-bred herself and had never got used to rural life.

Miss Pope looked disconcerted, but before she could answer an overall-clad figure appeared at the vicarage front door. "Oi, mum," called the figure, "telephone!" With a swift but clumsy gait Miss Pope cantered away up the drive to deal with the telephone. She was the vicar's sister. It was doubtful whether the Reverend Alaric Pope would have survived for long if he had not had a sister to deal with things.

Mrs. Prentice walked off towards her own house, one of the new ones on the main road at the other end of the village. The village was not picturesque, but in the sunshine of a fine May morning it had a gentler, brighter aspect than usual; the trees were newly in leaf and the sunlight mellowed the stone walls of the older buildings, which looked so bleak and grey in winter. Goatstock hill rose steeply to the east, but on the other side the ground levelled off, and there, across the canal, it was all open fields. Presently her view of the canal was blocked by Belmont House, a square, plain house standing by itself in a garden given up to trees and overgrown rhododendrons.

A low wall topped by iron railings separated Belmont House from the road, and peering in through the railings was Mrs. Minnis, who lived next door to Mrs. Prentice. This showed that Belmont House was still unoccupied.

Mrs. Prentice said good morning. She paused, and then added, "Marian is coming home today."

"Is it her week-end off?" asked Mrs. Minnis. "No, of course not, how silly of me, it's Monday today, isn't it? For a holiday then—how splendid for you! She gets good holidays, doesn't she? Now, poor Sonny—I mean Charlton—only gets a fortnight."

"Marian *needs* good holidays," said Mrs. Prentice. "Nursing is very hard work—and responsible. But this isn't a real holiday. Just a week's sick leave after influenza." She did not intend to disparage Charlton Minnis, who was Mrs. Minnis's only child; but no one could claim that his work was hard or responsible. Then, too, he came home every week-end, and Marian's free week-ends were rare occasions.

"I do envy Marian," Mrs. Minnis said gaily. "I always wanted to be a nurse myself, but my people would never hear of it! Thought it was *infra dig*, you know. Of course I was brought up very strictly. I sometimes think my old pater would turn in his grave if he could see what I've come to!"

Mrs. Minnis was in her early fifties, but when she spoke of her parents and her upbringing she always spoke as if they belonged to a very remote past—a past in which class distinctions were carefully preserved and domestic servants abounded.

"If he could see me doing the grates!" she went on.

'Or even just as you are now,' Mrs. Prentice thought; for Mrs. Minnis, a thin, flat-chested woman, favoured Dirndl skirts and embroidered muslin blouses, and had recently had her grey hair cut short and permanently-waved in shaggy little curls all over her head, which gave her the look of an elderly doll. Her cheeks were brightly rouged and her nails were lacquered dark red and this morning she was wearing, on top of the muslin blouse, a brick-red reefer jacket.

"Well, I must be getting on," Mrs. Prentice said aloud. But Mrs. Minnis clutched her by the arm and drew her towards the railings.

"Just look! They must have plenty of money."

Against her better judgement, Mrs. Prentice peered through the railings. Behind them was a privet hedge, but it was straggling and half-dead, and Mrs. Minnis had chosen a place where there was a big gap. Through the gap she had a clear view of the front of the house, in all its glory of fresh paint and clean stone walls.

"White paint!" Mrs. Minnis said. "That's an extravagance, isn't it? They must come from the south."

White paint for exterior work was not much used in Goatstock, because it got dirty so quickly.

"Mrs. Dunstan comes from London," said Mrs. Prentice. "I believe she used to stay here when she was a child."

Belmont House had formerly belonged to a retired major-general who had chosen Goatstock for his home because it was the cradle of his race. He had lived to be nearly ninety; but neither Mrs. Prentice nor Mrs. Minnis had known him well because after his wife's death he became a recluse, scorning the newer residents in the village and consorting only with the Daglishes, who had lived there for years and shared his antipathy for the modern world. In the last years of his life Belmont House had been sadly neglected, its walls smothered in ivy and its doors and window-frames rotting under peeling paint. But since his death Mr. Duffy the builder had been at work with his entire labour force; and last week two furniture vans had arrived. The house appeared to be ready for occupation.

"I hear they're moving in this week," Mrs. Prentice said.

"Tomorrow, I believe. She's a widow, you know."

"I know," said Mrs. Prentice, who often said she was no gossip but who usually contrived to know as much as her neighbours. "She is sharing the house with another woman, a relative, I believe. And there's a nephew as well."

"Really? How old is he?"

Mrs. Prentice had not discovered his exact age, but she had heard he was an engineer, which meant, of course, that he must be grown up.

"I hope he's nice," Mrs. Minnis said. "There are so few young men round here—I often think it must be dreadfully dull for Marian, now that your other two are married. When I was her age I had no end of a gay time! And of course for Harriet Finch too, though that doesn't matter so much. After all, it's up to her aunt. But I often think Marian must get awfully bored, with no one but Sonny to take her out. I mean Charlton."

By the rules of the game Mrs. Prentice ought to have protested that there was nothing Marian enjoyed more than going out with Charlton Minnis. Mrs. Prentice, however, was annoyed by the insinuation that her daughter found home dull, and annoyed too by the way in which Mrs. Minnis spoke, as if she was a close personal friend instead of a mere next-door neighbour.

"You forget," she said coldly. "Marian is engaged to be married."

Mrs. Minnis took no notice of the rebuff. She was—as she often proclaimed—a woman who could be friends with everybody, and it did not worry her that her friendships were sometimes one-sided affairs.

"Of course I haven't forgotten," she said cheerfully. "But then he's *abroad*. Being engaged isn't the same thing, is it, when the man's abroad? When I was engaged to Hugo he used to take me out all the time."

To this Mrs. Prentice made no answer. She was still indignant, but in spite of it she could not help feeling there was some truth in Mrs. Minnis's words. Moreover, she did not altogether approve of Marian's engagement, though she would never have admitted this to an outsider.

"I see they've got the curtains up," she said, to change the subject. They both turned back for another look through the railings, and Mrs. Minnis pointed out that the curtains were hung only in the ground-floor windows. The upstairs did not matter so much, said Mrs. Prentice; on the ground floor people could stare straight in at you, if you sat in an uncurtained room with the light on. Mrs. Minnis argued that the upstairs rooms were bedrooms, and that it was even more important to have curtains if you were dressing or undressing.

"Oh, but they're quite big rooms," said Mrs. Prentice. "One could keep well away from the windows."

Mrs. Minnis stuck to her point. It wasn't that one could be seen, it was just the feeling that one *might* be seen. Of course she was probably being ridiculous, but then she had been brought up in the country, in a house where there wasn't a road within miles, and now that she lived right on the road she always had that feeling. Hugo and Sonny thought she was absurdly sensitive, but she couldn't help it.

"Your house isn't as close to the road as this one," said Mrs. Prentice. "Or at least, you've got a good thick hedge in front. This place is dreadfully exposed."

"Yes, isn't it? I can look right into the dining-room. *And* the lounge. What's that tall thing at the back of the room—is it a grandfather clock? It's very broad for a clock, but surely it isn't a cupboard."

"Where? I can't see it."

They moved closer together, and Mrs. Minnis put her arm through the railings, pointing her finger to show Mrs. Prentice where to look. "There," she said. "No, more to the right. There!"

Suddenly something prompted Mrs. Prentice to glance up at the bedroom windows. She saw with horror that they were no longer, as they had been a minute ago, a row of empty frames. One of the frames now held two ladies, who stood side by side gazing out.

Not only gazing out, but gazing down, as though they were as interested in Mrs. Minnis's pointing finger, or in what it pointed to, as she herself had been. Oh, worst horror of all, surely the taller one was laughing!

"Sst, sst!" she cried softly, glowing with embarrassment. Mrs. Minnis looked up, exclaimed shrilly, and jerked her arm back. In her haste she somehow managed to ruckle up the wide cuff of her coat sleeve, and this became wedged between the narrow bars. There she stood, her arm held in the railings as if they had been a pillory; the word pillory at once flashed into

Mrs. Prentice's mind because it was a place where one was exposed to public ridicule.

"Help me, help me!" Mrs. Minnis begged, tugging at her sleeve in a way that did no good at all. Mrs. Prentice's first, cowardly impulse was to abandon Mrs. Minnis to her shame and to make her own retreat as quickly as possible; perhaps, if she kept her head down, the owners of Belmont House would not recognize her when they saw her again. But her better self rejected this plan, which in any case would not have been successful because Mrs. Minnis would have spread the story everywhere, and she went to her neighbour's assistance. It was easy enough, once Mrs. Minnis extended her arm, to smooth out the rumpled cuff and set her free, but it took a little time.

During this time neither of them dared to cast a glance at Belmont House, and as soon as Mrs. Minnis was free they hurried off along the road, Mrs. Prentice keeping her head down and Mrs. Minnis staring across the road, with rapt interest, at Goatstock Hill. After twenty yards they reached the big clump of rhododendrons at the corner, and knew that no watcher at the upper windows could now observe them. They stopped, and exchanged cautious looks. Each would have liked to accuse the other of leading her astray; but each was conscious that she needed, above all, reassurance and sympathy, and that she could only obtain it, in this crisis, from her fellow culprit.

"How aw'fly embarrassing!" said Mrs. Minnis, taking refuge in a childish voice and a giggle. This way of escape was not open to Mrs. Prentice, who was statuesque and unadaptable and who had long ago given up thinking of herself as a frolicsome schoolgirl. She had to face the fact that she had committed a social blunder.

"I've no idea they were there," she said.

"I'm sure no one saw them arrive. They must have come late last night."

"Of course I wouldn't have *dreamed* of stopping if I'd known they were in the house."

"Of course not," Mrs. Minnis echoed virtuously. "I thought the house was empty. It looked empty, didn't it?" she added, as if she had been led astray by a piece of trickery on the part of Belmont House. "All the windows shut, and no smoke from the chimneys. They really ought to have a fire going, it must be awfully damp."

"But what shall we *do*?" Mrs. Prentice interrupted. "It will be so awkward meeting them—I'd meant to call, as soon as they were settled, but I'm sure they would remember me. And yet if I don't call I'm bound to meet them somewhere, and that will be just as bad."

Mrs. Minnis had a happy thought. "Perhaps it wasn't them after all. Perhaps it was the maids!"

For a moment a ray of hope gleamed, but then Mrs. Prentice shook her head. Two resident maids seemed unlikely, and if the watchers at the window had been local 'dailies' she would have recognized them. Besides, it was even more unlikely that a new arrival would have succeeded in getting daily help straightaway.

"Let alone *two*," said Mrs. Minnis, impressed by this reasoning—and rather thankful, now that she had had time to think about it, that her struggles with the railing had not been witnessed by Mrs. Glint or Leah Townley, who would have carried the tale to all the people they worked for. Looking on the bright side, it was really a good thing that the witnesses had been strangers to the district.

Looking on the bright side was a habit with Mrs. Minnis, who resolutely believed in making the best of things. If she had been shipwrecked on a coral reef in the tropics she would have rejoiced that she was not on an iceberg in the polar seas; and so, as they walked away from Belmont House, she soon began to congratulate herself—and Mrs. Prentice—on the comparative mildness of their ordeal.

"Why, we might have been in the garden!" she said. "I went in last week, just to have a look round. Now that *would* have been awkward—if they'd come into one of the downstairs rooms and found us peeping through the windows. It was lucky we were outside in the road, wasn't it?"

"Yes," Mrs. Prentice said faintly, thinking what a dreadful woman Mrs. Minnis was. Peeping through the windows, indeed! Well might her old father turn in his grave, if he could hear his carefully brought-up child uttering such remarks.

But she did not rebuke Mrs. Minnis, for in her slow way she had already perceived that she and Mrs. Minnis could not afford to differ. They were partners in crime, or, if not in crime, in a dreadful *faux pas*, and they must stick together. If she were to annoy Mrs. Minnis the silly creature would be quite capable of telling the whole story, just to get her own back.

"I think we had better keep this to ourselves," she said, when they had reached the gate of Mrs. Minnis's house. Mrs. Minnis replied that she wouldn't dream of mentioning it to a soul, not even to Hugo or Sonny.

"Perhaps, after all, they won't recognize us," said Mrs. Prentice, indulging in wishful thinking. Her private hope was that they might not recognize *her*; it hardly seemed possible that anyone could fail to recognize Mrs. Minnis, whose Dirndl skirts and windswept curls made her a local landmark.

"I don't suppose they saw us for more than a second, really."

"So if we just say no more about it . . ."

"Rather!" said Mrs. Minnis, reverting to her schoolgirl self. "After all, one doesn't want to own up to a thing like that, does one?"

"No, indeed."

They parted with smiles. Mrs. Minnis pushed open her front gate, which had the name of the house—*Kandahar*—painted on it in large green letters, and disappeared down the asphalt path that led to the back door. Mrs. Prentice walked on to the next gate, a solid oak one with wrought-iron hinges. The difference between the two gates was not unlike the difference between Mrs. Prentice and Mrs. Minnis; Mrs. Prentice did not feel superior to her neighbour, but she felt solider, more firmly rooted and less showy. A name inscribed in green paint was not at all to her taste; the name of her own house was embossed in small gothic letters on a bronze plate.

The Prentices' house was the last of six or seven which stood on the main road, at right angles to the road that led to the centre of the village. These houses had been built after the first world war, and unlike the older part of the village they were built of shiny red brick. They all had a profusion of gables and bay windows, and their gardens were full of flowering shrubs, and surrounded by *thuya* and privet hedges, to give seclusion. Between Mr. Prentice's house and its immediate neighbour *Kandahar* there was also a brick wall, seven feet high. The previous owners had called the house Balbus Villa, perhaps in allusion to the wall, but the Prentices had changed it to Balbus Cottage. Though a villa might be right and proper for Balbus they both thought it sounded too suburban for Goatstock.

Mrs. Prentice had a persistent fear of burglars, and before leaving home she had shut the ground-floor windows and locked the door. As she walked up the path, searching in her bag for her latchkey, a voice hailed her; she looked up, and saw her daughter Marian sitting on a suitcase in the porch, with an expression on her face that suggested she might have been there for some time.

"At last!" Marian exclaimed. Her voice was reproachful, but an affectionate kiss showed that she was not really angry, only a little impatient. Mrs. Prentice broke into flustered explanations; she had no idea it was so late, she hadn't expected that Marian would catch the early bus—and surely it must have arrived before its time? But Marian answered that she had been there at least twenty minutes, and asked, half-jokingly, what her mother had been doing all the morning.

"Gossiping in the village shop, I suppose, and forgetting all about me."

"Oh, dear, no—well, not exactly," Mrs. Prentice replied. She could not tell Marian what she had been doing, but she was incapable of extemporizing. "I met Miss Pope." She paused, trying to remember what she and Miss Pope had talked about, and after a moment it came back to her. "She says we're going to be a New Town."

It was fortunate that Miss Pope had told her this news, for Marian was so interested in it that she made no further enquiries as to how her mother had spent the morning.

"What—here in Goatstock?" she said. "Of course there have been rumours about it for ages, but I didn't know it was settled. Is it definite?"

"So Miss Pope says. She's very much against it. She says Goatstock will be swallowed up."

By this time they were in the kitchen, and Marian had begun to peel potatoes for lunch. "I know one person who'll be pleased," she said. "And that's Harriet."

Mrs. Prentice thought that this hardly mattered, and that Miss Pope was a far better judge of the general good than Harriet Finch. But she did not say so, because Harriet was Marian's friend and it did not do to criticize one's daughter's friends.

"Harriet has always wanted to live in a town, but of course she can't because Lady Finch won't budge. It will be like the mountain coming to Mahomet."

Mrs. Prentice laughed. She did not quite understand what Marian meant (for surely it was Mahomet who went to the mountain?), but she was glad to see her daughter so gay and cheerful. Marian was looking extremely well, in spite of her hard life and the dreadful hospital food in the Nurses' Home.

"Of course it won't matter to me," Marian went on. "I shall be married long before the New Town gets itself built. It won't be built for years. You'll have to take lots of photographs and send them out to me."

She spoke casually, and her voice was as cheerful as ever. But Mrs. Prentice found it hard to make a casual, cheerful reply.

She had nothing against missionaries, and no doubt Hubert was an excellent one. She had nothing against Africa. But why couldn't Marian be like other girls? Other girls did not get engaged to missionaries; other girls did not propose to spend their married lives nursing the heathen under the burning African sun.

No, not the heathen. They would be Hubert's converts. But it was the same thing.

"My photographs never seem to come out," she said.

CHAPTER III

THE PEOPLE who lived in Goatstock spoke of it as rural, but it was only a few miles from a manufacturing town. If it had not been for the steep and rugged hill to the east Goatstock might already have been engulfed by Reddrod, which lay beyond that hill and which was a by-word for ugliness, dirt and progress. The hill kept the Reddrod suburbs at bay, and its long ridge made a dividing line between the smoky, industrial part of the county and the fertile agricultural plain to the west. Protected by this geological rampart, Goatstock had remained a village.

It was a long, narrow village, bounded by the hill on one side and the canal on the other. To the south was the main road, with an efficient hourly bus service to Reddrod, or, in the other direction, to a small country town which people never visited unless they wanted to buy the gingerbread cake which was its sole claim to fame. The newer houses in Goatstock were all built on or near this main road, and the other end of the village remained much what it had been fifty years ago.

Here, in what might be called the slums, lived Lady Finch and her niece Harriet. No one knew for certain whether Lady Finch was very hard-up or very mean, but they lived in a plain little stone house whose windows needed painting and whose roof sagged alarmingly in the middle. It was called Urn Cottage; it was old, and had always borne this name, and neither Lady Finch nor Harriet minded, but Mrs. Prentice thought it was rather a peculiar name and one with morbid associations. She had once suggested to Harriet that the name was probably a corruption of heron, and that Heron Cottage would sound much nicer; but Harriet had replied, with a sort of mad logic, that her aunt simply doted on the goldfish.

The house stood a little above the road, and was approached by a short flight of steps and a stoneflagged path. There was quite a big garden behind it, but in front there was only a small plot of grass, at the top of the steps, and in the centre of this plot an extremely unornamental square pool where Lady Finch kept her goldfish. Lady Finch was the widow of a baronet, and this gave her a certain prestige in a neighbourhood where titles were rare, but her numerous interests, of which goldfish-culture was probably the least unusual, made people say she was eccentric.

One was never quite sure of one's welcome at Urn Cottage, and if Marian went uninvited she always approached it with caution. Of course Harriet would be glad to see her, but it was as well to make sure that Harriet was at home. This evening she stood for a minute at the top of the steps, wondering whether to ring the bell or yodel outside Harriet's bedroom window. But just then Harriet came round the corner of the house, carrying a watering-can, and shouted a greeting.

"Good," said Harriet. "Good to see you again. And we've had such a tiresome day. I need a respite."

Marian laughed. Harriet looked as if she had had a tiresome day; her fair, silky hair was tumbling over her eyes and her hands were streaked with mud.

"You're awfully unkempt," she said.

"Why didn't you come sooner?" Harriet demanded, putting down the watering-can and splashing the water over her shoes as she did so. Marian replied that she had only got home yesterday.

"That's an age. I suppose parental claims come first. But I wouldn't know about that, being an orphan."

Harriet had a strong sense of drama, and as she spoke she instinctively assumed the face and bearing of an orphan—a pathetic, neglected orphan, alone in the world. It was easy for her, for she was small and thin and could look meek enough when she chose. But Marian rather disapproved of this play-acting, and she pretended not to notice.

"I came as soon as I could," she said. It was not quite true, but Harriet accepted it.

"There's masses of news," she said cheerfully, abandoning her orphanhood. "Just a minute while I water the goldfish and then we'll go in and talk."

She poured the water into the pond. Marian thought the goldfish were very dull creatures, neither pets nor useful. She had often said so before, but that did not stop her from repeating it. Harriet protested that they were very intelligent.

"In their own way," she added. "I mean, they are intelligent fish, not intelligent human beings." She looked across at Marian and laughed. "You think they should be a dog, don't you?"

"A dog?"

"An adoring dog. That's what people who live in the country ought to keep. And useful hens, and perhaps a sleek tabby cat."

Instead of which the Finches had goldfish, and bees, and a tortoise. The bees belonged to Lady Finch, the tortoise was Harriet's, and they shared the goldfish between them.

"Perhaps I will have a dog, one day," Harriet went on. "A large dog with a long pedigree, to give me moral support. An elkhound, or perhaps a Great Dane."

Marian was just going to say that these would cost too much to feed, when she saw that Harriet was joking. It was tiresome that she always made fun of conventional country customs, such as keeping a dog or going for nice walks.

She sometimes thought Harriet had a faint touch of Lady Finch's eccentricity, but one couldn't say it ran in the family, for they were not related by blood. Harriet was the daughter of Sir Michael Finch's brother; her parents had died young and Lady Finch had brought her up. Perhaps it was being brought up by Lady Finch that had made Harriet what she was.

At this point she remembered her manners and asked after Lady Finch's health.

"Oh, she's fine," Harriet answered, leading the way into the house. "At least, she is now. This morning she had the toothache. That is why it has been such a tiresome day."

"Poor Lady Finch," Marian said firmly.

"Poor thing indeed. But you know what Aunt Finch is like with the toothache. A raging lion. And treating it with herbs, when anyone else would have gone to the dentist."

As a student nurse with a scientific outlook Marian could not approve of Lady Finch's faith in herbs and nature cures. She shook her head.

"But it worked," Harriet said. "I am at a loss to account for it, but it worked. The toothache went. And now she's doing something to the bees, so we can have a good gossip."

The interior of Urn Cottage was as shabby as the outside, but it was a moderately comfortable house. The sitting-room had bookshelves all along one wall, and the other walls were hung with drawings of plants, done in pen-and-ink with botanical accuracy, the work of Lady Finch herself. There was a thick but very ugly carpet, a sofa which appeared to have strayed out of a Regency drawing-room and to have suffered considerably in the move, and a couple of leather-covered armchairs built on such a generous scale that one had to squeeze past them to reach the farther end of the room.

Harriet and Marian sat together on the sofa, and Harriet lit a cigarette. "Why don't you smoke?" she asked. "Hubert isn't here."

Marian had given it up when she became engaged, because Hubert did not smoke and rather disliked seeing a woman smoking. He could tolerate it in a man, and he wasn't in the least narrow-minded; it was just that he didn't like to see it. She had explained this to Harriet, and now she explained it all over again.

"But he *can't* see you. He's in Africa."

In some ways Harriet was very dense.

"I love Hubert," Marian said earnestly. "If you love a person, you want to do what he wants."

"Yes, but it ought to work both ways. If Hubert loves you, he ought to want to do what *you* want. Or at least not to stop you doing what you want."

"You don't understand."

"Of course," Harriet said, pursuing her theme, "it might become ridiculous. Two people, madly in love, each wanting to do what the other wants. Suppose one of them wanted swing music, cocktail parties, and late nights, and the other wanted Beethoven quartets and a cloistered existence. Then true love would simply make each of them change—to please the other— and they'd be no better off."

"I don't see—"

"The Beethoven fan would become a swing fan, and *vice versa*. You gave up smoking to please Hubert, and for all we know he may be puffing away like a chimney in Africa, to please you."

"Of course he isn't," Marian said indignantly. "Hubert wouldn't be so silly."

Marian was a pretty girl, but her normal expression was placid. Some people would have called her phlegmatic, and though Harriet was not one of them she could not help reflecting that it suited Marian to be flushed and indignant. She hoped Hubert would sometimes contrive to upset his beloved; though it did not seem likely. She had only met Hubert once, when he came to stay with the Prentices before leaving for the mission field, and he had seemed to her a dull but very amiable young man. Serious, calm, good-natured, like Marian herself, and a clergyman into the bargain.

It was a pity, Harriet thought. Marian was too solemn already, and she needed someone to stir her up. She couldn't be really in love with Hubert. Love, to Harriet's dramatic mind, was fire and fury, a heightening of all the emotions, a condition in which one suffered jealous agony as well as ecstatic happiness. Marian was marrying Hubert for no particular reason, or for some humdrum reason which wasn't the right one, and in so doing she was ruining her life. She would vegetate in the wilds of Africa, getting duller and duller, and producing children with a double inheritance of dullness. She would turn the heathen—and herself—into models of dreary mediocrity.

"No, no!" Harriet cried aloud, revolted by this picture. Though she made fun of Marian she was very fond of her.

"What's the matter?" Marian asked. "And do pull your skirt down, Harriet. Suppose anyone looked in through the window."

"No one will."

But at that moment someone did. It was only Lady Finch, but it gave Marian a shock all the same. A sudden glimpse of a beekeeper, veiled and armoured for the fray, might give anyone a shock.

"Bother," said Harriet. "Aunt Finch must have been routed. She always comes to the front door when she's routed—the bees call the chase off when they get to the corner of the house."

She pulled down her skirt. Marian patted her hair and prepared to stand up. After a short pause Lady Finch came into the room, and by way of greeting announced rather crossly that the bees had got inside her veil and stung her twice on the chin.

She was a tall woman, with a haggard weather-beaten face, a dominating nose, and a mass of densely black hair. Even without her Wellington boots, elbow-length gauntlets and long green veil, she looked rather odd and not a little alarming. In spite of a long acquaintance Marian never felt quite at ease with Harriet's aunt; though Lady Finch was usually kind to her and had once told Harriet who gleefully passed it on—that Marian's basic instincts were remarkably pure.

At the moment Lady Finch was not interested in Marian; she was telling Harriet about the goats. It was the proximity of the goats that had put the bees in a bad temper, for it was well known that they couldn't bear goats. She had warned the farmer what would happen, if he allowed his goats to graze in that field.

"Poor goats," Harriet said.

"I meant to finish the spring-cleaning today, but I'd only done three hives and then I had to stop. Now I shall swell," Lady Finch said fussily, peering at her chin in the looking-glass that hung over the fireplace.

"It doesn't show much."

"It will be worse tomorrow. I shall look a perfect fright."

"You can stay indoors," Harriet suggested. "No visitors allowed, in case they should have nervous breakdowns. It would be a first-class excuse for getting rid of Miss Pope."

"I can't possibly stay indoors. It would interfere with my programme."

Marian and Harriet exchanged a quick glance. Lady Finch was a woman of many interests, and her days were divided like a school timetable, the hours named and numbered in advance. There were social duties—she did not enjoy these, but believed they were necessary—and domestic duties; there were also bee-keeping and scientific gardening and Yoga exercises and Planned Reading. But her chief interest at present was in the book she was writing and the research it entailed. This took so much of her time that the rest of the programme was often disorganized, and in consequence, every now and again, there would be a period of hyper-activity which she described as 'catching up with things'.

Such a period was now overdue, and Harriet's glance expressed apprehension; for when she was catching up with things Lady Finch, like a galloping horse, was difficult to check. The danger, however, was not immediate. Lady Finch had her plans for tomorrow, but they were plans which had been made at the beginning of the week, and the timetable still held good.

"It's my day for collecting," she went on. "And I've got to go and call on Mrs. Dunstan at Belmont House. Only afternoon I can fit it in."

Marian wanted to say that it was too soon to call; for she had been brought up to know the rules and was aware that one must give people time to settle down. But one did not say such things to Lady Finch, who had her own rules.

"Mother was wondering about them," she said instead. "She wondered whether—"

"Whether they're respectable? Of course they are. They're the old man's nieces."

"Not both of them. It was Mrs. Dunstan that got left the house."

"Yes, yes, Harriet, I know that. I suppose she was his favourite, but Dora Duckworth's a niece as well. They're first cousins, and of course they are also first cousins of Francis Heswald up at Heswald. General Heswald was a younger brother of Francis Heswald's father."

Neither Marian nor Harriet could see that this made Francis Heswald, Mrs. Dunstan, and Dora Duckworth into first cousins, but they were quite prepared to take Lady Finch's word for it.

"Dora Duckworth," murmured Harriet. "I imagine her as small and fat, waddling a bit when she walks. Something like Jemima Puddleduck."

"And there's a nephew as well," said Lady Finch. "But I don't suppose he will be living at Belmont House—he's probably just staying there to help them with the moving in. Pity. He might have done for Harriet."

"Is he a Duckworth?" Harriet asked. "I don't think I could marry a Duckworth. Not if he was small and fat, and waddled."

In Marian's home the acquisition of a husband was not a subject that was openly discussed, at least between parents and children, and she was often disconcerted by Lady Finch's candour. But no one could accuse Harriet of over-eagerness to acquire a mate; on the contrary, she was almost too ready to find fault with the candidates her aunt suggested.

"He's a Dunstan," said Lady Finch. "No relation to the Heswalds of course."

"He's an engineer," said Marian, unable to resist adding her mite of knowledge.

"A very respectable profession," Harriet said approvingly. "Almost as good as being a missionary."

Marian gave her a reproachful look. If they had been alone she would have spoken in defence of missionaries, but she was not going to say anything in front of Lady Finch, who had a whole chain of theories about the natural goodness of the untutored savage and the necessity for leaving him to go his own way uncontaminated by western civilization. It was, of course, all rot; but to argue with her was simply a waste of time. She had tried it once, and had found herself up against Jean-Jacques Rousseau and a host of other authorities; and although she knew Lady Finch was talking nonsense she had been unable to produce good convincing arguments to refute her. So she contented herself now with the reproachful look, to show Harriet that missionaries were not a subject for jest.

Hands off missionaries, Harriet said to herself; and once again she was struck by the change that had come over her friend. Though serious by nature, Marian had been ready enough in the past to laugh at Harriet's jokes and to talk freely about everything. There had been no reproachful looks, no suggestion that certain subjects were sacred, or—worse still—beyond Harriet's comprehension. The change could be dated from the fatal day when she became engaged to Hubert.

Few people would have cast Hubert for the role of evil genius, but that was how Harriet pictured him. He wasn't, of course, evil in himself, but only in the effect he had had, and was having, on Marian. He was developing her worst qualities, making her smug, solemn, and intolerant, a fitting wife perhaps for a missionary (Harriet's views on Foreign Missions were strongly influenced by her aunt), but a poor sort of human being. It was a great, great pity; and something ought to be done about it.

Harriet was young, and she believed in action. She was impulsive and warm-hearted, and she seldom paused to consider whether her friends really wanted to be rescued from entanglements or prevented from taking false steps. It was enough for her that they stood in need of help.

But the notion of rescuing Marian from Hubert's evil genius was new, and she had not yet thought how it could be done.

"You'd better come with me," Lady Finch said suddenly, breaking a silence that had become a little strained.

"But where?"

"To call on those people at Belmont House. They might be nice friends for you."

"So they might," Harriet agreed. "Especially the nephew, if he doesn't waddle."

It was at that moment that she had her great idea.

CHAPTER IV

PROMPT AS Lady Finch was in the performance of her social duties, she was not the first caller at Belmont House. Miss Pope got there in the morning; but then, as she made haste to explain, she was not a 'real' caller.

"I just thought I'd pop in," she said, "to see if you wanted any help. I do feel one ought to be neighbourly, especially when you're strangers in a strange land."

Miss Pope was tall and thin—so thin that her legs looked like sticks and her long, scrawny neck appeared to contain more vertebrae than other people's necks. But she had a beaming smile and a loud, cheerful voice; not a bit like a parson's sister, thought Julia Dunstan, who pictured the sisters of the clergy as meek, diffident women dressed in grey or pastel shades.

Unlike these wraiths Miss Pope wore a bright blue cotton frock and did not lack self-confidence. She had already introduced herself, and without plainly asking to come in had contrived to enter the house. Perhaps her long experience of parish work had taught her how to gain admittance; anyway, they were now in the morning-room. Julia apologized for its untidiness, and Miss Pope replied that she could see they were not yet straight, and renewed her offer of help.

"There's always such a lot to find out, when you come to a new place. Now, how about tradesmen—and milk? You ought to get your milk from Scott's Dairy, and your rations—"

"Oh, Mr. Duffy arranged all that for us," Julia said hastily. Mr. Duffy was the builder and decorator who had been renovating Belmont House.

"Duffy's quite a useful man," said Miss Pope. "But I wouldn't trust him too far. He's hand-in-glove with some rather undesirable—er—racketeers." She produced this word with an air of pride, and Julia Dunstan looked suitably impressed—though she could hardly believe that racketeers were numerous in Goatstock.

"We're camping out at present," she said. "We brought lots of tinned food with us, and we're living on that." They were also living on eggs, supplied by the useful Mr. Duffy, but it obviously would not do to say so.

"Have you got any help? You'll need it, in a house like this. I must say I was surprised when I heard you were coming here. It seems such a big house for two women."

"But my uncle left it to me. It's so wonderful to have something left to you. I've never had a home of my own—and it seemed as if it was *meant*."

"Yes . . . I see," said Miss Pope, puzzling over the remark. Mrs. Dunstan was a widow, and apparently quite well off. How did it come about that she had never had a home of her own?

If Julia had been questioned she would have had to admit that she had had several homes. But they were all rented flats or bungalows in foreign lands, which was not at all the same thing as owning a house. She felt this strongly, though she found it hard to convince other people that the distinction existed. Moreover, she had never expected to inherit Belmont House and the legacy had fired her imagination, which, if it had a fault, was too readily inflammable. She heard mysterious overtones in the legal phrases of a will; she saw the hand of Fate guiding her to Goatstock.

There were many things to support this romantic fancy. The fact that, at the time of her uncle's death, she was looking for a house; the fact that her cousin Dora had had to give up her job and was at a loose end; the fact that her own doctor had advised her to live in the country. All these facts, and several others, were at the back of her mind when she declared to Miss Pope that it was *meant*.

With any encouragement she would have said more; but Miss Pope's puzzled smile checked the confidences. Miss Pope was clearly a practical woman who had come to offer practical help, and references to telepathy or the hand of Fate might antagonize her.

"But we shall certainly need some help in the house," Julia said, striving to be practical too. "We haven't got anybody yet, except my old nurse who lives with me—of course she's rather past work, poor dear, but she does what she can."

Miss Pope did not belong to the stratum of society that has old nurses at its beck and call, but she nodded comprehendingly.

"I expect she likes to feel she's of use," she said.

"Yes," Julia said, rather doubtfully. Of course, Nanny was useful, and no doubt enjoyed feeling useful, but her usefulness was embarrassingly concentrated on her employer. Sometimes she seemed to be pretending that Dora did not exist.

"My cousin is a great help, too," she said. "But I don't want her to slave away at housework. I can't believe she really likes it, though she pretends she does."

Miss Pope was too polite to ask the question that hovered on her lips. Was Miss Duckworth sharing the house—or was she perhaps a paid companion, a secretary or housekeeper? Julia gave her no help, though she went on to speak of her cousin in a way that showed they were tremendous friends.

"I don't know what I should do without her," she said.

A little later, she was leaving the house, Miss Pope encountered this paragon of a cousin. They met on the doorstep. Mrs. Dunstan introduced Miss Duckworth and explained that she was a keen gardener; but Miss Pope hardly needed the explanation, for she could recognize a fellow enthusiast when she met one. She herself had little time for gardening, she said, but she simply loved it. Dora Duckworth replied that she loved it too. Her earth-stained hands showed that she had already been at work.

There was only time to exchange a few words, and then Miss Pope had to fly. She had stayed longer than she meant to, and Alaric wanted lunch early that day because he had to go to Reddrod on the two-o'clock bus. But they must come to tea, she said, and see *her* garden—not that it was much to look at—and meet one or two of their neighbours. How about Tuesday next week?

The ladies accepted her invitation, raising their voices to do so because Miss Pope, by then, was nearly at the gate. "Half past four," she called over her shoulder. They nodded and smiled; they were newcomers and did not realize that the tail-end of every conversation with Miss Pope was always conducted in shouts while she hurried off to her next duty.

". . . look forward to seeing you!" screamed Miss Pope. Her long thin legs bore her out of sight. Julia stepped back into the hall and Dora followed, shutting the door behind her.

"I'm sure she's very nice," Julia said. "It's lucky we're both Church of England, isn't it? She quite took it for granted. It would have been awkward if we hadn't been."

Julia was so clever at dealing with awkward situations that she sometimes amused herself by imagining hypothetical ones and thinking how she would handle them. But Dora could not see the fun of this; her way of dealing with an awkward situation in real life was to ignore it altogether, and she was laughingly scornful of people who were hurt or offended by what she called 'trifles'.

"I liked her," she said firmly.

"Oh, so did I," Julia agreed. "But I'm not sure whether she liked me. I think she liked you best, anyway. It wasn't till she'd seen you that she asked us to tea."

Her voice was wistful; it mattered a good deal to Julia that people should like her.

"Of course she liked you," Dora said. "Don't worry, Julia, you've got lots of charm. People always like you."

Julia was reassured, though less by her cousin's words ('lots of charm' hardly sounded an asset, when Dora mentioned it) than by a sudden inward conviction that she and Miss Pope had something in common. What it was, she could not yet determine; but she wondered if Miss Pope was really as practical as she looked.

Her musing was interrupted by Nanny, who came into the hall and asked accusingly if Mr. Robert was back yet with the fish or if she was to do eggs again for lunch.

Until fairly recently, Nanny's name had been Gladys. In the more distant past she had been house-parlourmaid to Julia's Mamma, and had combined this task with acting as nurse to Julia when there was no one else available. She was genuinely devoted to her charge and had continued to send her Birthday and Christmas cards long after they parted, to which Julia had responded by sending presents from the eastern country where she had spent her married life. This generosity had been unexpectedly rewarded; for when, after her widowhood, she returned to England, she found Gladys, elderly but still active, panting to serve her. To Julia's romantic mind only one thing was lacking; and with a touch of creative genius she turned Gladys the house-parlourmaid into Nanny the dear old family nurse.

Even Dora, when it was explained to her, accepted the metamorphosis; partly because Nanny, out of loyalty to Julia, refused to answer to the name of Gladys.

In reply to Nanny's enquiries Dora said they had better have eggs, as Robert had a lot to do in Reddrod and would probably be late.

"Would you fancy eggs, Miss Julia?" Nanny asked, exactly as though Dora had not spoken. "Or will you wait for the fish?"

"Eggs, I think, Nanny."

Nanny retreated into the back premises. Dora looked at her cousin. "I must learn to hold my tongue," she said lightly. "It isn't a bit of good my saying anything when you're here."

"Poor Nanny, she doesn't mean it. You see, it's just because she was my old nurse, and so she spoils me. You mustn't mind, Dora."

"I wasn't minding, I was laughing," Dora protested.

Julia felt slightly disappointed. Difficult situations, jealousy and hurt feelings, were things she could cope with; after all, if people *minded* it proved, in a way, that they were fond of her. But if they didn't mind—if they simply laughed—it didn't prove anything.

Perhaps, however, Dora was simply pretending not to mind. She would have to have a talk with her some time, and find out what she really thought about Nanny.

She would also have to have a talk with her nephew, Robert, and explain how important it was to her not to be kept waiting for meals. 'It's this stupid gastric tummy of mine', she would say; for she wouldn't like Robert to think she was just being fussy.

But even as she rehearsed this talk to herself her nephew Robert opened the front door and thrust his way into the hall, somewhat encumbered by parcels, a double-crown size portfolio, and a bounding dog on a lead.

"Sorry," said Robert, missing his aunt by inches. "I didn't know you were just inside. Could you let Taffy off the lead—it's twisted round my wrist. . . . That's better." Taffy, to celebrate his freedom, ran round in circles barking. Robert propped the portfolio against the wall and offered Julia a damp parcel, wrapped in newspaper and rapidly disintegrating. "Only haddock, I'm afraid," he said. "But it's beautifully fresh."

Robert was her late husband's nephew, and like all the Dunstans he was tall and good-looking. For this Julia could forgive him a lot. She took the parcel and explained smilingly that it was too late to cook the fish for lunch today, so he would have to put up with eggs again. Robert said that didn't matter at all; the fish was so fresh that it would certainly keep till tomorrow, or else they could have it for supper.

This was not quite what he had been meant to say. An apology for his lateness, a hope that all these eggs would not disagree with his aunt, would have sounded better. But Julia again forgave him. She remembered how important it was to think good thoughts; and she remembered too that her cousin Francis Heswald was coming to see her that afternoon. Lunch must not be further delayed or she might not have time for the post-prandial rest, the change into more becoming attire, and the careful new make-up, all of which were essential to the success of this reunion.

Francis Heswald had been one of her earliest admirers; and she had not seen him for nearly twenty years.

Heswald was a village some miles to the north of Goatstock and well beyond the fringes of industrialism. It had no main road, no hourly bus-service, no church, in fact it was merely a collection of cottages, one or two farms, and a small general shop. At the end of its narrow street were the lodge gates of Heswald Hall, and close beside them the bailiff's house, now inhabited by Francis Heswald and the competent married couple who looked after him. Since he had managed to let his ancestral home, at a fair rent, to the county council—who used it as a home for Deprived Children—he was able to live in comfort, if not in luxury.

Everyone said it was quite absurd of Francis to go on living at Heswald. True, he still owned the land, but the farms and the Hall were let; he had nothing to do. He was a bachelor. He belonged to historical and antiquarian societies and was supposed to be writing—or perhaps to have written—a book about early rent-rolls or some other abstruse mediaeval subject. Few of his local acquaintances believed that this task was either necessary or profitable. Even if he should find a publisher for it, they said, he was not likely to find readers.

Mr. Heswald had been much surprised to receive a letter from Julia Dunstan, informing him of her return to Belmont House, and inviting him to come to tea with her and Dora. His interest in remote family history did not extend to contemporary relatives and he had long ago lost touch with his cousin Julia and his cousin Dora, who used to stay at Belmont House when they were young girls. He knew that his old uncle had bequeathed the house to Julia, but he had not expected that she would come to live there, since he believed her to be married to a rich businessman and living in Calcutta or possibly in Colombo. But it appeared that she was now a widow.

He arrived at Belmont House rather earlier than he had meant to, and a good deal before he was expected. The door was opened by a small, elderly female in a drab-coloured dress, and for a moment he supposed that this must be either Dora or Julia, prematurely aged by a hard life or tropical sunshine. But before he could question her the elderly female said the ladies were in the drawing-room, and turned to lead the way across the hall.

As it happened, only Dora was in the drawing-room; Julia was upstairs getting ready. This time Francis Heswald made no mistake; and indeed Dora, in spite of grey hair and a complexion which had been left wholly to nature, was still easily recognizable as the Dora of twenty years ago.

The first moments were a little awkward; neither of them knew how to talk to a first cousin who was almost a total stranger. Dora felt it would be a mistake to rush straight into reminiscences of the past, and after the first greetings she said the garden was in a dreadful state but she was going to enjoy living at Belmont House.

Francis Heswald asked politely if she meant to live there permanently.

Of course the house belonged to Julia, Dora explained, but they were going to share it.

At this point she paused for a brief struggle with her conscience. 'Sharing the house' suggested that they were sharing the expenses; whereas in fact Julia was paying for everything. But if she mentioned that, it made her sound like a poor relation, a mere hanger-on, which of course she wasn't. She hated to think of herself as a hanger-on.

"I mean, the house is really too big for Julia, so she asked me to live with her," she said hurriedly. This was true, and her conscience felt easier. Pausing no longer she began to tell Francis about Robert, who was Julia's husband's nephew and a recently qualified engineer; but whether he lived permanently at Belmont House would depend, of course, on whether he could get a job in the neighbourhood.

"Of course," Francis Heswald agreed, mesmerized by the phrase. He said no more, for he was unaccustomed to making conversation and while he sought for a subject Dora was off again. She told him about the dry rot in the attic and the way the rain came in under the scullery door; she told him about the immersion heater and the electric cooker. She just stopped herself from telling him about the pale pink bath and other fittings in Julia's new bathroom, because it occurred to her that these were not the sort of things one mentions to unknown cousins. But it did not matter; there were plenty of other things to talk about, and by now she was beginning to feel more at home with Cousin Francis.

Francis Heswald, however, was far from feeling at home with his cousin Dora. He seldom paid social visits, and although he sometimes went to tea with the head librarian in the county town, or with one of his fellow antiquarians in London, the talk on these occasions was formal and scholarly. Dora's conversation, by comparison, was like the chattering of chimpanzees at the zoo.

It would have been difficult to refuse Julia Dunstan's invitation, but he wished now that he had thought of an excuse. Cousins were all very well but it was ridiculous that he should be expected to waste his time listening to all this nonsense about sinks and cupboards and stair carpets. He glanced surreptitiously at his watch.

"*There* you are!" Dora exclaimed suddenly, interrupting the stream of her own remarks. Francis Heswald turned round. There in the doorway stood his cousin Julia, who struck him immediately as being a great improvement on his cousin Dora. He could not have explained this (for he was the last man in the world to be impressed by outward appearances), but it was so. Perhaps it was just because she was small and quiet, and looked a little shy, in contrast to the tall, noisy, overbearing Dora.

"Well—Francis," Julia said, advancing into the room almost reluctantly. "It has been a long time, hasn't it?"

Francis Heswald was not so stupid as to tell her that she hadn't changed; but he thought she had changed very little. On her side Julia was rather disappointed in Francis, but comforted herself by the reflection that at least he was not bald. Grey hair, after all, was quite distinguished—in a man.

"I've been telling Cousin Francis all about the house," Dora said. Julia thought this explained why Francis had been peeping at his watch when she entered the room, and she at once changed the subject.

"But I want to hear about Goatstock," she said pleadingly. "About who lives here, and what they are like. A candid view between cousins."

Francis might have dealt with this by saying he was a recluse, but he hesitated to make so churlish a reply. The momentary silence was broken by the jangling of a distant bell and the thumping of a not so distant knocker.

"Gracious, who can it be?" cried Dora.

"We cannot tell," Julia said. "I hope not callers."

Dora said it couldn't be callers, it was much too soon and anyway it was too late.

If he had been alone with her the idiocy of this remark would have turned Francis against Dora for ever, but Julia's gay laugh was so affectionate, so uncritical, that his own contempt diminished. It was clear to him that Julia liked Dora, even though she laughed at her.

"She means that it's too soon after our arrival, and too late in the afternoon. Callers, you know, shouldn't call after four o'clock."

"That's what I said," Dora declared.

"These callers do not appear to know the rules," Francis Heswald said, listening to the voices in the hall and the tread of approaching feet.

"I'm afraid they don't," Julia said regretfully; and to his surprise he found himself sharing her regret.

Nanny opened the drawing-room door, and ushered in Lady Finch and Miss Harriet Finch.

CHAPTER V

LADY FINCH and Harriet were wearing very dressy hats, and Lady Finch was also wearing a feather boa, wound round her neck two or three times in order to conceal as much as possible of her swollen chin. Both the hats belonged to Lady Finch, and the one which had been lent to Harriet was a brown chip-straw model with a royal blue satin ribbon swathed round it and hanging down behind in puggaree fashion. Beneath this extravagant hat Harriet looked child-like and subdued. Lady Finch, on the other hand, looked every inch a dowager, and Julia and Dora both came to the conclusion that she must be the leading lady of these parts.

Francis Heswald was acquainted with Lady Finch, but he did not know her very well. He was somewhat startled when he heard her speaking of him, to Julia, as a fellow author. He had not known that she was an author, and could hardly believe it. But Julia was greatly impressed.

"Two authors!" she cried. "We shall never be able to live up to Goatstock. Dora, did you know that Francis writes books?"

Dora did not, and asked if they were detective stories. While he was enlightening her Francis felt bound to admit that his book was not yet published (although two scholarly monographs, and several contributions to learned journals, entitled him to call himself an author); but he added, rather smugly, that there was a publisher waiting for it. At that Lady Finch turned away from her hostess and demanded to know who the publisher might be.

"Because I shall need one myself," she said, "as soon as my book is finished. Yours might do."

Francis Heswald was rather annoyed. Julia and Dora had assumed that all authors had the same status, and now Lady Finch was assuming that the publisher of an erudite historical work would be equally ready to publish romantic female fiction. He was sure fiction was her *métier*, and he didn't doubt that it would be romantic. He permitted himself a faint, ironic smile.

"They're specialists," he said. "They also publish a lot of school text-books and classics, but I don't suppose your book is written to instruct the young."

"Indeed it is," said Lady Finch. "It's written to instruct everybody. It's intended to be both an inspiration and a practical guide."

"Fresh food," said Harriet from under her hat.

"I had thought of that for a title. But it lacks dignity. Don't you agree, Mr. Heswald, that a book's title should be dignified?"

"I suppose so," he answered lamely, making a rapid mental re-assessment of Lady Finch and her *métier*. *Fresh Food* did not sound like a romantic novel; but on the other hand Lady Finch did not look capable of writing a practical guide to anything.

"Then I thought of calling it *Hedgerows, Highways, and Healthy Stomachs*. But Harriet thinks that is rather ambitious."

"Ambitious, I said."

"We could judge better," said Julia, "if we knew what your book was about."

Lady Finch sat up in her chair, cleared her throat, and began to tell them. She had forgotten that this was a first call on strangers and that she had meant to stay only fifteen minutes. An opportunity to speak about one of her major interests was not to be missed.

Hidden under her hat, Harriet sighed. Aunt Finch at least was getting some fun out of the afternoon, since her new neighbours were encouraging her to talk about her pet hobby; but she, Harriet, was getting no fun at all. Fresh food was no novelty to Harriet; she heard too much about it at home, and not only heard about it but lived on it. The valuable plants which were to be found in every copse and hedgerow were also to be found, in great variety, in Aunt Finch's garden, where Scientific Gardening caused them to flourish abundantly. Aunt Finch believed that people ate the wrong sorts of food, and her book was designed to enlighten them and to show how easy it was to live cheaply, agreeably, and healthily on what Nature provided.

'Finch on Nettles', Harriet said to herself. It would be quite a good title, authoritative and yet intriguing. But she had not come to Belmont House to listen to Finch on Nettles. She could do that at Urn Cottage.

She had come to inspect the nephew; and the nephew wasn't on view. Perhaps he was painfully shy, or perhaps he was a superior person who despised social gatherings. She realized that she had probably been over-optimistic about the nephew, but it was disappointing that her optimism could be neither confirmed nor disproved. One glance—even a brief glimpse of him out in the garden—would have given her some idea of his possibilities.

"Their roots are remarkably succulent," said Lady Finch. Harriet's thoughts had strayed so far from fresh food that these words had for her no context, and it looked as if the rest of Lady Finch's audience had been equally inattentive. There was an awkward pause, as if everyone was waiting for someone else to make the right comment. In this silence the opening of the door sounded unnaturally loud, and the entry of Robert Dunstan had an unnatural importance. Unnatural, that is, for everyone but Harriet.

"My nephew," Julia explained, unaware that her visitors were perfectly capable of identifying him. Grateful to Robert for arriving at that moment and interrupting the interminable lecture, she drew him into the circle and made him sit next to Lady Finch.

'He will do,' Harriet thought. Mentally contrasting this tall, handsome young man with the insignificant Hubert she decided that, as a counter-attraction, he had excellent qualifications. Her plan for rescuing Marian from Hubert's evil influence had been hardly more than a dream, but now it began to seem feasible. Elated, but outwardly composed, she sat listening, appraising, and working out her campaign.

Robert Dunstan had been prepared to meet Julia's cousin Francis Heswald, but he had not been prepared for the elderly gorgon and the unnerving child. He supposed they had come with Francis, and he felt quite sorry for his aunt for having such ghastly relations in the neighbourhood. It just showed how careful one ought to be about vetting one's kith and kin before settling down in their vicinity.

"We were talking about food," said the gorgon. This was the only lucid statement he could catch, for she immediately embarked on a long rigmarole about sorrel, nettles, and different varieties of wild vetch, none of which, to his mind, ranked as food at all.

"Yes," he said politely. "Yes, I see."

It was not the gorgon who repelled him so much as the child sitting opposite. Apart and a little withdrawn, she kept on staring at him from under the brim of her absurd ex-garden party hat with an intense but impersonal curiosity which made him feel like something in a zoo. If he could have persuaded himself that she had taken a sudden fancy to him it would at least have been flattering, but there was nothing in that cool gaze to warrant such an assumption.

Misled by the hat, which made Harriet look like a child in fancy dress, he put her down as a schoolgirl, and tried to reassure himself by supposing that she was at the awkward age. Probably her staring and her silence were simply forms of schoolgirl *gau-*

cherie like the giggles and shrieks he had observed in the younger sisters of his friends. Nevertheless he was relieved when the clock struck five and attracted Lady Finch's attention.

"Dear me, I have stayed longer than I meant to," she said, rising to her feet with no particular haste. "You must forgive me, Mrs. Dunstan—but this is such an important subject to all of us that enthusiasm is never wholly out of place."

No one contradicted this statement, though no one agreed with it. Lady Finch proceeded to say good-bye to her hostesses, and then paused to say a few friendly words to Francis Heswald, remembering that a fellow author might prove a useful acquaintance when it came to choosing a publisher. While this was going on Harriet turned to Robert.

"Are you living here?" she asked.

He did not care to commit himself, but honesty compelled him to say that he was staying at Belmont House for the present.

"Then we shall meet again. You must come to tea," she said kindly. "Are you interested in bees?"

"I know nothing about them."

"Perhaps you like goldfish. Or tortoises? I have a sweet tortoise called Michael, after my uncle. My uncle is dead."

Robert felt—and looked—baffled. He did not know whether to congratulate her on her tortoise or commiserate with her over her uncle's death. After a short pause he said that tortoises weren't really in his line, either. Nor, he added firmly, were goldfish.

"To the outsider goldfish seem dull," Harriet said. "I have a friend who thinks exactly as you do. She always says our goldfish are very stupid pets."

'And you are stupid, too,' she thought sadly, awarding him a mere five marks (out of ten) for conversational ability. Remembering, however, that it was Marian he had to suit, she fired off another question.

"Do you like dogs?"

Yes, Robert liked dogs. The mention of dogs seemed to raise his spirits. He told her he had a dog of his own, a Corgi puppy; its name was Taffy and it was a very intelligent dog, though a bit undisciplined at present.

"And you take him for nice walks, I suppose?"

Her voice was innocent and polite. Nevertheless, it suddenly occurred to Robert that he had been gravely mistaken. She wasn't a schoolgirl, she wasn't shy and awkward; on the contrary, she was very much at her ease. To add to his confusion, he suspected that she was laughing at him.

"Nice walks? Oh, I see—nice walks," he answered rapidly. "Yes, I do. I take him for nice walks."

The shock of finding himself wrong—totally and absurdly wrong—seemed to paralyse his mind and, at the same time, to stimulate his tongue; he heard himself babbling on like a brook in spate. Nice walks, the niceness of dogs, Taffy's particular endowments—it all came pouring out in a flood, while the bewildered inner Robert asked himself how he could possibly have been so blind. For now that he looked at Harriet, seeing her as it were for the first time, he found her extremely attractive. In spite of the dreadful hat she had become a girl whom he longed to know better.

"Come, Harriet," said Lady Finch, moving at last towards the door. Meekly Harriet turned to bid everyone good afternoon; meekly she followed her aunt, stopping to pick up the gloves Lady Finch let fall, one after the other, as she passed out of sight.

Dogs, Harriet was thinking; dogs unlock his tongue. Robert's conversational output on dogs was quite startling. She awarded him another mark, for quantity not for quality, and thought how lucky it was that Marian too was fond of dogs. Right from the start they would have something to talk about.

"Poor Francis—what a visitation!" Julia exclaimed, as soon as the door had shut behind the callers.

It was instinct in Julia to soothe the ruffled feelings of any man who might have been even slightly inconvenienced by the behaviour of other, less considerate women. She even remembered to throw a quick sympathetic smile at Robert. Robert was looking dazed, but Francis—and this was more important—was looking cross.

"I ask you to tea and let you in for a crusade!"

"Not your fault," Francis replied. A moment ago he had been thinking on other lines, but his cousin's distress, her touching acceptance of the blame, melted his heart.

"I never expected callers. So stupid of me. I shan't dare to ask you again until I'm quite certain that everyone who could possibly call on me has got it over."

"I hope you won't postpone it as long as that," he said. Even as he spoke it occurred to him that this was rather unnecessary; attractive as Julia was, he had other things to do than take tea with her. But somehow it seemed natural to reassure his cousin, and natural too that the reassurance should take the form of a compliment. He congratulated himself on having brought the words out so neatly. The grateful smile with which Julia rewarded him rounded off the little incident to perfection, and left him with the happy knowledge that he was not only a man who could pay compliments but a man whose compliments were appreciated.

"What about tea *today*?" asked Robert, on whom these verbal felicities had made little impression.

Julia remembered that Dunstans were always hungry, and suggested that he should go and tell Nanny they were ready in case she hadn't heard Dora letting the callers out. There was no real need for this, for the efficient Dora would certainly see to it herself; but it gave Robert something to do.

It also took him out of the drawing-room. When they were alone she was able to tell Francis how very, very glad she was to see him again. It was absurd to be sentimental about the past, but she had spent some of her happiest times at Goatstock and the people she had known there still mattered to her far more than people she had met since.

"But you are almost the only survivor," she said plaintively. "I suppose they were all Uncle James's friends—the generation before us. Or else they've sold up and gone to live in nooky cottages in the south. That seems so defeatist, doesn't it? I'm glad you're obstinate enough to stick to Heswald."

Francis realized that Julia knew little or nothing about the difficulties of continuing to inhabit one's ancestral home when one had neither the money nor the staff to keep it up. But he found it easy to forgive her ignorance, because her views on nooky cottages in the south appealed to him. He had a stubborn conviction that people ought to live in their own county, even though they could no longer afford to live in their own homes.

He explained that Heswald Hall was let and that he had moved into the bailiff's house.

"I know that—Mr. Duffy told me. Still, you haven't run away."

She was laughing, but it was a sympathetic laugh; and again he had the pleasure of feeling that he was admired and respected.

The return of Dora and Robert, followed by Nanny with the tea, put an end to this agreeable duologue. At tea the talk was general, with Dora's voice taking the lead. Julia presided over the tea things, but she seemed quite content that Dora should direct the conversation.

Now that he had had time to get used to it Francis Heswald found he was amused, not annoyed, by the loud amiable chatter of his cousin Dora. In some ways she had changed less than Julia; she had grown older, but she had not grown up. She was still the beaming, sturdy niece whose visits to Belmont House had given so much pleasure to her Aunt Mary, and he was almost surprised to notice that her teeth were no longer fettered by a gold band. It was true that she had worn the gold band only for a short period, but she was so vividly the Dora of that particular time that he felt she ought to be wearing it still.

"Uncle James must have been so lonely, after she died," Dora was saying. "Dear Aunt Mary . . . I was so fond of her."

A favourite aunt, Francis perceived; and this was just as it should be, because Dora had undoubtedly been Aunt Mary's favourite niece. But Uncle James had apparently preferred Julia. Odd, he thought, very odd that Uncle James should leave her Belmont House, when he hadn't seen her for years and could not have known that she would want to live there. It was not what one would have expected of Uncle James, a disciplinarian who, in his lifetime, had made a point of treating all his nieces and nephews alike. Puzzling over this uncharacteristic behaviour, he made perfunctory replies to Dora's sallies and forgot to drink his second cup of tea.

This absent-mindedness, Julia thought, was a good sign, since it showed that Francis accepted them and was no longer troubling to be formally attentive. Probably that was how he ate his meals at home, solitary and unhurried, brooding over remote historical problems while the tea grew cold in his cup.

It was a good sign; but that did not mean that absent-mindedness and a solitary aimless existence were good in themselves. Francis had possibilities, and he must be encouraged to lead a fuller life. After all, he was a Heswald, and there had been plenty of distinguished Heswalds in the past—not scholars, certainly, but important people in the county and even beyond it. There had been the Cavalier who got his head cut off, and the judge who was accused of taking bribes (but triumphantly exonerated), and Uncle James, who was a general, and probably many others unknown to her.

It was too late for Francis to become a judge or a general—or a Cavalier—but it was not too late for him to begin to lead a fuller life. Julia's lively interest in her neighbours often led her to the conclusion that they ought to lead fuller lives, and also compelled her to listen to their troubles. She listened very sympathetically; though her late husband had sometimes complained that she was too eager to listen, and that strangers in railway carriages ought not to be incited to reveal their secret sorrows, no matter how sad their faces looked. But then her late husband, a true Dunstan, believed in keeping himself to himself.

Her interest in Francis, however, was warmer and more personal than this generalized benevolence. He was her cousin; he was the head of the family; and he had been the first man to admire her. She had never been in love with Francis, but she had always been fond of him—or so she now told herself—and she looked forward to presiding, like a modern Egeria, over his concerns.

Something which she called intuition informed Julia that Francis, like the Dunstans, would reject encouragement and good advice if they were proffered too lavishly or too soon. Her married life had taught her that good intentions—even the best—were not enough; they were liable to be misunderstood. And Francis, of course, was a bachelor, and probably set in his ways; he would not welcome cousins who threatened to interfere with his aimless, but peaceful, existence. Though she cherished good thoughts towards humanity in general, Julia could not rid herself of the knowledge that men—and especially mature bachelors—were dreadfully selfish.

The afternoon, however, could be counted a success, and she was fairly certain that Francis liked her. He seemed to like Dora too; although Dora had clearly done the wrong thing by badgering him to bring plants and cuttings, whenever he was passing, to fill up the neglected garden.

"Yes, you must come again," Julia said, when Francis took his leave. But she said it lightly, without emphasis; there was no demand, in the gentle voice, that he should drop in 'whenever he was passing'. She stood at the door for a brief moment as he got into his car, and then turned back to the house, leaving Dora to wave energetic farewells. This friendly but casual parting was quite to his taste; it mitigated a lurking fear, which had assailed him during tea, that with any encouragement she might become possessive and sentimental.

He felt that he had misjudged Julia; and, perversely, he felt that a little more warmth, an invitation more definitely phrased, would not have been out of place between cousins so lately re-united.

CHAPTER VI

IN THE DAYS that followed Julia was too busy to think much about Francis and her plans for his future. There was still a great deal to be done to Belmont House; she had moved in as soon as the builders and decorators had finished their tasks, and now she was blissfully 'making a home of it'. This meant spending a good deal of money; for no house, in Julia's eyes, could be looked on as a home until it had been luxuriously equipped with handsome carpets and curtains, pictures and china, and linen and towels to match the colour schemes of the various bedrooms.

Because her married life had been spent in foreign parts, and her widowhood in furnished flats, Julia had few household possessions. She was able to indulge in an orgy of buying. She made expeditions to the county's largest city, she made a flying visit to London for some special curtain material which could not be found elsewhere, and she frequently drove over to Reddrod in search of little things, such as door-mats or extra ash-trays, which had somehow been overlooked.

"I call it awfully extravagant," Dora declared, surveying the two dozen hand-painted dessert plates with which Julia had returned that morning. "You've *got* a dessert service. And anyway, who uses them nowadays?"

"Well, perhaps it was just a wee bit extravagant," Julia admitted. "I saw them in the antique shop, when I was looking at the knife-box, and I realized at once how lovely that deep blue would look in the dining-room."

"*What* knife-box?"

"Not to use, Dora—they're much too precious for that. To stand in a row along the back of the sideboard. They'll look marvellous against that dark oak. Such a heavenly colour!"

The plates had wide blue borders, and in the middle of each was a picture of a bird. "All different," Julia cried triumphantly. "Look! The robin, and the bullfinch, and the—what's this bird, Dora?"

"A sparrow."

"Oh no, not a sparrow, they wouldn't put sparrows on a hand-painted dessert service. I think it's a—a falcon."

"Or possibly a black-browed albatross; it certainly looks rather bad-tempered," Dora said lightly.

Julia might have resented this mockery of her newest and most beautiful acquisition. But she remembered that Dora had had a hard life, had always had to work for her living and probably had never been able to afford pretty things such as these. She couldn't help feeling envious, poor Dora, and it was natural enough that her envy should lead her to disparage Julia's purchases and to suggest that they were a waste of money.

Thinking this, Julia wondered if Dora was really happy at Belmont House. She had already learned that Dora was proud of her independence; reminiscences of her former hard life were sometimes phrased like reminiscences of a better, nobler existence, and she seemed to have the curious idea that comfort could be demoralizing if it were not the result of one's own endeavours. Perhaps she felt that the comparatively unearned comfort in which she now lived was corrupting her.

Or perhaps, on the other hand, she was not comfortable enough. This seemed to Julia more probable; and later in the day she became involved in an emotional scene with Nanny, whose marked partiality for herself must be curbed lest it left Dora, physically as well as mentally, out-in-the-cold. With veiled references to her cousin's hard life she begged Nanny to treat Dora and herself exactly alike, and in particular to draw Dora's bedroom curtains at night and fill her hot-water bottle. But Nanny, whose devotion allowed no margin for rivals, took the request in quite the wrong spirit.

"You know very well, Miss Julia, that I've got my hands full," she retorted. "One of me isn't enough for a house like this, and I thought Miss Duckworth was here to help."

"So she is," Julia said hastily, remembering the careful explanations she had given Nanny to account for Dora's coming. "But it isn't as if—well, you see, she's my cousin—"

"And no help at all, if she's to be waited on hand and foot. No doubt you're very fond of her, Miss Julia, but you might spare a thought for your poor old nurse."

Julia gave a soft, reproachful cry and begged Nanny not to misunderstand her. But it was too late; for Nanny, bristling with annoyance, had begun to talk about her rheumatism and the way her knees clicked when she ran up and down stairs, and the time it took to get all round the house doing the work she was there to do, without doing extra jobs for those that could well wait on themselves.

"Then leave my room," Julia said with misguided kindness. "I can easily do my hot-water bottle myself. I'll get an electric kettle."

"The idea! Anyway, what does Miss Duckworth want with a hot bottle this weather? It's different for you, Miss Julia dear—you that have lived in those foreign places and miss the hot climate. But she never seems to feel the cold—always going round opening all the windows as if to say I didn't air the rooms properly!"

This was clearly a grievance. There were several other grievances, and they all came pouring out; for Nanny, as the weeks
went by, was becoming more and more like the tyrannical, privileged old nannies of fiction and less and less like a well-trained
house-parlourmaid. Julia listened and sympathized, and told
herself hopefully that this was a demonstration of Nanny's devotion to herself, for which she ought to be grateful. Nanny's resentment of Dora was perhaps a form of jealousy; and although
she found it difficult to be grateful she managed to feel sorry for
her grumbling, hard-done-by retainer.

"I didn't realize, when we first came here, that there would
be so much for you to do," she said.

"It's not the work I do for you, Miss Julia, that I mind. It's—"

"But now I see that it's far too much for you. We must get
someone to help," Julia said quickly.

Nanny sniffed, and said—with evident reference to Dora—
that there was help *and* help, and some sorts were no better than
a hindrance. But after some discussion she more or less agreed
to allow another paid domestic in the kitchen, if one could be
found, and Julia thankfully retreated.

True, she had not won her point—for no appeals to her kind
heart would persuade Nanny to fill Dora's hot-water bottle—but
she had done her best and satisfied her conscience.

News travels fast, and it soon became known in Goatstock
that Mrs. Dunstan was furnishing Belmont House with prodigal
splendour. Except for the Wilmots at Canal Lodge, who were
said to be rich, but who were also notoriously stingy, no one in
Goatstock had much money; and therefore the arrival of this
Croesus in their midst caused a considerable stir. The owners
of small shops hoped for her patronage, and the champions
of deserving causes hoped for handsome subscriptions. It was
generally felt to be a good thing that Belmont House should be
occupied by someone who was qualified to play a leading part
in local affairs, and those of Julia's neighbours who believed in
social customs hastened to pay calls.

Some, accomplished in the formalities, produced cards. Others, for whom the technique of paying calls was a lost art, simply

introduced themselves on the doorstep to Nanny; like Francis Heswald they had come to accept it as probable that the door would be opened by the lady of the house, but unlike him they were impulsive friendly creatures who burst into speech without waiting to make sure of her identity.

Mrs. Minnis was one of these. In impetuous goodwill she outdid her neighbours, and she contrived to seize Nanny by the hand and to utter words of ardent greeting, before she could be checked. The discovery of her mistake so unnerved Mrs. Minnis that when, a few minutes later, she found herself face to face with the real Mrs. Dunstan, everything she had meant to say—and had, in point of fact, already said—went clean out of her head.

"Of course you've seen me before, well, sort of," she blurted out. "Only you weren't meant to. I felt quite awful about it."

Julia looked at her visitor, who was wearing a pink-and-white merry-peasant dress with puffed muslin sleeves, and a small pink hat perched on top of a mass of shaggy grey curls. Something about her seemed dimly familiar; but surely she could not have forgotten a previous meeting with this distinctive figure.

"Have I?" she said. It seemed unkind to probe for details of an encounter that had left Mrs. Minnis feeling awful. "Perhaps on board ship," she murmured vaguely, and without waiting for an answer she went on to say how glad she was that never again would she be forced to take long sea voyages.

Mrs. Minnis regretted her hasty words, for it was clear that Mrs Dunstan had not recognized her. At the same time she felt piqued; it was slightly mortifying not to be recognized. Her feelings were too much for her, and she burst into a loud, nervous giggle.

"I got stuck in the railings," she announced abruptly.

As Julia said afterwards, that broke the ice; one cannot remain on formal terms with a woman who positively glories in getting stuck in other people's railings. Now that she had confessed it, Mrs Minnis overcame her initial nervousness and settled down to establishing herself as a tomboy character, a gay and friendly person who, despite an old-fashioned up-bringing, had never been a slave to convention.

"I'm afraid I shock people dreadfully," she confided. "I shocked Mrs. Prentice, that day—though really it was just as much her fault as mine."

Julia and Dora had heard of Mrs. Prentice from Miss Pope, who described her as such a nice woman and greatly respected in the village. They had wondered why this excellent creature had not been to call on them. Now, realizing that Mrs. Prentice must have been the stout, flustered lady who detached Mrs. Minnis from the railings, they understood her aloofness.

"Of course Mrs. Prentice is terribly conventional," Mrs. Minnis went on. "But people in the north *are*, don't you think? They're all so—so stodgy and reserved."

Julia was interested in this theory, but Dora said what about Lady Finch? Mrs. Minnis replied that Lady Finch didn't count, because she was mad. She then proceeded to give them a sketch of local society, with brief accounts of Mr. and Mrs. Wilmot, Miss Daglish and her old brother, and that other brother and sister, the Popes, at the vicarage. Of course they were all nice people, but somehow—what was the word?—stodgy. Perhaps it was because they were mostly middle-aged or elderly. Really there were no young people in Goatstock, no one for Sonny, she meant her son Charlton, to talk to at week-ends, except Marian Prentice and Harriet Finch; and anyhow Marian was seldom available because she was engaged to a missionary and training to be a nurse, and Harriet wasn't Sonny's type.

Battered by this flood of information, Julia clung to a name she remembered and could identify. Mrs. Wilmot had called on her two days ago, and stood out in her memory as having beady eyes and a knowledge of etiquette. And in addition, hadn't she claimed to possess a husband and a son?

"The Wilmots," she hazarded. "I believe Mrs. Wilmot told me she had a son . . . but perhaps he's not living at home?"

"Oh—poor James. Yes, he does live at home. But of course he doesn't count," Mrs. Minnis said. For a moment Julia and Dora took this to mean that poor James, like Lady Finch, was mad; but Mrs. Minnis went on to say that Mrs. Wilmot was ridiculously, absurdly possessive and ruled her son with a rod of iron, never allowing him to entertain his friends—not that he had any—or to join in local activities. He couldn't call his soul his own.

"Why does he put up with it?" Dora asked.

"He has to. They have plenty of money, but she has the managing of it. He works in his father's business and I believe he doesn't get a penny for it except what she gives him. It's odd, but he's devoted to her. Of course, he's got a very docile nature."

She pronounced it dossle, but they knew what she meant. Julia's kind heart went out to poor James, who at once became a candidate for a fuller life.

"He'll never get married," Mrs. Minnis said. "She's so possessive that she'll never let him. Now I just couldn't behave like that to Charlton, but then we're not like mother and son. We're just good pals."

"How wise of you."

"And, of course, I speak frankly to him. I tell him right out that I expect him to get married one day. I think men being bachelors is a great mistake."

The latter sentence was addressed to her present listeners rather than to the absent Charlton, but before they could reply Mrs. Minnis hastened to qualify it. She didn't disapprove of all bachelors, only the affluent, idle ones who got set in their ways and fussed over their health.

"Worse than . . ." She was going to say worse than spinsters, but in the nick of time she remembered that Miss Duckworth was a spinster. "Worse than real invalids," she extemporized. "Because there's nothing the matter with them."

"Don't you feel sorry for them?" Julia asked. Mrs. Minnis shook her head vigorously, tilting the pink hat from its perch. Unlike Julia she did not cultivate sympathy.

"I don't feel sorry for—well, look at Francis Heswald!" she exclaimed. "Why should one be sorry for a man like that?"

Owing to some curious failure in the local intelligence, or more probably to a failure on her part to listen to what other people were saying, Mrs. Minnis had not grasped that Mrs. Dunstan and Miss Duckworth were first cousins to Mr. Heswald. She did not take much interest in relationships and family pedigrees, and although she knew vaguely that they were connections of old General Heswald, the late owner of Belmont House, it had somehow never occurred to her that they might also be related to the Heswalds of Heswald Hall.

There was a short pause. Julia and Dora exchanged glances; it was perhaps their duty to enlighten her, but they longed to know more. Mistaking their silence for ignorance, Mrs. Minnis proceeded to tell them who Francis Heswald was, and what he was like.

He thought of nothing but his own comfort, gave himself airs, and was dreadfully snobbish. Although he lived so near Goatstock (and Heswald itself was nothing but a few cottages), he simply ignored the Goatstock residents. He had once left her, Mrs. Minnis, standing by the roadside in a shower of rain, when he might easily have stopped and offered her a lift. And another time, when she and Hugo and Sonny had been picnicking at the Roman Camp beyond Heswald Hall, he had popped up from nowhere and been abominably rude to them, telling them that they had no business to light a fire there and it might do a lot of damage, and even spread to the heather.

"As if we were trippers!" Mrs. Minnis exclaimed. "And, anyway, our fire was perfectly safe—it was on a bit of pavement where they'd been digging for Roman remains."

After this outburst Julia and Dora did not dare to claim Francis as their cousin. Presently Mrs. Minnis decided that her call had lasted long enough, and departed with many promises of seeing them again soon.

"You must come to tea," she said. "Or perhaps a little evening party. I'm afraid I'm awfully scatty—I never plan things in advance. It seems so much more fun when it's all on the spur of the moment!"

"And if it's a spur-of-the-moment invitation we can always plead a prior engagement," Julia said to Dora, when they had got rid of Mrs. Minnis and were sitting down to their own tea.

"Not so easy in a village. Everyone knows whether you are at home or not."

"Well, we could be truthfully not at home. We could drive over to see Francis."

"Poor Francis! How disagreeable she made him sound."

"It was pique," Julia declared. "I understood her so well. He ignored her, and she resented it. One can tell from her appearance that she wants to be noticed. No one who didn't crave to be noticed would dress like that."

But this was lost on Dora, who never thought of clothes as a guide to character. For her, clothes were divided into two categories, 'smart', and 'comfortable', and she prided herself that her own were comfortable.

"Of course, he ought to have stopped and given her a lift," she said. "I quite sympathized with her about that."

"I expect he never saw her. Probably he was driving along in a brown study, thinking about his book," argued Julia. Her own sympathies were wholly with Francis (or any man) as opposed to tiresome women like Mrs. Minnis.

Dora remarked that people who drove cars in a brown study were a danger to themselves and others. At this point, perhaps fortunately, they were joined by Robert, who had been out for a walk and was now ravenous for tea. While Julia plied him with scones and jam and Nanny's little feather-cakes Dora told him about the recent caller. They both knew he went for walks in the afternoons in order to escape callers, but they put this down to his being shy.

"And she has a son," said Dora. "About your age, I gathered. He's working and lives in lodgings, but he comes home for weekends. You must get to know him."

Robert said nothing.

"He's called Charlton."

"Or else Sonny," said Julia. "I suppose he was Sonny in childhood, and she kept on forgetting and alluding to him as Sonny still."

"Poor mutt," said Robert. "But I believe he's a bit of a joke, anyway. Could I have another cup of tea, Julia?"

By her own wish Julia had relinquished the title of aunt; she said it was ageing, and in any case she was Robert's aunt only by marriage. But sometimes, as now, she wished Robert would not be so casual and off-hand; he ought to remember that she was in a sense his aunt, and that she was housing him and had paid for quite a lot of his education. Obviously, if he knew something about the Minnis family he must have made acquaintances in the village, and he should have mentioned it. She and Dora had supposed, all this time, that he was just taking Taffy for walks.

"Who told you about Charlton Minnis?" she asked.

"Harriet," said Robert. Seeing that his hearers looked blank, he added, "Harriet Finch."

"That funny little thing," Dora said tolerantly, remembering Harriet Finch as the girl in the silly hat. Robert scowled, and Julia perceived that Dora was being tactless. Though she could not imagine what he saw in Harriet she leaned forward and asked sympathetically if he had met her out on a walk.

"Yes," said Robert. Under the pressure of further sympathetic questions he said he had been to Urn Cottage, where the Finches lived. Yes, Harriet had asked him to go. Yes, it was quite a small house. Yes, Harriet lived there alone with her aunt. Yes, like him she was an orphan.

Julia had already returned Lady Finch's call, but the Finches had been out and she had seen no more than the exterior of Urn Cottage. It had not impressed her.

"Mrs. Minnis said Lady Finch was mad," Dora said.

To this Robert answered nothing at all. He did not care for Lady Finch, but he did not feel inclined to agree with Dora; usually they got on pretty well, but he could not immediately forgive her for speaking of Harriet as a funny little thing.

He had forgotten his own first impression of Harriet, for by this time they had had several meetings, and the more he saw of her the more he liked her. He remained sulkily silent, and presently, his own hunger satisfied, went off to give Taffy his dinner.

"What an odd boy Robert is," Dora exclaimed, as soon as he had left them.

Julia sighed. At another time she might have defended Robert but it had been an exhausting afternoon and she was tired.

"I'm afraid he *was* rather surly, but he's at a difficult age," she said. It was the best she could manage; and in her heart she felt that he did not deserve even this extenuation.

"Anyway, it's a good thing he has begun to make friends," Dora said cheerfully. She stood up and shook herself, as she always did when she had been sitting still for an unusually long time, and announced that she was going out to do a bit more gardening before supper. It was a shame, she remarked, to waste a perfectly good evening like this lounging indoors.

Left alone, Julia dallied for a while with an old dream of retiring to some warm desert island or to a single-roomed stone cottage in the middle of a great forest. She fondly believed that she had the hermit's temperament and could live without human companionship, drawing spiritual nourishment from the beauties of nature. At times like these—times when the smooth surface of her present life was ruffled by threatening breezes—the thought of this solitary life was very tempting.

But it could not be. She could not leave her world, because she was needed. She felt herself responsible for other people—for Robert, who was an orphan and dangerously good-looking and who had yet to be launched on a career; for Nanny, who was old and depended on her; for poor Dora, who had had such a hard time and who must be gently weaned from her bad habits of snorting and banging doors, because otherwise she would never be really popular. And these were not all; there was also Francis Heswald, who was simply wasting his life.

Julia had not liked Mrs. Minnis and had not believed all she said, but she could not help feeling that there was some truth in the things she said about Francis Heswald. Although, as his cousin and well-wisher, she would defend him in public, she privately agreed with Mrs. Minnis that he ought to take more part in local affairs and local society. That she should dream of a hermit's life for herself and deplore it for Francis did not seem to her illogical; after all, she had not gone to her island, because the world needed her. It needed Francis, too, and he had now become another of her responsibilities.

The desert island, the forest-shrouded dwelling, had played their parts. Julia was ennobled by the vision of her simple unworldly life in these solitudes, and she could not fail to perceive that there was also a certain merit in abjuring her own wishes for the sake of others. The two sensations combined pleasurably; she decided—with a swift return to practical standards—that Belmont House suited her.

'After all,' she thought, going upstairs to relax in the pink bathroom and try the new bath-salts she had bought that morning—'after all, it's where I was meant to live. Uncle James realized that, though I didn't. It's my native heath.'

CHAPTER VII

"Come in," said Miss Pope. "No, not in the church-room, Millicent. We're having the meeting in the dining-room today, because it isn't really a church matter. Alaric thinks it makes a clearer distinction in people's minds if we have secular meetings in the dining-room."

Mrs. Prentice turned away from the church-room—a large room built on at one side of the vicarage and linked to it, rather oddly, by a greenhouse-passage in the Gothic style—and crossed the hall to the dining-room. Miss Pope was already greeting another arrival, and Mrs. Prentice had lost the opportunity of asking whether Mrs. Dunstan and Miss Duckworth were to be at the meeting. She had meant to ask it straightaway; but then, if they were coming, how could she find an excuse for going home again? Her life, hitherto so simple and easy, was now complicated by her fear of meeting the newcomers on whom she had not called, and by the impossibility of explaining her reasons for not calling on them.

She peeped round the half-open door. The dining-room was empty except for Mr. Daglish and his sister, who were sitting side by side in a corner of the room. They appeared to be asleep. The room faced north-east and even on this hot summer afternoon retained the characteristic atmosphere of all the vicarage rooms, dampish, sanctified, and smelling faintly of cabbage.

'But it can't be cabbage at this time of year,' Mrs. Prentice thought. She remembered that the vicarage was supposed to be haunted by an Evangelical ghost, the shade of an early incumbent who had practised plain living and high thinking, and she wondered if the cabbage smell also had a supernatural origin. Perhaps he had lived on cabbages. Pondering this problem, she trod on a loose, creaking board, and woke the Daglishes from their nap.

They woke with dignity, and greeted her as if no snores had passed their lips.

"We chose this corner for the view," said Miss Daglish. "Come and sit here, you can see the hill."

Doing as she was bid, Mrs. Prentice looked sideways through the narrow arched window; its borders were filled with stained glass, but through the central section she could see Goatstock Hill against a clear blue sky.

"Very nice," she said.

Miss Daglish sighed. "It's sad to think it may not be there much longer."

"You mean, the New Town?"

Miss Daglish nodded. That was what the meeting was about: to consider the threat of the New Town, and what action, if any, could be taken by the inhabitants of Goatstock to avert this catastrophe. Mrs. Prentice, whose mind was slow but practical, thought that Miss Daglish was over-stating her case; for even if the New Town was *here*, surely Goatstock Hill would still be *there*, they could not take it away—or could they? Uncertain what modern planners could achieve, she said cautiously that it would mean great changes.

"Mabilla remembers Goatstock before they built the new road," said Mr. Daglish. "There have been a lot of changes since then. Not all for the best."

He was an elderly man, but younger than his sisters, of whom the last survivor was Mabilla—the Miss Daglish who sat beside him. The family had lived in Goatstock for a long time, and Mr. and Miss Daglish were therefore entitled to take an interest in its future, but Mrs. Prentice could not help feeling they were rather too obsessed by the past. She thought this because she knew that they looked on all the newer houses (of which her own was one) as horrible excrescences which ought never to have been built.

The room was filling up. Lady Finch was there, with Harriet, and Mr. and Mrs. Minnis, and Mrs. Wilmot with poor James sitting meekly beside her. Two late-comers hurried in, shepherded by a short, squat figure who announced that Miss Pope was just fetching Mr. Pope and would be with them in one moment, and would they please draw up and sit round the table. This squat figure was Miss Brigg, Miss Pope's useful friend. She lived by herself in lodgings over the baker's shop, but seemed to spend all her waking hours at the vicarage, or working for good causes sponsored by the church.

Mrs. Prentice felt happier; for the meeting was about to start, and Mrs. Dunstan and Miss Duckworth were not there. She moved her chair towards the table, and contrived to separate herself from the Daglishes and to find a place next to the vacant chair at the end, which would be occupied by Miss Pope. A moment later the vicar and his sister entered the room, and when everyone had wished Mr. Pope good afternoon, and all had been assured of his pleasure at seeing them there, they got down to business.

It was all quite informal, Miss Pope explained. Just a small private gathering, so that they could find out one another's views and perhaps make a few plans of their own. After all, town-planners were not the only people who could make plans.

Several people laughed at this little joke, and Miss Pope paused to allow the laughter to die down. This was a mistake, for Mr. Minnis took advantage of the pause to begin a speech of his own. Mr. Minnis was a long-winded speaker, a man whom it was difficult to stop. In a great many words he asked if the meeting was really necessary, and if it was quite certain that Goatstock, that charming rural spot which they all had good reasons to love (and he listed the reasons in detail), was to become a New Town?

"Oh yes, I assure you it's all settled," Miss Pope said hurriedly. "Of course nothing has been announced yet—no public announcement, I mean. But Alaric heard it from the Bishop's chaplain at least a month ago when he was lunching at the Palace. It was—when was it, Alaric?—yes, it was the week after Easter."

Mr. Pope coughed uneasily. When he told his sister of the Bishop's chaplain's news he had not foreseen that she would spread the information all over Goatstock and publicly proclaim its origin at his own table. Still, it was true; though the chaplain had not said, in so many words, that it was all settled. He had said there was a strong probability of its happening.

"A strong probability," Mr. Pope said aloud—but softly. He meant these words to be a qualification of his sister's bold statement, but those who heard him supposed that he was upholding her, perhaps because it was usual for Mr. Pope to agree with his sister. A murmur of dismay, and disapproval, went up from the meeting; hitherto no one had quite believed in the New Town, but if the news came from a source so trustworthy as a Bishop's chaplain it was obviously a thing to be taken seriously.

"My sister lived in a New Town in the south," said Mrs. Wilmot. "But she had to move. She couldn't put up with it."

"But we can't all move. Where should we go?" Mrs. Minnis cried despairingly.

Harriet suggested that they should found a New Village and emigrate to it *en masse*. "Like the Pilgrim Fathers when they were persecuted."

"That's what all those men with poles were up to," said Miss Brigg, referring, not to the Pilgrim Fathers, but to the surveyors and their henchmen who had been observed, more than a year ago, wandering about the neighbourhood. "I knew they weren't up to no good."

"If they build new streets it will seriously interfere with our gardens," said Lady Finch. "And gardens, properly cultivated, mean health. It's a retrograde step."

"Why should it interfere with the gardens?"

"Naturally, in a town, there must be streets. And they can't build streets through our *houses*, so they will have to run them through the gardens."

"Perhaps they'll pull the houses down."

Cries of protest, cries of wrath, rent the air. Miss Daglish said she would never give permission; if their house stood in the way of a street the street would have to encircle it, that was all. Mrs. Minnis said brightly there was a church in London like that, the Strand went round it on either side. Harriet said the New Town would look very funny.

Mrs. Wilmot, who through her sister's experience could count herself an authority on New Towns, began to explain what town-planning meant. It wasn't a case of giving one's permission—they simply took what land they wanted, even when it was a brand-new orchard with a wall round it and valuable fruit trees inside, such as had belonged to her sister. She made it clear that the Daglish residence—which was well known to be in an advanced state of decay—would not stand a chance. It would be razed to the ground.

The meeting became rowdy. Everyone was talking at once, except Mrs. Prentice who was listening to Mr. Minnis telling her a long and improbable anecdote about storks. That they nested on houses she already knew, but she did not know how they had appeared on the hypothetical rooftops of New Goatstock. "Very remarkable instance of sagacity," said Mr. Minnis. "If I hadn't seen it for myself I shouldn't have believed it." Not having seen it for herself, Mrs. Prentice felt under no obligation to believe it, but charity forbade her to say so.

"But all this is beside the point," Miss Pope cried loudly, rapping on the table to gain attention. "We are not here to discuss what we shall do if the New Town comes. We are here to prevent its coming!"

These were brave words, but they did not produce a brave response. "How can we stop it?" Lady Finch asked crossly. Mr. Minnis suggested that in due course, when the plans had been publicly announced, there would be an opportunity to raise objections.

Miss Pope retorted that it would then be too late. Once things had been publicly announced, she said, the Government was simply determined to carry them through, and objections would not get a fair hearing.

Unfortunately, Mr. Minnis's suggestion was received with murmurs of approval, especially from those who felt that the meeting had lasted long enough. Everyone liked Miss Pope, but everyone knew that she was an enthusiast and that she would keep them sitting round the table for hours, arguing about plans, unless some reasonable way of escape could be found. The procrastinating phrase, 'in due course', offered such an escape; and it was eagerly applauded.

Mrs. Wilmot looked at her watch and said she must be going. Other people followed her example. The danger that threatened Goatstock was a serious matter, and required careful consideration, said Mr. Minnis, but they would do better to meet again, when they had had time to think things over. Probably they could get up a petition; but that, of course, would need a lot of organization.

The Daglishes, breathing tremulous defiance, left with the Wilmots. The others soon followed, until only Mrs. Prentice and the ever-faithful Miss Brigg remained as audience to Miss Pope. Miss Pope still had plenty to say, but the interruptions of leave-taking rather interfered with her eloquence.

"So disheartening!" she exclaimed, as the door closed behind the Finches. "I had counted on getting some really constructive support—but you see how it is. People simply aren't prepared to co-operate!"

"Lady Finch was right, I reckon. There's nowt to be done," said Miss Brigg.

"But there *must* be something," cried Miss Pope. "The trouble with Goatstock is that there is no one to give a lead. I don't count. I haven't the—the right personality."

It was only on rare occasions, when things had gone wrong, that Miss Pope lost confidence in herself. Mrs. Prentice and Miss Brigg hastened to assure her that she had an excellent personality and that they didn't know what the village would do without her. But Miss Pope refused to be comforted.

"I ought to have asked Mrs. Dunstan," she said. "But then she's only just come—and it seemed a pity to tell her about the New Town when she's so looking forward to living in a village."

Mrs. Prentice, for reasons of her own, approved of this considerate attitude, but Miss Brigg pointed out that Mrs. Dunstan and Miss Duckworth would have to know sooner or later the fate that awaited them.

"Perhaps, if I had asked them today, it would have made a difference," said Miss Pope. "I do feel that Mrs. Dunstan is just the sort of person we want in Goatstock. Someone who can give us a lead."

At this prospect she looked happier. Her enthusiasm was not confined to 'causes', it extended also to people, and when she thought of Julia Dunstan, so prosperous, so sure of herself, so delighted with Belmont House and its surroundings, it seemed to her that the village had gained what it had long needed—a leader who would command respect and get things done.

"All geese aren't swans," Miss Brigg said belligerently. "I liked Miss Duckworth all right, but t'other one, I wasn't too sure of her. A bit too honey-mouthed for my liking."

Miss Brigg believed in saying exactly what she thought. Her homely face shone with soap and virtue, and she was a pillar of the church, more useful than many such ornaments in that she would turn her hand to anything. But of course, thought Miss Pope, she was difficult; she was touchy, rather given to fault-finding, and terribly suspicious of new people. There was no need to feel discouraged merely because Mary Ellen Brigg disapproved of Mrs. Dunstan; at the same time, one must not allow her to think that one shared in her disapproval.

"Oh no," she said hurriedly. "I'm sure that's not true. Mrs. Dunstan has a very charming manner and I'm sure she has a charming nature, too. Pleasant manners aren't necessarily insincere."

"Happen you're right," said Miss Brigg. "Or happen you're not. All I say is, she's glib. And I didn't fancy her hat—if you could call it a hat."

Saying exactly what she thought always put Miss Brigg in a good humour, whatever it did to her listeners, and now she announced that she would get the tea and they were just to sit back and rest their feet. She marched out of the room. Miss Pope turned to Mrs. Prentice, who had been asked to stay for tea after the meeting was over, and began to speak of something else. But as soon as she was sure that Miss Brigg was safely occupied in the kitchen she confided that her useful friend was really something of a trial.

"She means so well, and you mustn't think I don't appreciate all she does. She's a wonderful woman. But sometimes it seems as if it is more her house than mine."

"Yes, I was rather surprised when she said she'd get the tea."

"That's exactly it. And coming in, the day I had Mrs. Dunstan and Miss Duckworth here, and the Daglishes and Mrs. Wilmot, and just staying—to help, she said. It's true she has a lot of meals with us, and I suppose she has got into the habit of dropping in."

Mrs. Prentice uttered sounds of sympathy. She did indeed feel sorry for Miss Pope, whose tea party, so carefully planned to introduce the newcomers to Goatstock's worthiest residents, had been spoilt by the intrusion of Mary Ellen Brigg; but she could not help reflecting that her friend had brought it on herself. All geese *were* swans to Miss Pope, at any rate when she first met them; and none had been more swan-like than Mary Ellen.

When the Popes had first come to Goatstock, seven years ago, Mary Ellen had been a loyal but humble church-worker, a background figure who would never have dreamed of dropping in at the vicarage uninvited and staying to tea—let alone of ordering the late vicar's wife to sit back and rest her feet. It was Miss Pope who had made a fuss of her and raised her to the position of family friend. But of course one could not say so.

"That's when she saw the hat, I suppose," Mrs. Prentice said instead.

"What hat?"

"The hat she didn't fancy. If you could call it a hat." Some part of Mrs. Prentice's mind had been occupied with the hat ever since Miss Brigg had mentioned it.

"Oh . . . oh, the *hat*!" said Miss Pope, wrenching her thoughts away from the butter ration (how reckless Mary Ellen was with butter!) and the even graver problem of Alaric's peril. She had not dared to breathe a word about that, even to Millicent Prentice, but she had lately begun to fear that Mary Ellen's frequent visits had a purpose quite other than mere friendship.

"What was it like?" asked Mrs. Prentice.

"Mrs. Dunstan's hat, you mean? Well, it was only half a hat, really—"

"Half a hat?" Mrs. Prentice echoed in surprise.

"Just a bit of ribbon across the head—like this," said Miss Pope, gesticulating. "And a little bunch of feathers, well, not exactly a bunch, a—an arrangement of feathers at each side."

"How did it stay on?"

"I don't know. But it looked very nice."

"I can never understand how people keep these flimsy little things on their heads," said Mrs. Prentice. "I'm sure I should feel quite miserable if I didn't have a hat that came well down."

She expected that Miss Pope would agree with her. Miss Pope's hats, like her own, were solidly constructed, with a good deep crown and a proper brim. But Miss Pope was not attending; her eyes were fixed on the half-open door and she seemed to be listening to what was going on outside.

"The kettle must have boiled by now," she said fretfully.

"Oh, she'll be here any minute," Mrs. Prentice answered. "I heard her crossing the hall just now. I expect she's gone to tell your brother it's ready."

"Yes," said Miss Pope. She hesitated. "Millicent," she began.

But the confidence remained unspoken. At that moment there were more footsteps, the sound of Miss Brigg's loud laugh, and then Alaric Pope appeared in the doorway, followed shortly afterwards by Miss Brigg with the tea tray. Tea at the vicarage was not a drawing-room meal, except when Miss Pope gave formal tea parties; at other times both she and Alaric preferred the comfort of a firm table on which they could prop their elbows and their books.

Mrs. Prentice knew this. She was not surprised that they should sit round the table for their meal, but she was surprised by the abundance of the meal itself. Miss Brigg had done wonders in the time; there was a plate of hot scones, a plate heaped with bread-and-butter, a plate of chocolate biscuits and another of macaroons. There was also a sad-looking cake, with a piece cut out of it, which was what Mrs. Prentice had been expecting; for whenever she stayed to tea at the vicarage this cake, or one exactly like it, appeared on the table, flanked by a few plain biscuits or sometimes by four pieces of bread-and-butter—one each for herself and Miss Pope, two for Alaric. But today Alaric was provided with a boiled egg, and in addition to jam there was a freshly opened jar of meat paste. Good manners restrained Mrs. Prentice from commenting on this unusual quantity of food. She noticed that it seemed to come as a surprise to the Popes themselves.

"Is this egg for me?" Mr. Pope asked modestly. It was a pointless question, for the egg had been placed in front of him and could hardly have been intended for anyone else.

"That's right," said Miss Brigg. "I knew it was church council tonight, so I reckoned you'd better make a good tea, for you're sure to be late back by the time they've all done talking."

"An undeserved benefaction. But not unwelcome." Picking up his spoon, Mr. Pope devoured his egg wolfishly, and went on to make a hearty meal. "These biscuits are delicious," he observed. "Much better than our usual fare."

"They were left over from the tea party," Miss Pope said, rather coldly. "I put them away in a tin, and I'm afraid I forgot about them. But Mary Ellen knows her way about the kitchen better than I do."

"True, true. And how she spoils us."

Even Mrs. Prentice, whose mind worked slowly, perceived that there was a fallacy hidden in this remark. But Miss Brigg, her plain face wreathed in smiles, received it as no more than her due.

"I know what men like," she said.

CHAPTER VIII

JULIA WAS SITTING in front of her dressing-table, holding a hat in her hand—or, according to the village opinion, half a hat—and wondering if she should wear that one or her little white straw.

"Or perhaps *no* hat," she said, looking at herself and thinking that the Reddrod hairdresser wasn't so bad after all. She and Dora were driving over to Heswald to have tea with Francis that afternoon, and Dora had just come into her bedroom to tell her it was time they were starting.

"Tie a scarf round your head," Dora suggested. "What does it matter—we're not going to a garden party!"

It mattered a great deal, but Julia did not say so. Dora was a very nice person, but she had her limitations; she would not have understood that before encouraging Francis Heswald to lead a fuller life it was necessary to gain his interest, and even if this had been explained to her she was quite capable of arguing that a sensible man like Francis would not be interested in clothes.

Julia knew better. Deciding in favour of the white straw, she settled it carefully on her head. In the looking-glass she could see Dora's reflection—Dora with her calm good-humoured face, her grey hair brushed vigorously night and morning but otherwise left to nature, and her striped silk summer frock hanging loosely from her shoulders. Dora hated clothes to be too tight; and this frock was the very reverse of tight.

"I gave up all that business years ago," Dora said tolerantly, watching her cousin apply her lipstick. "I don't even possess such a thing."

Julia, a prey to generosity even when she was concentrating on her own appearance, offered to lend Dora the lipstick so that she could see what a difference it made. But Dora laughed and said she couldn't be bothered.

"At our age it seems rather a waste of time," she added. "Come on, Julia—we've wasted enough time as it is."

As they walked downstairs Julia could not help feeling it was in some ways a disadvantage to live with a cousin who scorned all aids to beauty, and who was also one's exact contemporary. If Dora would only take a little trouble she would be quite handsome; but as it was she looked far older than her years. That made it all the more galling that she should say 'at our age', because it was definitely misleading. But unfortunately there seemed no way of stopping her.

It was the first time they had visited Heswald. Francis had been twice to Belmont House, but had been unable to entertain them in his own house because his staff—Mrs. Sable and her husband—were busy with the spring-cleaning. He seemed to think this was a perfectly good reason for postponing an afternoon visit; which just proved—as Julia said later—that he must be completely under his staff's thumb.

"Or thumbs," said Dora. But Julia shook her head. With a married couple it was always one particular thumb, and in this case it was undoubtedly Mrs. Sable who ruled the establishment. A man would not have taken spring-cleaning so seriously.

The drive to Heswald charmed them both. They recognized forgotten landmarks and reminded each other of trivial incidents of the past. They stopped the car twice to gaze at views which old General Heswald had specially favoured—though now that he was no longer there to point out their beauties these views seemed strangely uninteresting. At last they came to a steep hill, and as the car topped it they saw the distant moors, and in the foreground the village of Heswald, looking much as it had looked twenty years ago.

"Except that it looks smaller, somehow," Julia said. "And rather bleak and remote. I used to think Heswald was a pretty place."

As they approached the village, however, her imagination got to work on it, and by the time they arrived she had decided that it was a village of great character, having a sort of sturdy independence which was exactly suited to its remote situation and to the stone-walled, rainswept fields that surrounded it. Not that they were rainswept at that moment—it was, in fact, a perfect June day—but wind and rain were needed to complete the picture.

The bailiff's house was just beyond the wrought-iron gates which led to Heswald Hall. It was a small house, standing close to the road behind a low stone wall, and rather overshadowed by trees at the back and sides, which had been planted to hide it from the eyes of the Heswalds when they gazed out across the park. It had not mattered to the Heswalds of those days that their bailiff's house should be dark and damp; and apparently it had not occurred to the present Heswald to cut the trees down.

"It's the first thing I should do," Julia whispered to Dora as they walked up to the door.

"What?"

"Open it all up—let in some light and air. It's not a bad little house, if it wasn't so dripped on."

Dora pointed out that the house wasn't being dripped on just then. But Julia was still seeing the landscape in its winter mood of stormy splendour, though she was now resolved that winter should not endure. The sunlight that was to transform the house was a symbol of the brighter life that awaited its owner, when he had been persuaded to play his proper part in the world.

Francis Heswald opened the door to them, and since Dora at once engaged him in talk Julia had time to look about her. The house smelt of soap and furniture polish, proving that the spring-cleaning had been no myth, but it was rather dreary. The passage in which they found themselves was lined with book-shelves, and the dining-room, glimpsed through an open door, was furnished with a massive table and chairs which must have come from Heswald Hall, and papered with a hideous brown wallpaper which turned it into a cave of melancholy. It must be very bad for Francis's digestion, Julia thought, to eat his meals in a room like that.

But the room to which he led them was not so bad. It was at the back of the house, with a french window looking out on to a small lawn. He explained that it had been the bailiff's office, and that he had enlarged it to make himself a library where he could work undisturbed.

"It's charming," Julia said enthusiastically. "And what a lot of books! I'm dreadfully ignorant, but I mean to do a great deal of reading, once I've settled in. I shall know where to come for books!"

"I'm afraid you may not find much to interest you here," Francis replied. He did not like lending books, and the suspicion crossed his mind that Julia had only that moment decided to do a great deal of reading. But this unworthy thought was quick-ly forgotten; he had been looking forward to his cousins' visit, and now that they were here he found it even more agreeable than he had expected. Since they were his cousins, they could ask questions about the past, and he could talk about Heswald's palmy days without the fear that he might be thought conceited.

Francis, of course, was as well aware as Julia that there had been distinguished Heswalds in the past. He had no wish to emulate them; in a sense he felt that, simply by being their de-scendant, he had a share in their prestige. He liked to talk about them, but since good breeding did not permit him to talk about them to outsiders it was a pleasure he could seldom enjoy. With his cousins, however, it could be enjoyed to the full; for the fine achievements of the Heswald family were their heritage as well as his own.

He was quite surprised to find that it was time for tea. Julia and Dora, on the other hand, had been wondering when tea was going to appear. They had been invited for four o'clock, and they could not guess that Francis had absent-mindedly said half past four to Mrs. Sable and that Mrs. Sable, to mark her distrust of cousins turning up from goodness-knew-where, had decided to keep them waiting for it.

"Tea . . ." said Francis, when Mrs. Sable finally came to announce it. "Oh yes. I said we'd have tea in the garden."

They stepped out through the french window. The garden was very small, no more than a narrow strip of lawn between the house and its enclosing trees, with a flower bed running under the wall of the house, and another one between the lawn and the rough ground where the trees grew. The latter could hardly be termed a flower bed, since it contained only weeds and a few anonymous and sulky-looking plants which appeared incapable of blossoming.

The keen gardener Dora saw at once that this was because the bed was so much under the shade of the trees. The plants got no sun. She remembered what Julia had said when they first saw the house, and decided that there was some truth in it, and that, as Francis was clearly no gardener, it might be kind to tell him what was wrong.

"Julia and I both thought the house looked awfully dark when we arrived," she began briskly. "Because of those trees so close behind it and round the sides. Julia said the first thing she would do would be to cut them all down."

This was awkward for Julia, who a moment ago had been agreeing with her cousin Francis that his house was beautifully sheltered and private.

"Oh no, Dora, not all of them!" she said quickly. "Just one or two—to let in a little more sunlight. I thought, from the front, that they were closer," she explained to Francis. "I didn't realize you had this little garden at the back."

"You said the house looked dripped on," said Dora, to whom tact was practically an unknown quality.

Dripped on, thought Francis . . . she said the house looked dripped on. The dank, unpleasing associations of this phrase filled him with indignation.

Julia could not explain that she had been visualizing the house in a symbolically desolate landscape, but she protested that she hadn't meant quite what she said. She had only meant that perhaps in winter it might be melancholy for poor Francis to listen to the wind sighing through the trees and to the rain— well, yes—dripping from their branches.

"But only in winter," she said pleadingly. "In summer it's perfectly sweet. It couldn't be nicer."

But here Dora disagreed with her. It would make all the difference to the garden if some of the trees were cut down, because then Francis could have a herbaceous border in that long bed where nothing grew at present.

"We had better have tea," Francis said, shepherding his cousins towards the table and chairs which had been set out (rather unfortunately, he now felt) in the shade of his largest tree.

The chairs were comfortable wicker ones, and the table was covered with a white cloth edged with torchon lace. There was a silver teapot, the cakes were home-made and looked appetizing, and the cups and plates were blue and gold Crown Derby china. Though Francis lived the simple life it was obvious that he did not live in squalor.

"How delightful this is!" Julia exclaimed. "Tea in the garden seems so English, and yet we so rarely get a day that's absolutely right for it."

"And somehow in one's own home one never takes the trouble."

"Oh, but *I* shall, now that I've got a house—and a garden. I can't tell you how much I'm looking forward to living in Goatstock and being anchored and secure. Of course," Julia added pathetically, "I've never really had a home of my own until now."

Francis, busy with the tea cups (for he had decided to do the pouring-out himself, in case either of his cousins should feel slighted by the other's being given the place of honour), did not immediately answer this remark. Dora was making overtures to a white cat which had come round the corner of the house and was stretching itself upon the lawn. Julia, clothed for a moment in sad silence, sat wistfully smiling at her own thoughts.

"The houses you occupied when you were abroad," said Francis, courteously handing her a tea cup, "were they not homes?"

This question, faintly critical in its implications, was not the response she had expected from him.

"Puss, puss!" said Dora.

"Well, naturally they were homes, in a way," Julia admitted. "But it was all quite different. Oh, I know I'm explaining myself very badly; but it's—well, it's a feeling I have about Belmont House."

"Puss, puss! Come here, Pussy."

"The cat's name is Snowball," Francis said. "But it is Mrs. Sable's cat and it won't come here. It is extraordinarily unresponsive to suggestion."

"Of course, it's silly, but I feel that I was *meant* to live at Belmont House."

Julia did indeed feel this, and it was by no means the first time she had mentioned it. She spoke with genuine fervour, thinking of Uncle James and the mystic bond between them, and seeing herself as a storm-tossed wanderer who had at last found peace. Her eyes shone with faith and awe.

But Francis, like the cat, seemed extraordinarily unresponsive to suggestion. He did not ask sympathetic questions, he showed no wish to hear more about her mystic intuitions. He said, rather dryly, that it must be agreeable to inherit a house that suited one, and begged her to try a cucumber sandwich.

Julia ate the sandwich out of courtesy. Cucumber was one of the things she was supposed not to eat, but she could not hurt Francis's feelings by refusing it. Her kind heart also compelled her to nibble at a piece of rich plum-cake and to echo Dora's praise of its excellence. They talked about gardening, about the country round Heswald and the state of the roads. It was a conversation between mere acquaintances.

By the time tea was eaten Francis's indignation had lessened. Listening to his cousin Julia's flutter of explanations, observing how charming she looked when slightly agitated and abashed, he found it easy to forgive her for criticizing his house. But at the same time he was seeing her in a new light. She was charming, certainly, and still inspired the cousinly affection he had felt towards her from the first, but the new light showed a great deal which he had not seen at their earlier meetings.

In spite of living a quiet life and meeting few people, he prided himself on being a good judge of character, and it had been a shock to find himself wrong about Julia. Now he rallied; for, after all, he had not been deceived—or only for a short time. He forgot that it was Dora who made him suspect Julia's sincerity, and he remembered instead that right at the beginning of the afternoon, when she had professed a love of reading, he had had his suspicions. His judgement had not been at fault.

Julia was glad that Francis had recovered his good humour. Perhaps his silence and formality had been due to shyness, or to anxiety about the tea. He entertained so seldom that a tea party must be quite an ordeal. She congratulated herself on having eaten the cucumber sandwiches and the plum cake; though her digestion might suffer it would suffer in a good cause, and Francis could not but feel that his tea party had been a success.

"Won't you show us the rest of the house?" she asked.

The tour of the house led to more reminiscences, for there were things which had come from Heswald Hall, some of which Julia and Dora dimly remembered; in particular a stuffed golden eagle in a glass case and a portrait of the Cavalier who had been executed. The portrait, a small blackened painting of a rather ugly man, had been to the child Dora an object of romantic veneration, and when they had been over the house she went back for another look at it. Julia and Francis were left alone.

"You've done wonders," Julia said. "It's just the right house for you. It's pleasant and comfortable and civilized."

Francis had a bland smile for these compliments. And dripped on, he thought.

"Of course bachelors always do."

He was startled by the unexpected mockery in a voice which he had just been comparing to the cooing of a dove.

"Do what?" he asked.

"Wonders. Or wonders are done for them. Bachelors can hardly help becoming selfish and lazy, when they get their own way in everything. Life, for a bachelor, is just too easy."

"Nonsense," he retorted, showing more displeasure than he meant to. It was on the tip of his tongue to add that widows too had an easy life—particularly rich widows like Julia—but he restrained himself.

"I was only joking," she said meekly. The meekness alarmed him. Had he sounded irritable or absurdly thin-skinned? He hastened to put this right by admitting that there might be a grain of truth in the joke.

"I dare say I do get my own way, more often than is good for me," he declared. He did not believe this, but he spoke with good-humoured conviction.

"I dare say you do. And of course the worst of ease and comfort is, that you get into a rut."

"No," said Francis. Again he was aware of sounding shrill. "No," he repeated a tone lower. "I am not in a rut."

"Oh, but you are. You're wasting your life."

"What do you mean?"

"You're wasting your talent, your brains—your heritage," Julia said earnestly. "You are a clever man. You ought to be out in the world—playing your part in the world. You ought to lead a fuller life."

A little earlier he would have dismissed the tribute to his brains as blatant flattery. But her candour on the subject of selfish bachelors—a subject which he could not help taking personally—had rather blurred his picture of her as a woman who only wished to please. He smiled; and though he shook his head in protest it was clear that this gesture was dictated by modesty, rather than by disbelief.

"I have no talent for the affairs of men," he said. The smooth, well-chosen words impressed them both, and Julia gazed at him with admiration. It was perhaps a kindly intervention of providence that brought Dora noisily into the room before she could ask him exactly what he meant.

". . . so we saw all over the house," said Dora. "And he's still got the picture—the one I was telling you about. You must come with us and see it, next time we go."

The idea did not appeal to Robert, who was interested neither in history nor in other people's ancestors. But he answered politely that he would love it.

"And you'll love the country up there," she went on, speaking as if Heswald was a hundred miles away. "It's right on the edge of the moors. Quite different from the country round here."

"Round here isn't going to be country much longer," Robert said.

"Julia, did you notice that the stuffed eagle had a claw missing on its right foot? I'm sure it used not to be like that."

Julia said she had only noticed it was very dusty and moulting a bit on its back. "I suppose Mrs. Sable can't get the glass case open to dust it."

"Of course she can't, the case is sealed up."

"I must say the rest of the house was as clean as a new pin."

"Oh, Francis is well looked after," Dora agreed.

Robert glanced from one to the other of his aunts (for Dora, though no relation, held an aunt-like place in his thoughts) with what he believed to be well-concealed scorn. Decapitated ancestors, moulting eagles—of what interest were these, compared with his momentous news? But they hadn't even listened to him.

He coughed. Julia turned towards him and noticed that something was wrong.

"Are you starting a cold?" she asked. "You'd better try a cinnamon lozenge."

"No, no," he said hastily. "But listen, Julia, there's going to be a New Town."

"Is there? Where?"

"Here. Goatstock is to be it, I mean it will be Goatstock, and it will stretch in every direction."

Their reactions, this time, were all that could be wished. They uttered loud cries, beginning with incredulity and passing on to horror and lamentation. Dora pointed out that it would ruin the village.

"But I'll probably be able to get a job," Robert said cheerfully. "I mean, they're bound to want engineers, aren't they? It'll be much better than trekking off to the tropics."

This remark, for all its heartless egotism, had a strangely calming effect on Julia, who suddenly saw the New Town as an asset. It would need more than engineers; it would need guidance, leadership . . . a director or controller to launch it on its civic career. Someone, of course, of good standing, with a name acceptable to the county.

"Yes," she said. "Yes, I suppose there are bound to be some good jobs."

And Francis's erudition, she thought, his familiarity with pipe-rolls and burgesses and charters, would certainly come in useful.

CHAPTER IX

"A CHARITY MEETING for the Aged Animals' Pension Fund," said Lady Finch, reading aloud from the invitation card in her hand. She sniffed; she did not like Mrs. Wilmot, from whom the invitation came, and she took a poor view of any schemes for reform and improvement which might interfere with her own. In a place like Goatstock the potential supporters of such schemes were limited in number, and a new demand on their sympathy— and their purses—might easily have a damaging effect on existing ones.

"I didn't know she was fond of animals," she said bitterly. "I don't think she does much for the R.S.P.C.A."

Harriet was making toast for breakfast. It was a task that needed attention, for the bread they used (made of a special flour from wheat grown without artificial fertilizers, stone ground, and containing all its original elements) produced toast of a brick-like texture if not closely watched and removed at the critical moment.

"Perhaps these are selected animals, personally known to her," she suggested. "Or chosen by vote, like the aged governesses."

"I suppose we shall have to go. Mrs. Wilmot will be so cross if we don't."

Lady Finch was too resolute a character to mind annoying her neighbours, but experience had taught her that one had to support other people's charities if one wanted them to support one's own.

"But I shan't give more than one-and-six," she said.

"What does she mean by 'a charity meeting'? Perhaps there will be side-shows and things to buy."

"Oh no. That's a garden fête. This will be a meeting with someone to tell us all about it, and afterwards they'll hand round a plate. And tea, I suppose."

"I wouldn't count on it."

No one in Goatstock really liked the Wilmots. There was a certain amount of sympathy for poor James, who was so ruled and possessed by his mother; but it was a slightly contemptuous sympathy. Poor James was getting on for forty, and it was felt that a man of forty ought to be able to stand up for himself. As Mrs. Minnis had said, it wasn't as though he was all *that* delicate.

"Anyway, it's not till next month," Harriet went on. "And Marian will be home then for her holiday. We could all go together, they're sure to be asked."

She carried the toast to the table, and they sat down to breakfast. Lady Finch read the paper, munched her toast fourteen times, and drank herb tea. Harriet looked out of the window, drank milk (which she disliked only less than herb tea), and thought about her plans for Marian.

Today was important. It was a Saturday, and Marian was at home for a week-end. Next month, when she had her holiday, there would be opportunities for her to see a lot of Robert, but today they were to meet for the first time. First meetings, as Harriet had learned from many novels, were extremely important.

She had thought of asking them both to tea, but this seemed too dull and ordinary. Everyone had tea parties; and Aunt Finch's parties were decidedly below the average on account of the tea itself, with its herbal fragrance, and the peculiar nut sandwiches and other delicacies which she insisted on making. Then, too, Aunt Finch would be present, talking about nettles or equal pay for women and ruining the romantic atmosphere Harriet hoped to create. A tea party at Urn Cottage would be a poor beginning. But what different one could she devise?

An expedition, a picnic, an escape from Goatstock and its humdrum inhabitants, seemed the best thing. It had been difficult to arrange this, for the Finches had no car, and although the Prentices had one it was used, on Saturday afternoons, to take Mr. Prentice to the golf course at Ormington. But Harriet had discovered that Robert liked swimming, and by showing great enthusiasm for this pastime she had persuaded him to borrow his aunt's car so that they could drive forty miles to the coast and swim in the sea.

She had not yet told him that Marian would be accompanying them, but she had seen Marian yesterday evening, as soon as she arrived home, and had arranged to pick her up this morning at eleven o'clock. Marian, too, liked swimming, and although her conscientious nature made her hesitate about leaving her mother alone (for Mrs. Prentice did not play golf and looked forward to her daughter's free week-ends), this hesitation was pooh-poohed by Mrs. Prentice herself, whose own conscience was not wholly at ease. She could not forget that Mrs. Minnis had pitied Marian for having such a dull time at home.

"Shall we take lunch?" Harriet had asked. "Or buy some buns somewhere?" She looked a little anxious; she looked like an orphan; and the Prentices remembered that she *was* an orphan, and that any lunch originating from Urn Cottage would have to be approved by Lady Finch and would probably be very nasty. Mrs. Prentice had risen to the occasion and said she would provide a picnic lunch for both of them.

"What about . . ." She paused. To say 'Robert' seemed too familiar, when she had not called on them; to say 'Mr. Dunstan' sounded absurd. And tomorrow Marian would meet him, and perhaps she would be asked to Belmont House later on, and how in the world was one to account for not calling! Obsessed by these difficulties, Mrs. Prentice left the sentence uncompleted.

But Harriet understood her, and replied that it would be wonderful if she could provide lunch for Robert as well. He had said
he would bring some sandwiches, but he had also said that Mrs.
Dunstan's old Nanny was a difficult character and never gave
him quite enough to eat.

Yes, thought Harriet, neglecting her breakfast and gazing
out at the sunny garden—yes, it couldn't be better. A fine day,
good and sufficient food—for Mrs. Prentice was an excellent ca-
terer—and the enlivening prospect of a picnic by the sea. She
looked forward to it with pleasure; to the expedition itself as
well as to the furthering of her plans. She thought herself very
clever to have contrived it.

Shortly before eleven she arrived at Belmont House. The car
was out on the road, and Robert and Mrs. Dunstan were standing beside it. She was greeted with warmth by Robert, and with
a pleasant smile by Mrs. Dunstan, who hoped they would enjoy
themselves and wished she was coming too.

A planner with more experience than Harriet would have
paused to reply to these courtesies before rushing on with the
plan. But Harriet had an impetuous nature.

"Yes," she said, "it's going to be a heavenly day. Robert, I saw
Marian Prentice last night and I asked her to come with us."

"Marian Prentice?" he asked coldly. Julia heard in his voice
the threat of what she called Dunstan-sulks, but Harriet, intent
on sounding casual and spontaneous herself, heard nothing.

"My friend Marian," she hurried on. "I've told you about
her—she's training to be a nurse and she's at Reddrod Hospital,
only now she's got a week-end off. And she loves swimming—
she's an awfully good swimmer, but she hardly ever has time
for it. So of course she'll be tremendously glad to come with us."

For a moment Robert did not speak. He had been looking
forward to this picnic with Harriet, who was a queer creature but
somehow attractive and amusing. Now, however, she seemed
only queer, a girl so backward that she could not distinguish
between the merits of a tête-à-tête and a family outing. He used
the term family outing with contempt; it symbolized the kind of
picnic that this was going to be.

"Is that Mrs. Prentice's daughter?" Julia asked. Harriet said it was, and then said no more about Marian but began to talk to Taffy, who was sitting in the car to make sure it should not go without him. This, too, was part of the plan; she had determined not to describe Marian or praise her, because that always put people off.

Like anyone else, Julia found it hurtful to be ignored, and this second rebuff was more painful than the first because Harriet, swinging round to address Taffy, had actually turned her back on her would-be rescuer. Julia remembered what a good aunt she had been, lending Robert her valuable car and trying to smooth over an awkward moment with small talk so that they should start off happy; and at the sight of Robert's scowling face and Harriet's ungrateful back she felt inclined to leave them, to retire to the house and let them quarrel or not as they pleased.

But she could not do it. Her talent for handling difficult situations could not be denied; it was her duty to stay. She moved to Harriet's side, and remarked pleasantly that she had not yet met Mrs. Prentice but had heard she was a very nice woman.

"Hasn't she called on you yet?" Harriet asked in surprise.

"Not yet, but I hope she will."

"I'm sure she said she was going to."

"I suppose we'd better get off," Robert said abruptly.

Julia repeated her wish that she could go with them. She reminded them of what a fine day it was, and prophesied that the sea would be warm. She amused them by being comically fussy and exacting promises that they would not bathe for an hour after they had eaten; and with remarkable good-nature she restrained herself from making Robert promise not to drive too fast. Her intuition told her that that kind of fussiness would not have at all a good effect.

As a result of Julia's tactful gaiety the atmosphere grew lighter. Robert resigned himself to making the best of things, and Harriet, who had been slightly daunted by his long silence, was reassured. They got into the car, Harriet waved her hand as they drove off, and Julia, smiling and waving after them, retained to the last the expression of a benevolent aunt without a care in the world, though her doubts about Robert's driving were increased by the manner of his departure. There was really no need for him to accelerate like that.

"What a lovely morning!" shouted a voice behind her. It was Miss Pope, approaching rapidly on her long thin legs and bursting into conversation, as usual, the minute she presumed herself within earshot. "Was that your nephew in the car? How fast he drives!"

"He does indeed," said Julia. By this time Miss Pope was at her side. They smiled at each other, and Julia's heart warmed to this nice, understanding woman. She explained that Robert was taking Harriet Finch and Marian Prentice for a picnic by the sea. Miss Pope said it was very kind of her to lend her car, really remarkably kind because after all it was practically *new*, wasn't it?—and a new car cost a lot of money in these days. Julia agreed that it did.

Their concern over the car, and their apparent indifference to the safety of its occupants, might have struck an outsider as callous. But Miss Pope was too dazzled by her new friend's swan-like attributes to perceive any fault in her; and Julia could have argued that her zeal for Robert's happiness included, naturally enough, a wish that he should not hurt himself. Or his companions either.

"Come and have coffee with me," she said, when they had chatted a little longer.

Miss Pope shook her head. "I can't. I have to pay some visits." These, clearly, were calls of duty. "And I mustn't be late because Alaric wants lunch early today."

Alaric's meal times, Julia thought, were as variable as the weather. It must make life at the vicarage very difficult.

"Will you have to get back to cook it?" she asked, raising her voice slightly because Miss Pope was already on the move.

"Not today. I have a girl—Leah Townley—twice a week, and she can do ordinary cooking. Plain vegetables, boiled fish . . . that sort of thing."

Julia felt rather sorry for Alaric, condemned twice a week to this insipid diet.

"And then of course there's my friend Miss Brigg," said Miss Pope, stopping suddenly about twelve feet away and turning round. She hesitated, with a look on her face that Julia knew well—the eager yet stealthy look of one who is about to make a confidential statement. Julia smiled back encouragingly. But even Miss Pope, who was accustomed to long-range conversation, evidently felt that confidences needed a certain proximity, and perhaps more time. She turned away again, saying loudly over her shoulder: "She comes nearly every day . . . a great help."

"Yes, she must be."

Miss Pope broke into a walk which was almost a canter, as if her conscience were driving her feet to make amends for having stayed so long. Her last utterance came floating back from the neighbourhood of the rhododendron clump at the corner.

"A wonderful cook . . . Miss Brigg."

But Julia, with a wealth of experience behind her, had a strong feeling that this was not what she would have said if they had been sitting close together over the coffee cups.

Robert stopped the car at the gate of Balbus Cottage and said he would wait in it while Harriet fetched her friend. Harriet thought that on the whole this was a good thing, since Mrs. Prentice was slow to begin a conversation but unrestrainable, like a steamroller, once she got going. She jumped out of the car, assuring him that she wouldn't be a minute, and hurried away up the drive. Robert, who had often heard this phrase on his aunt's lips, discounted its accuracy and lit a cigarette.

Just behind him a gate squeaked loudly. It went on squeaking until he turned round to see why. A young man, with an oil-can in his hand, was pushing it to and fro, frowning and listening to the squeaks and sometimes making a jab with the oil-can at the gate's hinges.

The young man wore horn-rimmed glasses, which together with the frown gave him a serious, intellectual air. Robert knew him to be Charlton Minnis; he had met him once before when he was out for a walk with Harriet, and they had exchanged a few brief remarks about the weather. He had not been impressed by Charlton Minnis; but now, noting his gestures with the oil-can, he felt the sudden urge to help which so often assails those who watch someone else being inefficient.

He got out of the car. Charlton Minnis looked up as he approached, recognized him with what was visibly an intellectual effort, and wished him good morning.

"Good morning," Robert replied. He could not very well snatch the oil-can away. He looked at the gate and saw at once that the oil was trickling down the woodwork instead of going where it was needed on the hinges. "Doing a good deed?" he asked amiably.

"It's *our* gate. I live here," Charlton Minnis explained. "At least, I'm home at week-ends. And Bobs—my mother—saves up all these dirty jobs for me because she thinks my pater isn't a practical man."

Robert grinned at this pleasantry, wondering to himself if Mr. Minnis, senior, could possibly be more unpractical than his son.

"It's pretty rusty, isn't it?" he said, putting his hand on the gate and giving it a push.

"Oh, it isn't the *rust*. The oil would see to that—and I've given it plenty. What's happened is that the gate has sagged a bit, and it's binding on its hinges."

"Uh?" said Robert.

"What you hear—that nasty squeak—is metal on metal," Charlton told him. "Not rust. It's madly annoying, but I'm afraid the only thing to do is to dig up the gate-post and straighten the gate so that it hangs properly."

Robert stared at the gate, then at Charlton to see if he was joking. But it was clear that he was not. He looked pleased with himself, as if by finding a theoretical reason for the gate's squeaking he had done all that was necessary; and indeed, to confirm this, he now turned away and put the oil-can down on a flat stone just inside the fence, and taking up a rag from the same spot wiped his hands carefully.

"That's our late cat's grave," he said.

Robert stepped inside the gate and picked up the oil-can.

"She was called Carmen—but I say, it's no use oiling the gate. I've *done* that."

"Just hold it open a minute," Robert said, bending to his task. He applied the oil where it was needed, and then seized hold of the gate and swung it vigorously. It moved without a sound.

"There," he said, with quiet triumph.

"Very odd," said Charlton. "I'm afraid it won't last, but perhaps it will do until we can get the post straightened."

His calm voice disposed of the subject; there was nothing for Robert to do but to put the oil-can back, wipe his own hands on the rag, and wish he had left Charlton Minnis to struggle alone. At least the episode had served to pass the time. He glanced at his watch, and scowled.

"Are you waiting for Marian? It's not like her to be late."

Robert explained that he was waiting for Harriet to collect Marian. "We're supposed to be going to the sea, to picnic and bathe. If we ever get started."

"Rum girl, Marian. She's engaged to a missionary."

"Oh," said Robert, with a sinking heart. Whether it was being engaged to a missionary that made Marian rum he did not know; but he thought it was not unlikely. She would be plain and pious, probably with her hair in a bun and protruding teeth. The picnic would be even drearier than he had feared.

He looked gloomily at Charlton Minnis, and suddenly he was struck by an idea. It seemed such a good idea that he did not wait to ponder it.

"Why don't you come with us?" he suggested.

If Charlton came, he could sit in the back of the car with Marian. They could talk to each other, discussing the heathen and theorizing over the cure of friction between metal surfaces. They could keep each other happy; or at any rate occupied.

"Bathing?" Charlton said doubtfully. "I haven't bathed this year. The sea will probably be cold, it's really too early—"

"No, it couldn't be cold," Robert insisted. "Not today—it's an absolute scorcher." With honeyed words he coaxed Charlton to accompany them, and finally Charlton accepted, and departed to fetch his bathing things and tell his mother where he was going.

No sooner had he disappeared than Harriet and Marian came hurrying out from Balbus Cottage, carrying between them a large basket which appeared to contain enough food for a week's camping. Robert walked back to the car and started to open the boot.

"The basket can go on the back seat," Harriet called. "We can all three sit in front easily. Oh—this is Marian."

This was not quite the introduction she had planned. But it couldn't be helped, and anyway the drive, and the picnic, were the things that were going to count.

"We shall need the back seat," Robert was saying. "There'll be four of us. I've just asked Charlton Minnis to come. While I was waiting—"

"Not *Sonny*!" Harriet exclaimed in a shriek. "But he's—"

"Sst!" said Marian, looking, in this moment of crisis, rather like her mother.

Charlton Minnis appeared at the gate of Kandahar. As he opened it, it uttered the mere ghost of a squeak, a tiny, thin sound hardly audible to a human ear. He paused, and gave Robert a smile which was both kind and commiserating.

"I was afraid it wouldn't last long," he said.

CHAPTER X

A DAY AT the seaside means different things for different people. For the inhabitants of Reddrod and the neighbouring industrial regions it meant cheerfully crowded beaches, deck chairs, a long pier encrusted with slot-machines, and an unfailing supply of ice cream. These amenities were provided by two large seaside resorts which occupied much of the country's coastline, and whose posters were to be found side by side on every railway station. The more northerly of these earthly paradises proclaimed itself to be bracing, and the other boasted of its mild winter climate, but in fact they were much alike, and except for the place-names emblazoned on their souvenirs none but a devotee could have distinguished between them.

For Harriet, Marian, and Robert, a day at the seaside meant picnicking and bathing at a spot as far removed as possible from the rest of the human race. It was important, therefore, to avoid the two towns and their satellite fringes of wooden bungalows and caravan sites, and to arrive at the sea roughly half-way between them, even though the coast, at that point, was flat and uninteresting. As Harriet explained, the dullness of the scenery was in its way a good thing; they would be certain to have it to themselves.

This proved true. The narrow lane petered out by a ruined cottage at the edge of some low sand dunes, and beyond them stretched a wide expanse of muddy sand, empty of life except for a few sea gulls in the far distance. For a minute or so they gazed at this scene in silence, and then Robert asked politely, "Where's the sea?"

"Over there," said Harriet, pointing hopefully towards the horizon.

"It's because of the tide," Marian added. "The tide must be out."

"It goes out a long way."

"I've never seen it like this before," Harriet said. "But it's partly the heat haze. If it wasn't so misty we should see the sea."

"That isn't a heat haze," said Charlton. "It's a sea fog. I expect it will be all round us pretty soon—it's obviously blowing in." He spoke with an air of authority, which instantly caused Robert to side with Harriet and declare the mist to be a heat haze, nothing more. Having committed himself to this opinion he was forced also to agree with Marian, who suggested that they should change into their bathing things and then have lunch on the beach and sun themselves and wait for the tide to come in.

"It must be as far out as it can be," she added sensibly. "So probably we shan't have so far to walk, after lunch."

She and Harriet then retired to the ruined cottage that stood where the lane ended, whose crumbling walls provided, as Harriet said, a modest retreat that was more symbolic than real. Robert and Charlton were left to undress by the car.

Charlton said it wasn't worth changing; the sea fog would make it too cold for bathing, and would also make it dangerous to walk far out on the sands. Enveloped in fog, one might lose one's sense of direction and wander for miles, ending up in the quicksands off Hooton Point. He had heard of a man, only last year, who had done that very thing; he had been bathing here alone—and that in itself was a very silly thing to do—and a fog had come down and the man had walked north instead of east and had got stuck in a quicksand and perished miserably. His body had never been found.

Robert saw an obvious flaw in this anecdote.

"How did they know what had happened to him?" he asked sceptically.

"His footsteps were traced to the edge of the quicksand," Charlton replied. "That was afterwards, of course, when the fog had lifted and his friends were searching for him."

"But the sea would have washed the footprints away."

"No, the tide was going out when he bathed."

"A very sad story," Robert said coldly. He turned away and began to get the lunch-basket out of the boot.

Marian and Harriet emerged from their shelter. Marian's bathing costume, Robert noted, was not one he would have expected a missionary to approve of, but Harriet was decorously clad in the navy-blue regulation-pattern-garment she had had at school.

"Come on!" Harriet cried, calling to Taffy and racing away along the sand. Robert, carrying the lunch-basket and an assortment of cushions and towels, followed more slowly, and Marian ran up behind him and begged to be allowed to help. He gave her the cushions, they walked side by side, and Charlton came languidly and reluctantly in the rear.

Robert glanced back; the loitering figure was out of earshot.

"He seems rather nervous," he observed.

"Has he been telling you about bathing accidents? You mustn't mind—"

"I *don't* mind!"

"Well, that's all right, then. Only Harriet should have warned you—he's always like that."

"But—they're not true?"

"Charlton's stories? Oh no," Marian said placidly. "We're not sure if he gets them out of books or if he invents them. Harriet thinks some of them are too fantastic to appear in print."

Her calm acceptance of Charlton's peculiarities seemed to Robert quite out of character; the prospective bride of a missionary should surely be quick to condemn lies as lies, not condone them as harmless inventions. He himself had no use for fantasy; a thing was either true or it wasn't, and if it wasn't, then it was a lie.

Her bathing costume, too, was out of character, and so were her hair and teeth; she was quite a pretty girl, and not at all the plain, pious creature he had envisaged. It suddenly occurred to him that Charlton's tale of her being engaged to a missionary was perhaps just an invention like his tale of the man in the quicksands—or, in other words, a lie. One could not very well ask her; but he glanced down at her hand and saw that she wasn't wearing a ring.

"It seems pretty pointless—inventing stories that no one believes," he said.

"But he doesn't know we don't believe them. It's awfully hard to prove him wrong, and one can't always be sure they're not true."

Robert shook his head dissentingly. He for one was not going to play up to Charlton by pretending to believe him, and he flattered himself that he could distinguish fact from fantasy.

"I think we've come far enough," Marian said. "We can have the picnic here, and walk down to the sea afterwards—there's no point in carrying the basket any further."

Robert thought they must have walked a good way, for the bank of mist was much nearer. But when he turned round he saw that it was no great distance to the sand dunes where they had left the car. The expanse of beach was narrower than it had seemed at first sight.

Far ahead, Harriet looked back and saw Robert and Marian putting down cushions and opening the basket. They were alone; some way behind them Charlton was advancing slowly, scuffling the sand with his feet. Things had gone well, and Charlton's unforeseen presence had not after all interfered with her plan for leaving them to talk to each other. But it was a pity Marian had not sat beside Robert in the car; somehow, in the confusion caused by Charlton's sudden appearance and her own vexation, Harriet had ended by occupying the front seat herself.

"Good dog!" she said to Taffy, who was frisking round her with a piece of driftwood in his mouth. "Good dog, excellent dog, useful dog!" These commendations were deserved, since a dog offers the best of excuses for running ahead and detaching oneself from the rest of the company.

But it was time to return, for Charlton had now reached the others; he was, as Harriet knew from experience, a man who needed a lot of attention, and she must hurry back and talk to him if Marian and Robert were to have any further chance of talking to each other. 'It's very noble of me,' Harriet thought, speeding back over the shining sand—'noble and disinterested of me to take all this trouble.'

The sand, however, reminded her of the Sahara, and the Sahara, though it was far from the scene of his labours, reminded her of Hubert because like him it was in Africa. Marian's evil genius, from whom she must be rescued; Marian's dull though worthy betrothed, with whom she couldn't be really in love. The thought of Hubert fortified Harriet in her nobility, and when she arrived, panting, at the picnic spot, she flung herself down beside Charlton Minnis.

"Why haven't you changed, Sonny?" she asked. "Aren't you going to bathe?"

Charlton said it was too cold, or rather, it would be too cold quite soon; the sea fog was coming in with the tide and they would be feeling pretty chilly by-and-by. He had given Harriet a reproving look when she addressed him as Sonny, and now, lowering his voice, he reminded her that he wished to be known as Charlton. Harriet replied meekly that it had slipped out, and it was very hard to remember not to say it when they had known each other as children.

"True, true," Charlton agreed. He took another sandwich, and began to talk about the past. He had the habit—inherited perhaps from Mrs. Minnis—of speaking about his own childhood as if it had taken place long ago in a golden age; the child Sonny, the apple of his mother's eye and phenomenally advanced for his years, might have appeared in the early chapters of a book of reminiscences written by an octogenarian. This child, quaint, solemn, intelligent, and—as Charlton admitted with a lofty smile—rather pampered, was not like the child Sonny whom Harriet remembered, except in the matter of being over-indulged; nor had his quaint yet intelligent remarks ever been uttered in her presence. But she listened with remarkable docility, encouraging Charlton whenever he paused, and urging him to further feats of reminiscence by saying, "Do you remember the time when . . . ?"

It was a conversation in which Robert could not join, even if he had wished to. A conversation about a shared past is boring for outsiders, and the picnic was soon divided into two camps, Harriet listening to Charlton, and Robert telling Marian about Taffy and Taffy's predecessors. While doing this he also managed to eat a remarkable quantity of food. Harriet dared not let her attention stray from the welter of reminiscences, but she heard snatches of the rival conversation, and noticed with satisfaction the amount Robert was eating. It seemed pretty clear that he was enjoying himself.

And surely, she thought, Marian must be enjoying herself too. Surely she could not fail to be attracted by this handsome creature who was talking about a subject so dear to her heart as dogs. It was a pity they could not talk about something more romantic, but at least it would show Marian that they had a lot in common; and, for someone of her temperament, that was important.

For herself, Harriet believed in love at first sight. She believed that one day she would meet a man and know at once that she had met her fate: age, eligibility, things in common, would matter nothing. But Marian, she realized, was different; she would never fall in love at first sight; she was too cautious, too reserved, to allow such a thing to happen. This did not mean, however, that she was incapable of falling in love, it only meant that one must be prepared to let her take her time.

Anyway, Harriet thought happily, the first meeting was being a success. And presently the tide would come in, and they would bathe, and Marian—an excellent swimmer—would appear to great advantage. But, considering what Robert had eaten, it would be better to remember his aunt's entreaties and wait an hour before bathing; it would be dreadfully unromantic if he got cramp and had to be rescued by Marian.

"Isn't it hot!" Marian exclaimed.

"Gorgeously hot."

"A perfect day for a picnic!"

Charlton looked over his shoulder and pointed out that the bank of fog was creeping nearer. But no one was listening. Even Harriet no longer listened, for one cannot be perpetually noble, and self-sacrificing natures, like selfish ones, need periods of recuperation. The hot sun, the pleasant feeling of repletion—Robert had not been alone in doing justice to the lunch—and the knowledge that all was going well, combined to make Harriet drowsy and relaxed. She lay face downwards, pillowing her head on a cushion and wriggling her bare toes in the sand. Presently the toes ceased to wriggle. Harriet was asleep.

For a time they all slept. A siesta after lunch, on a hot summer day by the sea, was an agreeable necessity for Robert, who still believed that the mist would disperse if they waited and who could not be bothered to go on talking to Marian—a nice girl, a pretty girl, but of course not a patch on Harriet. Taffy thought otherwise, he recognized Marian as a born spoiler of dogs, and with beseeching looks he planted himself beside her while she packed up the remains of the picnic. Charlton took off his glasses, first the sun-glasses and then the horn-rimmed ones underneath, polished each pair carefully, put them on again, and then lay back and closed his eyes. Marian strapped up the lunch-basket and settled herself comfortably on the warm sand. She did not really care for siestas and she wished she had brought a nursing text-book; but soon her thoughts were with Hubert in Africa, and while she was drowsily working out exactly what time it was at the mission-station the thoughts faded into dreams.

Sounds of dismay woke Robert; he opened an eye and had a hazy view of Harriet. She was sitting up, talking excitedly, and it seemed to him that he saw her through a mist of sleep. He blinked, rubbed his eyes, and looked again; his sleepiness had gone but the mist was still there, so dense that even at close quarters it hung like a veil between them. Sun and sky and sand had vanished, hidden by a white, impenetrable fog which gave to the picnic group the forlorn aspect of shipwrecked mariners on a very small raft. The clammy chill in the air suggested that they had been shipwrecked in polar seas.

"I thought I had better wake you," Marian was saying.

"You should have woken us sooner," Harriet retorted crossly.

"But it came up so quickly. I'd hardly closed my eyes . . ."

"I told you this was going to happen," Charlton said calmly.

"I'm freezing," Harriet cried. "Come on, let's get back to the car."

Robert stood up and looked cautiously about him. There was of course nothing to see, but he felt that some sort of gesture was necessary; he felt that he was responsible for Harriet's and Marian's safety, and although he had not believed Charlton's story about the quicksands he could not help remembering it, now that his prophecy about the fog had so tiresomely come true. They must walk east, away from the sea; and they mustn't panic. He put his hand to his ear, listening for the sound of breaking waves—for surely the tide must have risen by now—but it was impossible to hear anything through the babble of conversation around him.

"You can carry the basket," Harriet said to Charlton. "It's your turn—Robert carried it here."

"I wish I'd brought a jersey," said Marian.

"Charlton ought to take off his shirt and wrap it round you."

"I will if you're really cold. But it's a very thin shirt and there's not much warmth in it."

"Still, you're the only one who can afford to take off anything."

"Quiet!" Robert cried sternly. They were silent, looking at him in surprise and, as he fancied, in admiration. His natural modesty could not blind him to the fact that he was better qualified than Charlton to take command in an emergency; and the idea that Marian or Harriet might aspire to leadership did not occur to him. In a hushed, respectful silence he stood listening, but unfortunately he could hear nothing at all.

After a minute Harriet broke the silence to ask what he was doing. "Listening for the sea," Robert said; "we don't want to walk into the sea, do we?" Nor did he want to alarm his female companions by turning their thoughts towards quicksands and lingering death; for in this crisis the adventure stories he had read as a boy, and perhaps an inherited belief that women were the weaker sex, prompted him to chivalrous behaviour at which his everyday self would have shuddered.

"We don't want to, and we're not going to," said Charlton. "But it's no good straining your ears—if indeed one can do such a thing—because this fog simply blots out sound. Acoustically it's like layers and layers of cotton-wool. You might just as well listen for the quicksands."

He ought not to have mentioned the quicksands. Robert frowned, and looked up to see if he could discern a gleam overhead that might show him the position of the sun. While he was doing this Charlton, Marian and Harriet began to walk away.

"Wait," Robert commanded. "We must get our bearings first."

"We've got them," Harriet replied. "We only have to follow the trail. Clever Charlton has saved us from hideous death."

"He scuffled up the sand as he came," Marian explained. "He made a track."

"You and Marian walked delicately like Agag. But Charlton stamped like a bull of Bashan."

"Of course I knew this was going to happen. I took the obvious precaution," Charlton said blandly.

Harriet did not know Robert well enough to recognize the onset of Dunstan-sulks, but she soon perceived that he was out of spirits. The walk back across the sands hardly counted, since they were all feeling cold and unsociable, but by the time they had dressed and re-assembled at the car her own spirits and the spirits of Charlton and Marian had revived sufficiently to make Robert's dour silence noticeable.

"It won't be foggy as soon as we get inland," Charlton assured them. "We might drive back through Kestleton and have tea there. There's quite a good café by the water-mill,"

"Or what about Ormington?"

"No, Kestleton would be better. Ormington is painfully crowded on a Saturday afternoon."

Harriet did not argue; she foresaw that, wherever they had tea, it was not going to be a successful meal. The picnic was spoilt, Robert was cross, and Marian, with the best intentions, had assumed the bright kind face of a hospital nurse dealing with a fractious patient. Somehow Harriet knew that Robert would not respond favourably to this technique, or indeed to any technique. Tactful concern and breezy *bonhomie* would be equally wasted on him.

'What he needs,' she thought vindictively, 'is a good shaking!' But as social conventions made this impossible she had to content herself with sitting next to him, and thus preserving Marian from the disillusioning view of a profile rigid with thwarted chivalry.

"How lucky you asked Charlton to the picnic," she said. "Without him we might all have perished."

Robert was silent.

"And, of course, he's quite an asset in other ways. He talks, for instance."

A shade of sadness, a blush of shame—as Harriet remarked poetically to herself—seemed to creep over Robert's face, and although he made no intelligible reply he uttered a pained little grunt. At this she took heart. There were more ways than one of administering a shaking.

CHAPTER XI

JULIA STOOD with Miss Pope at the gate of the vicarage, looking up and down the village street. Miss Pope wore a sacking apron and had a smear of mud on one cheek; she had been planting out lettuces and had only emerged from the back garden to chase away a trespassing cat. Julia, who was passing, had stopped to hail her—a neighbourly but misguided action which had compelled Miss Pope to come down to the gate.

"I'm not fit to be seen," she said.

She did not really mind being seen in her sacking apron and laddered old cardigan, but she minded being torn away from the lettuces; there was so little time for gardening, and the soil, after a night's rain, was just right for transplanting them.

"Isn't it a heavenly morning?" Julia said. "After such a horrid wet night, too. May I come in and look at your garden?"

Miss Pope hesitated. But she was too used to interruptions—people wanting advice, or the key of the church—to show resentment.

"Yes, do come in," she said cheerfully. "Only there's not much to see, now that the rhododendrons are over."

The rhododendrons grew in large clumps round the lawn in front of the house. In the middle of the lawn was a circular bed filled with rose bushes. There were two big chestnut trees, and in one corner a weeping ash whose branches, sweeping the ground, made a rustling green tent. Between the garden and the adjoining churchyard an earlier incumbent, or his wife, had laid out a shrubbery, with a winding path cunningly flanked by evergreens to give an effect of remote solitude. But much of this shrubbery had been cut down to make a site for the churchroom, and the rest was now overgrown and impenetrable.

"It's a great pity," Miss Pope said, explaining this to Julia. "If only I had time to clear the path and thin the bushes I could make a lovely wild garden there. With clumps of iris, you know, and daffodils and wood anemones."

"There's a very good landscape gardener at Ormington. He's coming to us, later in the year, to re-turf the lawn and put up a pergola and advise us what to do about the hedge. You should get him to come here at the same time."

"Yes," said Miss Pope. She reflected on the slightly exasperating inability of the rich, however well-disposed, to understand how the poor live. However, Mrs. Dunstan was so kind that it was easy to forgive her. "I'll have to think about it," she said vaguely, as she led the way up the drive.

The ground at the back of the house was given up to vegetables, fruit trees, and an untidy dingle which had once been a rock-garden. Beyond it were rising fields, and the steep, bare slopes of Goatstock Hill, shimmering faintly in the heat.

"Lovely!" said Julia. "I don't know how you get anything done—*I* should be looking at the view all the time!"

Miss Pope was looking at the box of seedling lettuces, and at the nice damp soil waiting to receive them. But her admiration for her visitor tempered her regret at the interruption, and she suggested that they should sit down. A rustic wooden seat stood under one of the apple trees; it had been there for years but was seldom used because Miss Pope was usually too busy to sit in the garden and Alaric suffered mildly from hay-fever. As they approached it Julia noticed that it was green with lichen and exceedingly damp. Miss Pope noticed it too; she took off her sacking apron and with the gesture of a Raleigh she spread it along the seat.

"There! Would you like some coffee? Or a cigarette?"

Julia refused, protesting that she could only stay a minute and then she must fly. As she uttered these words it occurred to her that she was behaving just like Miss Pope herself. She stifled a laugh, and then, afraid that her companion had seen it, she said quickly:

"Do you think people who live in small places like this, and see a good deal of one another, tend to grow alike? I was laughing at myself—I feel so villagy and rural, sitting under an apple tree—not a bit the person I was in London!"

Miss Pope saw that it was meant as a joke. (How could dear Mrs. Dunstan think she was like Lady Finch or—or Mary Ellen?) She laughed; but then she sighed.

"Villagy and rural," she said feelingly.

"I suppose it won't be that much longer."

"Oh!" cried Miss Pope. "Then—then you *know*?"

Indeed she did, said Julia, her nephew Robert had told her about the New Town, and of course it had been a terrible shock at first but one had to get used to these things. Miss Pope was rather chastened by this reply, which was not what she had expected from such an enthusiast for village life. She was about to protest, to argue, when a voice from the house, loud, clear, and somehow accusing, shouted to know if it should put the potatoes on.

"Yes!" said Miss Pope, bellowing back. "Please," she added on a quieter tone, as if she did not care whether her gratitude got there or not.

"Is that your daily?" Julia asked politely. Miss Pope looked at her and this time it was a look that hardly needed encouragement.

"No, it's Mary Ellen," she said. "I mean, Miss Brigg."

"Oh yes. Your friend Miss Brigg."

"But she's not! At least, I don't know. She's a wonderful woman—such a good cook, so much better than I am. I oughtn't to say a word against her, only—And then she does the brasses, and mends the hassocks, and spends all that money on flowers. Arum lilies at Easter—you know what they cost!"

Julia did not; she was just going to say that she couldn't bear arum lilies in the house when she realized that they, like the brasses and the hassocks, pertained to the church. It was equally clear that Miss Brigg's demerits, whatever they were, had nothing to do with church activities. Miss Pope, after the first excited outburst, dropped her voice and glanced nervously over her shoulder.

"You see," she said, "she's always *here*."

"She comes here when you're busy and hangs round you?"

"No," Miss Pope said sadly. "She comes here when I'm out. At other times too, of course, but I shouldn't mind that. . . . You see, it's happening oftener and oftener—just when I've popped *out* for something, she drops *in*."

This time Julia did see. She saw Alaric, a weak man with an understandable distaste for boiled fish, and Miss Brigg, a ruthless opportunist with a light hand for pastry. She had met Miss Brigg, and her heart quickened in sympathy for Miss Pope, threatened with the triple loss of a brother, a home, and a career. She was happily certain that Miss Pope liked her; and this made her all the more deserving of help and sympathy.

"I'm sure Miss Brigg is a very good woman," she said. "Of course, that makes it difficult to—to discourage her."

"I'm so worried. I don't know what to do."

"You must be. But tell me a little more about it. Talking helps, you know."

Encouraged by this benevolence, Miss Pope forgot the wilting lettuces. Enthralled by another's perplexities, Julia forgot the hardness, and possible dampness, of the wooden bench. Their voices sank to a confidential murmur: Miss Brigg, peering out from the dining-room window, sniffed contemptuously and wondered what sort of silly fairy-tales *that* Mrs. Dunstan was reciting. She would have been surprised to know that the recital was being given by Miss Pope, and that its recurrent motifs of 'excellent woman' and 'snake in the grass' both applied to herself.

Miss Pope returned again and again to Miss Brigg's good qualities, in her capacity of pillar of the church, and was careful to add to every unfavourable comment the proviso that she might be mistaken. By this behaviour she salved her conscience; which was troubled, strangely enough, less by the denunciation of Miss Brigg than by the fact that she was denouncing her to a newcomer, a comparative stranger. It seemed to Miss Pope a little odd that she should find it easy to tell Mrs. Dunstan what she had not been able to tell Millicent Prentice. But it did not seem odd to Julia, who was used to being confided in, and whose expressive face and soothing voice elicited, in the end, a far more detailed story than Miss Pope had intended to relate.

It took so long that there was no time to discuss what should be done, but Julia invited her friend to have tea with her, on a day when she knew Dora would be out. Then they would have a really good talk, she said, and perhaps between them they would be able to think of something. She rose to go; Miss Pope walked down to the gate with her; and as they stood there saying good-bye a gong boomed sonorously from the vicarage, the noise rising in a steady crescendo which at once conjured up a picture of Miss Brigg's muscular arms.

"That's what she does!" Miss Pope complained. "I suppose she means well, but after all it isn't her house. Or her gong."

"It's a very powerful gong."

"Yes, isn't it? It came from our grandfather's house—but of course he had a park, so I suppose he needed something loud. I think I might just mention that to Alaric."

"About your grandfather?"

"No—about the gong. I could just laugh and say that Mary Ellen thought I was getting deaf. I mean, that might give him a hint that I didn't approve of everything she did."

"Don't—whatever you do—*don't* speak to him," Julia advised. "If he's not thinking of her in that way you'll put the idea into his head. And if he is, he'll only think you're interfering. Interfering for your own sake, I mean."

"But it's for *his* sake. He would never be happy, if—"

The gong began an encore performance, starting up with a muffled dirge in a curiously hesitant rhythm.

"And that's Alaric," Miss Pope went on. "You see—she's asked him to do it and he can't refuse. I'd better go."

She galloped away up the drive. Julia walked slowly back to Belmont House, thinking about the Pope-Brigg situation and how nice it was that people should trust her and seek her advice.

At home Dora, Robert, and lunch were awaiting her return. No booming gong reproached her for being late; though Robert showed signs of impatience, faint but, to the widow of a Dunstan, unmistakeable. Julia disregarded them, talked about the weather, and told herself that it was time Robert set about getting a job. It wasn't good for a boy of his age to live in idleness.

"Francis called this morning," Dora said casually. "He'd been over to Reddrod, and he came in on his way back."

Julia helped herself to salad. She said she was sorry to have missed him, but she had been visiting Miss Pope.

"He waited to see you," Dora said.

"Oh dear—was it something special?"

"Just a cousinly call, I think. We did our best to entertain him, didn't we, Robert?"

"*You* did," said Robert. "I dropped out pretty soon, but you were wonderful." He turned to Julia. "Dora took him all round the garden, inch by inch. 'This is where the pergola is going to be—here will be the lawn, here the first flower bed, here the second.' You could almost *see* the garden by the time she'd finished."

Julia laughed. She felt a little sorry for Francis, exposed to Dora's horticultural zeal with no one at hand to rescue him, but she realized that Dora had done her best. It wasn't her fault that she sometimes bored people.

"He seemed really interested," Dora said. "I believe he'd enjoy gardening if he once started. Of course he knows nothing about it."

"He does now. He must, after all that intensive tuition. And I expect you know a lot about heraldry by this time."

"Heraldry?" Julia asked.

"Don't be silly, Robert—it wasn't heraldry, it was family history."

"I wasn't really listening, so I'll take your word for it. Whatever it was, he was a mine of information."

Julia did not care for the tone of this remark. Robert had no business to laugh at a man who was older, cleverer, and better-mannered than himself; especially when that man was a Heswald. She said reprovingly:

"It's all very well to laugh, Robert, but Francis is a very able man. He knows a—a great deal."

"But what *about*?"

"Pipe-rolls," said Julia, snatching hastily at this impressive technical term, and then rushing on before Robert could ask what it meant. "And early county records, and mediaeval burgesses, and that sort of thing."

"But really, Julia, who cares what happened in fifteen-something-or-other? It's what's happening now that matters."

"In one way, yes. But—"

"And your cousin Francis doesn't know anything about what's happening now, any more than he knows about gardening. He hadn't heard a word about the New Town."

"He could hardly believe it," Dora added. "And he was absolutely horrified."

Julia could not help feeling that her nearest and dearest had behaved very tiresomely. She had hoped to tell Francis about the New Town herself, for she had known that it would need tact to persuade him that new towns, as opposed to mediaeval ones, had any merits whatsoever. She had hoped to arouse his interest, and later his enthusiasm; but it seemed all too likely that Dora's intervention had destroyed these hopes. Dora would have dwelt on the New Town's short-comings, its probable ugliness, its appropriation of good agricultural land (to say nothing of gardens), and thus would have prejudiced Francis against it from the start.

However, tiresome as it was that Dora should have forestalled her, she could not be blamed for trying to entertain Francis. Julia realized it, and with a slight effort she overcame her annoyance. She smiled at Dora and told her that she and Francis were true Heswalds in their cautious attitude to innovations.

"First you are horrified, then you're curious, and finally you'll say it was your own idea."

"I shan't say that about the New Town," Dora declared firmly. "But perhaps you're right about me and Francis. Now that I've got to know him I can see that we are rather alike. We seem to have a lot in common."

It seemed to Julia almost pathetic that poor Dora, so brusque and boring and ordinary, should compare herself with a clever man like Francis.

"You certainly hit it off," Robert remarked. "He was chatting like mad. So were you. And I could hear you both roaring with laughter when I was out in the field hunting for Taffy. I shouldn't have thought Cousin Francis could let himself go like that."

Neither would Julia. A little cloud dimmed her contentment, and her smile became anxious.

"I wish I'd been there," she said. "What were you talking about?"

"Oh, nothing much. I forget."

It was unlike Dora to be evasive. Julia was perplexed; for how could she have forgotten, in so short a time, a conversation so sparklingly successful? 'Both roaring with laughter' was of course an exaggeration; for Francis did not roar—he wasn't the type—and if there had been any roaring it had been done by Dora. But Francis must have been laughing, in a manner more or less obvious, or Robert would not have noticed it.

"You must have had an amusing morning," she said.

Dora suddenly thumped the table with her hand—a hearty gesture that set all the cutlery trembling. "Earning one's living!" she exclaimed. "That's what we were talking about. I was telling him about some of the funny jobs I've had."

A horrid suspicion smote Julia that this wasn't true, that Dora had invented it, and that they had been talking about something else which could not be revealed. Had they been laughing at Belmont House, or at her? It seemed dreadfully possible, because otherwise Dora would have had no reason to lie; and the thumping gesture, the well-timed recollection, were too emphatic to ring true. She tried to think she was being fanciful, but the suspicion remained. She looked at the hand-painted plates on the sideboard and remembered how Dora had made fun of them, calling the falcon a sparrow; she looked at Dora, who was eating strawberries and cream with gusto, and remembered, a little hazily, the proverb about biting the hand that feeds one.

"I quite forgot to tell you," Dora said suddenly. "A man turned up this morning about the advertisement. I said you were out, and he said he'd call again this afternoon."

Julia gathered up her straying thoughts. "But I didn't advertise for a man," she said. "A house-parlourmaid was what I put. I thought it sounded better than general help."

"Well, this is a house-parlour*man*. He says he has been one before."

"Did Nanny see him?"

"Oh yes, he went to the back door. He had references. He looked quite respectable."

"Too respectable," said Robert. "He's probably a thief in disguise."

But neither Julia nor Dora agreed with this. Dora said the man had honest eyes, and Julia was thinking that a house-parlourman might suit Nanny better than another woman. Moreover, he would give to Belmont House a certain air of distinction; she pictured him opening the door and ushering in guests, wearing a grey alpaca jacket and dark trousers, and striking a happy mean between the pomposity of a butler and the informality of a general help.

She stood up. She had felt, after Dora's suspicious remarks, the first throbbing symptoms of a headache brought on by worry, and she had meant to retire to her bedroom and rest. But this retreat was now impossible. She must interview the man and, if he proved suitable, coax Nanny into accepting his assistance. She must sit down with pencil and paper and work out exactly what his duties would be, because that would have to be settled with Nanny in advance, if there was to be any peace.

This was a task which ought to be undertaken by Dora, who was, perhaps, better qualified to do it. But Dora seemed to think she had done all that was necessary. She announced that she was going to have a busy afternoon in the garden, and strode off without waiting for Julia's reply.

Julia was left alone to wrestle with her headache, her doubts about Dora, and the list of a house-parlourman's duties. She reflected that Dora, hard-working though she was, worked only at the tasks she enjoyed; and she wondered whether, for the purpose of maintaining one's *amour-propre*, this really counted.

CHAPTER XII

FRANCIS HESWALD was a man who could forget all about his neighbours for quite long periods of time without feeling guilty or bored. Nor did he think himself idle. His book, and the correspondence and research it entailed, occupied him for several hours each day, and round these dedicated hours he had built up a comfortable routine so that the days went by on oiled wheels. In the mornings he worked, on fine afternoons he took a walk for the good of his health, and on wet ones he browsed happily in his library. Once a week, wet or fine, he left his work and drove into Reddrod, where he had his hair cut if it needed it and did the shopping. Mrs. Sable gave him a list of what was wanted, and although he pretended that the shopping expedition was a good deed, he secretly enjoyed it. He was a critical and careful buyer, and he prided himself on knowing just where to go for the cheapest and best of everything.

About a fortnight after his morning call at Belmont House he found it necessary to go to Reddrod on a Friday. He usually avoided Fridays, because they were market-days and the town was crowded, but on Thursday his car had refused to start; the mechanic who had been summoned had not arrived until late in the afternoon, and had then started the car at his first attempt and declared there was nothing wrong with it. The car's mulish behaviour and the mechanic's weary scepticism had combined to ruin the day for Francis, and although his temper had recovered by the following morning, he set out for Reddrod with less than his usual enthusiasm. He told himself that a less kind-hearted man would have expected his housekeeper to do the shopping, and to go to Reddrod by bus.

It was a wet morning, with a chill unsummery wind. The Reddrod pavements were thronged with large women in dripping raincoats, ruthless housewives whose determination to procure the best for their families led to a great deal of shoving and pushing round the market stalls which, by a time-hallowed custom, filled the square and part of the main street. On Fridays it was impossible to find a parking place in the street, and he had to leave his car in the station yard; Mrs. Sable had foreseen this and had given him a large basket to carry the parcels, but the basket, though useful, proved an encumbrance in the crowded, busy shops. Menaced by umbrellas, buffeted by other people's baskets and impeded by his own, Francis enjoyed himself less and less. He crossed off several items on the shopping list as being unnecessary (Mrs. Sable could surely improvise a pan-cleaner and a floor-cloth), and he decided, by way of respite from the rain and the crowds, to go and have a cup of coffee as soon as he had bought the fish.

Usually he patronized a small neat café on the Windish road, kept by two ladies who knew his name and treated him with deference. But today he chose the Café Royal, because it stood next door to the fishmonger and the other café was some distance away. He walked in, climbed the twisting stair to the first floor, and began to look about him for a vacant table.

The Café Royal dated from the early years of the century and had been considered extremely modern and artistic when it was first opened. There were large mirrors on the walls, and these mirrors were framed in embossed panels of *art nouveau* design, full of water-lilies twining improbably upwards as well as sideways on a background of tortuous lattice-work. The lattice motif was repeated in the jutting partitions which gave to the tables along the walls a spurious privacy. The place had originally been lit by gas, but now the ornate brackets carried electric bulbs, each concealed within a coloured glass imitation of a Japanese lantern. The waterlily panels on the walls, and the lattice woodwork, were painted in various shades of pallid green, and the table tops were green to match.

Francis Heswald looked at it with a disapproving eye. The place was crowded and noisy, the waitresses pushed past him impatiently, and he could not see an empty table, or even an empty seat. But the screens hid some of the tables from view; he moved slowly down the length of the room, and at the far end, in the last alcove, he saw a table for four with only the two inner places occupied. As he reached it the occupants looked up; they were Lady Finch and his cousin Julia.

"Francis!" Julia exclaimed. "Come and sit down and talk to us. Somehow you are the last person I would expect to meet here!"

She seemed pleased to see him, nevertheless; and he too was glad of the meeting, though he could have done without Lady Finch. It soon appeared that Lady Finch and Julia had arrived separately in Reddrod—Julia in her car and Lady Finch on the bus—and had met at the fishmonger's shop next door.

"I do not eat fish," Lady Finch explained, "but I was buying a pair of kippers for Harriet. Harriet is young, and I sometimes think a purely vegetarian diet does not suit her. She's so skinny."

"Oh no," Julia protested politely. "She has a very nice figure. Don't you think so, Francis?"

He was startled. He felt he did not know the Finches well enough to comment on Harriet's figure; nor could he remember having noticed it. Julia observed his hesitation and laughed.

"Don't you ever look at people?" she asked.

"She has not a nice figure," said Lady Finch. "She has no figure at all. But then no one has, nowadays."

"Well . . ." said Julia. She gave Francis a smiling glance, a glance that seemed to invite him to say something; but although he realized that a protest, if subtly phrased, would be in its way a compliment to Julia's own figure, he could not bring himself to utter it. He remembered, however, how trim and elegant she had looked, that day at Heswald. He permitted himself to disagree—though in silence—with Lady Finch's dictum.

"Well," Julia repeated brightly, "one might say figures have altered. We're all much—much flatter, nowadays, aren't we?"

"I'm not. I was fat as a girl, but since I started eating the right sort of food, I've found—"

"Not *fat*. Flat."

"My dear Mrs. Dunstan, women aren't flat. Not today or yesterday or any other day. The body beautiful—"

Francis was suddenly aware of a waitress standing at his elbow. "Coffee," he said loudly. "Coffee for three." He could see that the waitress was more interested in the body beautiful than in what was required to nourish it. "And bring some cakes," he commanded desperately.

"We've had ours," Julia said. "But I'd love another cup of coffee."

"Coffee is poison. Do you realize how much caffein there is in a single cup?"

"Then have some more malted milk," Julia suggested kindly. Lady Finch agreed to this. The waitress, disappointed, went away. Francis asked Julia if she often came to this café, and began to tell her about the other one, so quiet and select, on the outskirts of the town.

"One often has it to oneself," he said.

"How on earth do they manage to make a living?" Julia asked.

It was a point that had not occurred to him.

"No doubt they keep it as a hobby," said Lady Finch, poking at one of the cakes on the plate which the waitress had just set down. "There are many people with little to occupy their minds, and no worth-while interests, who *need* hobbies. Poisoning one's fellow-countrymen with artificial stimulants and food-substitutes is considered, I believe, a perfectly legitimate way of adding to one's income."

"But that's just what they won't do, if no one but Francis ever goes to their café."

"Which serves them right," Lady Finch retorted. "Don't take that cake, Mrs. Dunstan. Or that one." She poked them all in rapid succession. "They're all the same," she announced angrily. "It's the flour."

"But what's the matter with them?"

"Bleached flour. It won't keep, you know. One can always tell by testing the amount of resilience."

"I'll risk it," said Julia. She helped herself, and passed the plate to Francis. As a rule he disdained fancy cakes—it was one thing to drink coffee, and quite another thing to stuff oneself with café confectionery—but now, as a gesture of moral support for

Julia, he took an ornate pink one, garlanded with mock cream and rather dented on the top where Lady Finch had poked it. He hoped Julia would understand, and value, the gesture.

Julia did. She was touched; she remembered how she had eaten cucumber sandwiches and plum cake to please Francis, and it seemed to her both fitting and significant that he should now be eating a noxious-looking cake to please her. True, he had not actually begun to eat it; true, he might have taken it simply to annoy Lady Finch; but nevertheless her heart warmed towards him. He was her dear cousin Francis, and blood was thicker than water.

"Isn't this a wonderful place?" she said.

For a moment Francis strained the mystic bond of kinship to breaking point by looking blank, as if he thought his cousin had taken leave of her senses.

"The *décor*" Julia explained. "It's so unexpected. It's a survival of provincial Edwardian splendour, almost perfect except for the gas lighting. I wish they'd kept that."

Francis stared about him. Inspired by Julia's enthusiasm he began to see charm where before he had seen only pretentious bad taste. He smiled, and said it was a pity they could not dress the waitresses in long black frocks and frilly aprons and streamered caps to match their background.

"And us!" Julia cried. "I should be wearing a big hat with drooping plumes, and a feather boa. And of course I should have a magnificent figure, all in and out."

This time he took his cue. "I prefer you as you are." he said neatly. Julia laughed; Lady Finch raised her head from her malted milk and said:

"Gas lighting? There's nothing romantic about *that*. It's smelly and dirty and thoroughly dangerous. Did you know that old Miss Daglish's nurse, when she was a baby, set the nursery on fire through trying to curl her hair at a gas bracket? And she was bald for the rest of her days."

"No, I didn't," said Julia. "What a terrible thing."

Lady Finch wiped a milky moustache from her upper lip and pushed back her chair. She announced that she had some more shopping to do, and that since Julia had been kind enough to offer her a lift she would meet her at the car in twenty minutes' time if that suited her. Julia said it would suit her beautifully and the car was parked in the station yard.

"I know that," said Lady Finch. "If I hadn't known I couldn't have met you there, could I? You told me it was there when you first offered the lift."

"How stupid of me," Julia said humbly.

Lady Finch picked up her umbrella and shopping bag, and strode away down the room.

"I don't think she really likes me," Julia said to Francis. "And she never thanked you for the malted milk."

"She was too busy denouncing gas lighting."

"I didn't know what to say about that. I mean, it was a very sad story—about Miss Daglish's nurse—and yet it was so inappropriate."

"Very alarming for Miss Daglish, anyway."

"But, Francis, she wasn't there."

"You didn't listen. The tragedy took place in the nursery, and presumably the infant Miss Daglish was occupying it."

"No, no—she wasn't born. It happened to the nurse, when *she* was a baby."

"I can't agree," Francis said gravely. "If the nurse was a baby at the time, how could she be trying to curl her hair at a gas bracket? It's improbable that a baby would have curling tongs, or even hair."

"Well—perhaps you're right. But the infant Miss Daglish must have had hair, if the nurse was curling it."

"I didn't say that. The nurse was curling her own hair. The infant Miss Daglish was merely a horrified spectator."

"I hope the Daglish family forgave the nurse and fitted her out with a handsome wig."

Julia was pleased to see that Francis could take an interest in something which had nothing to do with charters or mediaeval burgesses. Francis was pleased to find that Julia could talk amusing nonsense, for it was a long time since he had known anyone well enough to indulge in this form of relaxation. They sat on in the emptying café, forgetting the wet morning and the shopping and Lady Finch waiting by Julia's car, until the un-Edwardian waitress reappeared to say that the table was reserved for early lunch customers and morning coffee was now off. Julia looked at her watch and exclaimed in dismay:

"She'll never forgive me! I shall pretend I remembered something urgent . . . fish—no, I've got that—it will have to be buttons or sewing-cotton . . . Francis, are you going to the Aged Animals' Pension Fund?"

"Not to my knowledge. What is it?"

Walking back to the station yard, Julia explained that it was a garden party—or so she supposed—and that it was being given by Mrs. Wilmot on Saturday week, and everyone in Goatstock was going to it. Francis said he had not been asked. He knew the Wilmots, but he seldom saw them; and probably they realized that he wasn't particularly fond of animals, aged or otherwise.

"But it isn't confined to animal-lovers—or Wilmot-lovers, either," Julia said. "No one wants to go, but I understand that Mrs. Wilmot's invitations are like royal commands and can't be refused. What a pity you're not going—I'm sure it would be much more enjoyable if we were both there. We should see the funny side of it."

Like other men, Francis firmly believed that he had a sense of humour. But few of his acquaintances seemed aware of it, and no one had hitherto detected in him an ability to see the funny side of tedious social occasions. He could not help feeling gratified by Julia's words; and he felt too that she understood him much better than most people. These feelings led him to say, with unexpected warmth, that he hoped Julia wouldn't give up her entire time to Goatstock and its inhabitants but would remember that she had a cousin no further away than Heswald.

"Of course," cried Julia, correctly identifying Francis with himself. "And I hope, now that we've settled in, you'll come and see us more often. When you can spare the time," she added tactfully.

"But you must come to Heswald," Francis declared. He was still elated by her recognition of his sense of humour, and the elation spurred him to attempt hospitable heights which normally he would have shunned. "You must both come and dine," he said cordially. "A small celebration to mark your return to your native heath."

"A dinner party? What fun! Of course we'd love to."

He had not really intended to give a dinner party, but he was now committed to it. For an instant he wondered what Mrs. Sable would say and whether she would co-operate; then, meeting Julia's happy anticipatory smile, he cast the doubt away. He felt in his pocket for the engagement book he always carried.

"When shall it be?" he asked boldly.

Whenever he liked, Julia replied; and qualified this remark by saying it had better not be before the week after next. He was rather glad of this, because he had already realized that it would take a little time to organize an entertainment of that kind. The family silver would have to be fetched from the Bank, the menu planned, and, of course, suitable guests chosen and invited. He flipped over the pages of the engagement book; Julia, standing beside him, could not help seeing that they were all blank for weeks and weeks ahead, with apparently not even a visit to a dentist or a tailor to break the dreadful monotony of his life.

'I must change all that, she thought. In her mind's eye she saw the empty pages peppered with important engagements, and heard Francis explaining to some would-be host that he was a very busy man. She found her own little book, and held it so that he could see what an engagement book ought to look like. It was true that a lot of the squiggles were books for her library list or the telephone numbers of shops, but the general effect was crowded and impressive.

Bidding Francis good-bye, she said that she hoped they would see him at Belmont House before long. It was nearly a fortnight to the day of the dinner party; and anyway, she added, the dinner party would not give them an opportunity for a nice, long talk, which she had been looking forward to for ages.

At these words he felt both flattered and alarmed.

"What shall we talk about?" he asked. Even in his own ears the question sounded faintly apprehensive, and he hastily added that there was nothing he would like better.

Lady Finch received Julia's apologies graciously.

"Please don't distress yourself," she said. "I had meant to be home early, to get the bees ready, but it's too wet to open the hives."

"Ready for what?" Julia asked.

"For their At-Home day, tomorrow afternoon. My demonstration, you know. I've invited the Reddrod and district B.K.A. and I'd planned to demonstrate my swarm-control system. But if it's as wet as this I shall just have to give them a talk."

Julia tried to look intelligent and sympathetic.

"Bee-keeping must be so interesting," she said. "You have to tell your bees everything, don't you? I've read about that somewhere."

"Death," Lady Finch said portentously. "That's the only thing that really matters. I believe some people tell them about other things, but I think one's quite safe if one sticks to death."

"Oh," said Julia. How gloomy for the bees, she thought, to hear nothing but tidings of death. For a moment her sympathy for human beings was diverted to the insect world. "But surely you tell them about weddings?" she asked.

"There never are any weddings," Lady Finch retorted. She chuckled suddenly and loudly, startling Julia out of her entomological reverie. "Though I hear there's going to be one at last. Yes, I mustn't forget to tell the bees—after all, he's a beekeeper himself."

"Who?"

"Alaric Pope. Mind you, it's supposed to be a secret; but I hear he's going to marry Miss Brigg."

CHAPTER XIII

A WET WEEK-END was as common in Goatstock as elsewhere, and the uninterrupted wetness of Friday, Saturday and Sunday caused no particular disappointment to anyone except Mrs. Minnis and Lady Finch.

Lady Finch was disappointed because her bees' At-Home Day was ruined; the demonstration could not be attempted, and only six people turned up to listen to her talk on 'Bee Stings as an antidote to Rheumatism'. (The six were all local beekeepers who dared not offend her by staying away, and who cravenly joined in her strictures on the effeminacy of the absentee Reddrod beekeepers.)

Mrs. Minnis was disappointed because she had planned to take Hugo and Sonny for a lovely picnic on Sunday; that is to say, they had talked about it at supper on Saturday, and afterwards Mrs. Minnis, with her usual optimism and a quite unusual forethought, had hard-boiled three eggs and prepared a sardine spread. These were not wasted; the Minnises ate their picnic fare in the diningroom, sitting on rugs in the window bay to make it more amusing; but even this humorous interlude could not redeem the day from failure. Mrs. Minnis was disappointed; and when she woke on Monday morning the sense of disappointment was still with her.

It was raining as hard as ever, and Hugo had to breakfast at eight, and it was Monday. Mrs. Minnis saw all the days of the week as differently coloured. Saturday was pink and Sunday was bright yellow, and Monday wasn't black—that would have been too ordinary—but a drab greenish-brown. She was an erratic housekeeper and there were no special chores to account for Monday's distasteful hue. Perhaps it was a relic of past Mondays in her childhood, in the fabulous country-house where each day was coloured by the moods of her autocratic papa.

At half past eight, when Mr. Minnis went out to start the car, a small patch of blue sky had appeared, and the violence of the rain was lessening. Mrs. Minnis, at the window, observed these signs and remarked to Charlton, who was finishing his breakfast, that it was going to be a fine day after all.

"What a shame it isn't yesterday!" she said. The disappointment still rankled; and at the back of her mind there lingered another relic of childhood, the idea that a disappointment could be neutralized by the advent of a lovely surprise—a box of chocolates, or, in extreme cases, a visit to London and a matinée. This belief, and the sight of the patch of blue sky, had a powerful effect; they gave Mrs. Minnis what she called a brainwave. As she announced it she hurried across to the kitchen dresser and seized a bit of paper and a pencil and began to scribble a list of what would be needed: sausage rolls and potato crisps, gin and sherry and orange squash. "Run and stop Daddy," she said to Charlton. "It's lucky he's going to Ormiston today—he can get all this stuff there. I'm not going back to Pergate and Heaton, after all that unpleasantness last time."

Pergate and Heaton were the grocers in Reddrod, who had jeopardized the last Minnis cocktail party by refusing to supply any more gin until their long-outstanding account had been settled.

"A party tonight?" Charlton queried. "But, look here, Bobs, it's *Monday.*"

Mrs. Minnis tossed her head gaily and besought her son not to be so stuffy. Why shouldn't they give a party on a Monday? That's what they could call it, she went on happily: a Monday-Party . . . or a Spur-of-the-Moment Party . . . or—yes!—a Welcome-Home Party. That was it—a welcome-home party for Marian Prentice, who was starting her holiday that very day.

Charlton showed no enthusiasm for this plan.

"I don't see why we should give Marian a welcome-home party," he said. "Surely that's up to the Prentices."

"But they never give parties. Oh, I know they ask people in for drinks, but that isn't the same thing when it's just about six of you and biscuits out of a tin."

"What I feel . . ." Charlton began.

But what he felt had to wait, for the distant slamming of a car door reminded Mrs. Minnis that Hugo was about to depart for Ormiston.

"Quick, quick!" she cried, flapping excitedly at her son as if he was a wasp. To escape the indignity of being flapped at Charlton turned and ran.

"Tell Daddy to come back to the house," Mrs. Minnis screamed after him. At this hour of the day it was impossible for her to go out-of-doors, because she was wearing last week's cotton-frock and a minimum of make-up. She waited anxiously in the hall, hoping that Charlton would be in time and that Hugo wouldn't be difficult. The Monday party had now become the most important thing in the world.

Mr. Minnis was seldom difficult. When they first met he had been captivated by Mrs, Minnis's gay, childish ways, her impulsiveness and her professed unconventionality; and although twenty-four years of matrimony had accustomed him to these characteristics his attitude of indulgent approval was by now as much a habit as being an *enfant terrible* was for his wife.

There was one difficulty, however, which had to be faced. "Shall I pay for all this stuff?" Mr. Minnis asked, standing in the hall and scanning the crumpled paper which Mrs. Minnis had thrust into his hand.

"We—ell, if you go to that shop in the High Street, Birtwhistle and Something, they might let you put it down. We haven't actually got an account there, but I've had things before."

"Um," Mr. Minnis said doubtfully.

Mrs. Minnis clapped her hands as if she had just had a wonderfully bright idea.

"I know!" she exclaimed. "Give them a cheque."

"Actually, Bobs, I'm not sure if they'd take a cheque. I don't think they know me."

It did not occur to either of them that this was perhaps just as well. If they wouldn't, they wouldn't, Mrs. Minnis proclaimed, but Hugo had better *try* to make them take a cheque, and he had better take some of the nest egg with him in case he had to pay cash.

The nest egg lived in a flat leather box hidden at the back of a drawer where Mr. Minnis kept his underwear; the box, to make it doubly safe, was wrapped up in a white silk scarf which had belonged to Mrs. Minnis's papa, and heavily padded with mothballs to put burglars on the wrong scent. The nest egg itself varied in size from month to month; and no part of it ever paid income-tax. Luckily it was at present quite large, so that Mrs. Minnis was able to add olives, Angostura bitters, and a bottle of whisky to the list, and later on to send Charlton down to the village shop for a hundred cigarettes to fill up the silver box that looked so empty on a packet of twenty.

Charlton should have returned to his work in Reddrod by the early bus, but in the excitement of the brainwave and the unpacking of the nest egg the bus had come and gone. He had not approved of the brainwave, but now, since there was to be a party anyway, he agreed that he might just as well take a day off and help to prepare for it. After all, he said, if he caught the later bus the morning would be pretty well gone before he got to the office and no one ever did much work on Monday afternoons.

"And you're only young once," his mother added gaily. Being a mother, for Mrs. Minnis, meant being good pals with Sonny and bad pals with the nationalized industry that employed him.

Charlton went off to telephone to the Coal Board—by speaking of his sub-sub-office as the Coal Board he amused himself and infuriated Harriet—and Mrs. Minnis washed up the breakfast things in a slapdash manner which left all the plates as greasy as they had been in the first place. Then she sat down and wrote two notes, one to Lady Finch and one to Miss Daglish, inviting them to Kandahar at six-thirty that evening. "Just a spur-of-the-moment party to welcome Marian Prentice back to Goatstock," she scribbled briskly—though the Prentices had not yet been invited. Lady Finch and the Daglishes were not on the telephone, but everyone else could be rung up and coaxed or bullied into coming. Mrs. Minnis did not think of it in these terms, but she had often noticed that guests were more easily obtained if they were rung up than if they were written to.

The Prentices lived next door; and a personal approach was even better than the telephone. She waited till Mr. Prentice had left the house (this gave her time to attend to her face and change her frock), and then she hurried round to the back door of Balbus Cottage and surprised Mrs. Prentice by walking in as if they were bosom friends instead of mere next-door neighbours.

A determination to be friends with everybody had carried Mrs. Minnis through many a more frigid reception; and Mrs. Prentice, on her knees counting the washing, was badly positioned for being dignified or aloof.

"Good morning," said Mrs. Minnis. "Isn't it a gorgeous day? I mean, it's *going* to be—it's practically stopped raining already and there's a Dutchman's pair of trousers over the garage roof. Look here, I've had a brainwave—at least, I hope it's going to be a brainwave, but it sort of depends on you—"

She paused, looking hopeful and eager. Mrs. Prentice rose to her feet and asked non-committally what it was.

"I feel *dreadful*, popping in at this hour," Mrs. Minnis assured her. "Of course I know you must be awf'ly busy—aren't Monday mornings ghastly?—only I just had to come because it's about tonight and you've simply got to say Yes!"

Mrs. Prentice's first thought, on seeing Mrs. Minnis at this unwontedly early hour, was that she had come to borrow something. She remembered the lawn-mower, which they had borrowed and left out all night in the rain, and the piece of rubber tubing, which had returned a foot shorter than it went; and she was quite determined to refuse Mrs. Minnis a quarter of margarine or a few spoonfuls of tea, because tea and margarine were never returned at all. It was difficult for her to look severe, but she strove to look uncooperative.

"I've got Marian coming home today," she said, "so I'm rather busy—"

"But that's it! That's what my brainwave is about!"

With gurglings and chirrupings Mrs. Minnis explained her wonderful idea: something to cheer us up after the wet weekend . . . have it out of doors because that will be more fun . . . a jolly welcome-home for Marian. The last inducement did not go down very well; Mrs. Prentice was incensed by the suggestion that Marian needed a warmer welcome than she would get in her own home, and she began to breathe deeply and rapidly, as if her lungs, like bellows, were fanning a fire which would presently burst into flames of indignation. But these signs of mute opposition only encouraged Mrs. Minnis to greater exuberance, exaggerated *bonhomie,* and loud, reiterated wails that it would ruin everything if the Prentices weren't there. Nor could Mrs. Prentice think of any good reason for refusing the invitation; and at last she was forced to accept it.

Mrs. Minnis skipped with joy. She lingered a little longer to tell Mrs. Prentice what a lovely party it was going to be; then she remembered that the other guests had yet to be invited, and hurried off to despatch Sonny with the notes and to telephone to Mrs. Wilmot, Mrs. Dunstan, and Miss Pope. It was not to be a large party—there was no time for extensive preparations—so she decided to ask everyone in Goatstock and no one outside it.

'Everyone in Goatstock' meant, of course, everyone who might, at some future date, ask the Minnises back, and Lady Finch and the Daglishes were included mainly for reasons of prestige.

There were two telephones at Belmont House, one in Julia's bedroom and one in a small alcove at the back of the hall. The alcove, where Uncle James had kept mackintoshes and gardening jackets and an Inverness cape, had now been equipped with concealed lighting and an upholstered stool, and on the shelf beside the green telephone was a pad for taking messages. Sometimes a green pencil could be found with the pad, but more often it was in Robert's pocket.

"You should tie it to the telephone with a piece of string," Dora said. But Julia thought that looked petty—as if one set an inordinate value on pencils, or as if the place was a boarding-house. She spoke to Robert about the matter, half-jokingly but with an undertone of seriousness, and the next day he produced five-and-a-half green pencils retrieved from various pockets, and put them in a neat row beside the telephone. A week later they had all disappeared again.

This time Julia blamed Carrington. Carrington was the house-parlourman, and in spite of his honest eyes she was not sure if she trusted him. Dora put it differently; in spite of his excellent references, she said, it seemed improbable that he had ever been a house-parlourman before. But whether or not he stole pencils, and whether or not he knew his job, Carrington had gained an immense advantage over the other applicants for the post. Nanny had taken to him.

There had been only two other applicants, both local women who had come to be interviewed; and Nanny had declared that she wouldn't have either of them in her kitchen. So Carrington had been engaged, and was now slowly learning his job; he seemed quite willing, though rather stupid, and Julia was alternatively vexed by his stupidity and pleased by his impressive appearance in the dark trousers and grey alpaca jacket with which she had provided him.

It was obvious—or at least it was obvious to Julia—that Carrington must sometimes enter the alcove where the telephone lived; the disappearance of the pencils proved it. Unfortunately he was seldom there when he ought to have been; he seemed deaf to the sound of the telephone-bell or antipathetic to this means of communication. Nanny shared his aversion (it was perhaps a bond between them), and if Julia and Dora and Robert were out the telephone rang unheeded.

At three o'clock on Monday afternoon Dora had to telephone the laundry. When she returned from this task she reported that there was a message written on the pad: Mrs. Minnis had rung up at ten that morning to invite them to a cocktail party that very evening.

"Carrington is coming on," she said. "Not only did he answer the telephone—he wrote it all down in block capitals and put p.p. Jacob Carrington at the end."

"But why didn't he *tell* us?"

"I suppose he thought we should read it on the pad."

"I don't mind people being stupid," Julia said kindly. "After all, they can't help it, poor things. But Carrington is so stupid that I sometimes wonder if he's quite 'all there'."

"If he isn't, he can't help that, either," Dora pointed out.

"No-o. But it's a bit hard on *us*," said Julia, implying that retainers who were not quite all there did not deserve the high wages and excellent food which Carrington was getting.

"Well, what about Mrs. Minnis? This must be the spur-of-the-moment party she hinted at. Shall we have a previous engagement?"

Julia thought it would look rather rude to refuse now, so late in the day. It would have been all right, she explained, to have refused straightaway, but now Mrs. Minnis's feelings might be hurt. It would look, wouldn't it, as if they had waited to see how they felt, or to see if anything better turned up.

Dora replied that Julia was making far too much fuss about Mrs. Minnis's feelings. "Of course, if you *want* to go, say so—it's all one to me. But I don't suppose she will really mind whether we're there or not."

Julia believed in kindness and forbearance, but nevertheless she was affronted by two things in this speech. To be told that she was making a fuss was bad enough, but to be told that Mrs. Minnis would not regret her absence was worse, because it implied that Mrs. Minnis did not like her. For a moment, regardless of forbearance, she allowed herself to look at Dora with a frankly hostile eye. The large pink face, the loose summer frock, the muscular arms and legs, were all in separate ways displeasing, and together they added up to a person Julia regretted having to call cousin.

"It isn't that I want to go. I think we *ought* to go. But if you would rather not, Dora, I'll go by myself."

Julia spoke with gentle dignity and with just a faint tremor in her voice. Unfortunately the tremor's faintness made it inaudible to Dora's insensitive ears, and she declared that she would certainly come too.

"I'll telephone now," she added, jumping up briskly. "Unless you'd like to do the telephoning?"

Julia shook her head.

In the interval which elapsed while Dora, at the telephone, explained and apologized for the delay and listened to Mrs. Minnis's repeated assurances that it didn't matter one bit, Julia had time to get her thoughts under control. She persuaded herself that Dora did not mean half she said; or rather, that her manner of speaking made the things she said sound harsher than she intended. Her voice, when she accused Julia of making far too much fuss, had been the voice of a rather intolerant head-girl criticizing the behaviour of some junior member of the school; it had exactly that tone of lofty contempt which one heard from youthful autocrats.

But lofty contempt, even though it was no more than an unfortunate mannerism, was irritating to live with. The desert island, the picture of a solitary hermit communing with Nature, undistracted by the presence of Robert, Nanny, Carrington or

Dora, hovered beguilingly in the background of Julia's mind, while on another level she debated what she should wear that evening. She wondered whether Mrs. Minnis's party would be worthy of her new dress; but since cocktail parties in Goatstock appeared to be infrequent she decided that she had better not miss this opportunity.

"At half past six," said Dora, re-entering the room in boisterous haste and banging the door behind her. "It's only a small party—just the locals—and it's going to be in the garden if it's fine. It's going to be a *lovely* party. She said so."

"The garden will be rather wet," Julia said thoughtfully. It was a better day than yesterday, but there had been several heavy showers; their own garden, seen from the window, glittered damply in transient sunshine.

"Yes, the grass will probably be sopping, so we'd better go in strong shoes. And strong clothes, too, because of all those rambler roses. I think I'll wear my old blue."

Julia did not argue; but the thought of Dora in strong shoes and her old blue, squelching about on a wet lawn beset by rambler roses, cheered her considerably. It also served as a warning. She determined to stay indoors, or at least in the loggia, and to refuse all invitations to look at the rockery, or whatever other objects of interest the Minnis garden offered.

CHAPTER XIV

AT SIX O'CLOCK it was raining heavily and the Minnis family, in various stages of undress, were hurriedly mobilized to clear the sitting-room—or, as they preferred to call it, the lounge— so that the party could be held indoors. But at ten past six the rain slackened, and Mrs. Minnis suggested hopefully that it was going to be fine after all. None of them wanted to clear the lounge; Mr. Minnis was in his shirt sleeves and had yet to mix the drinks, Charlton was half-shaved, and Mrs. Minnis, who had just had a bath, would need all the remaining twenty minutes to comb out her tangled locks and wriggle into her new suspender belt. With one accord they decided to abandon the Herculean task; after all, Mrs. Minnis said, the guests could shelter in the loggia if there was another shower. And that reminded her, she had not yet washed the other five glasses which had been put away on the top shelf.

As it turned out, there was no time to wash the glasses; but she dusted them quickly, confident that the insides would be clean because they had been standing upside down. Then she ran upstairs and started to dress; but two minutes later she had to run down again to light the oven and put the sausage rolls in to get hot. As half past six approached the sounds of frenzied activity in the Minnis home grew louder and louder; Mr. Minnis was opening and shutting drawers, hunting for the cork-screw, and shouting to Bobs to get the ice; Mrs. Minnis, upstairs on the landing, was lamenting the ladder which had suddenly appeared in her best nylons, and calling to Sonny to go down and help Daddy; Charlton, who was already downstairs, was dragging a massive carved chair, which normally lived in the hall, towards the french window that led to the loggia. The chair was too heavy to lift, and its progress rucked up the carpet and swept a number of coats from their pegs; they lay in a heap just inside the front door, ready to trip up the first arrival.

"What are you doing?" Mrs. Minnis cried from the head of the stairs.

"Old Mr. Daglish," Charlton explained. "He'll want somewhere to sit, so I thought I'd put this outside in the loggia."

"But—"

"Bobs, what's wrong with the fridge? It hasn't made any ice."

Mrs Minnis gave a cry of woe. "I turned it off!" she exclaimed. "I turned it off to de-frost it, and I forgot to turn it on again!"

It was a crisis, but the Minnises were used to them.

"Run next door, Sonny, and ask Mrs. Prentice if you can have the ice out of her fridge," said Mrs. Minnis. "And come back quickly and get that chair out of the way. No, *no*, we don't need it—the Daglishes aren't coming."

The Daglishes' refusal had annoyed her. It was absurd to say that they had another engagement, when one knew perfectly well they hadn't. But everyone else had accepted: the Popes, Mrs. Dunstan and Miss Duckworth and the nephew, Mrs. Wilmot and James (but not Mr. Wilmot, who could reasonably be excused because he was in London), and Lady Finch and Harriet. And, of course, the Prentices and their daughter Marian, for whom the party was being given. They would be arriving at any moment, and here she was with one stocking on and the other off, and the hall littered with coats, the dining-room door blocked by the chair, Hugo clamouring for ice....

"And, good heavens, the sausage rolls!" she cried, rushing to rescue them. Luckily they were only dark brown, not really burnt. Luckily, too, everyone in Goatstock knew better than to arrive punctually at a Minnis festivity. The early comers were apt to find themselves shifting furniture or arranging shrimps in pretty patterns on cream-cheese-covered biscuits.

Even Julia and Dora had heard about the hazards of arriving too early, and they waited till five to seven before setting out. Julia said they would take the car, though it was no distance, because she was sure it was going to rain again. Dora, wearing her strong shoes and armed with an umbrella, said that a drop of rain would not hurt them; but Robert, who belonged to the generation that does not walk if a car is available, sided with his aunt. Julia rewarded him by letting him drive.

"Really, it's hardly worth while getting *into* the car," Dora said, as they arrived at the gate of Kandahar.

"We're not the only ones," Julia pointed out.

A handsome, opulent-looking coupé was drawn up in front of them. Robert looked at it with respect and wondered aloud who owned it.

"That's the Wilmots' car," Dora said. "At least, it's *one* of their cars. They have two—an enormous limousine and this. I suppose this one belongs to poor James."

"He can't be as poor as all that," said Robert.

The front door of Kandahar stood open, and after knocking and ringing and attracting no attention they entered the house. A pile of coats heaped untidily on a chair in the hall suggested that it was quite a large party, and Julia was surprised, when they had made their way through the dining-room to the loggia (after glancing through other open doors at empty rooms in a state of extreme disorder), to find no more than ten people including the three Minnises.

So far, no one ventured into the garden. The guests were huddled together at the open side of the loggia, like a group of nervous ducklings on the edge of a pond (pond, thought Julia, was an apt description of the dripping garden), while Mrs. Minnis, glamorously attired in a white *broderie anglaise* dress with a red belt and red-heeled shoes to match, scurried about with plates of food and urged everyone to step out into the lovely sunshine.

Dora, always a good guest, and incurably inquisitive about other people's gardens, was the first to obey her. Her example gave courage to the others; James Wilmot and a pretty, placid-looking girl followed her down the steps and along the puddle-strewn path towards the sun-dial, and were pursued by Charlton Minnis with a tray of drinks. Lady Finch went as far as the foot of the steps, where she stood talking to a small, quiet man who looked as if he would rather have stayed at home. Julia had just decided that the pretty girl must be Marian Prentice, and was wondering if the small, quiet man was her father, when Mrs. Minnis clutched her by the arm and said vivaciously:

"You know Mrs. Prentice, don't you, Mrs. Dunstan? Oh, but *surely* you do! Anyway, I needn't introduce you—'cos after all, you must know her by sight!"

The gay giggle that accompanied this sally was meant to remind Julia of the shocking episode of the railings, which had now become, in Mrs. Minnis's eyes, a delightful bit of devilry.

"Have a sausage roll," she begged, holding out a tray of dark, tough-looking morsels. Julia refused, but Mrs. Prentice, flustered and anxious, was easily mesmerized into taking one. Mrs. Minnis skimmed away to greet the Popes, who had just arrived. Mrs. Prentice drew a deep breath and burst into floods of conversation.

Small talk, as a rule, did not come easily to her; at least, not at cocktail parties, where she usually drank tomato juice and suffered from tight shoes and a feeling of sad isolation. But now, out of nervousness and dismay, she took big gulps of the strange, strong cocktail Mr. Minnis had thrust into her hand,

and talked—as if to stave off disaster—about the weather, the village, how nice it was in some ways to live in a village, and yet how much one missed a town . . . the weather in winter, muddy roads and no proper pavements . . . how nice Belmont House looked. . . .

From the outside, she nearly added; then, sheering off in horror from this gaffe, she found herself back with the weather, so nice at this time of year though of course not this particular evening.

At that point she absent-mindedly took a bite out of the sausage roll instead of drinking the last of her cocktail, and so was reduced to silence. Julia, seizing her chance, said that she was glad to meet Mrs. Prentice, and added that her nephew Robert had already met Mrs. Prentice's daughter Marian, when they went for the picnic.

"Which wasn't a great success, but that was the fault of the weather," she said. The reference to the weather steadied Mrs. Prentice; it suggested that Julia's conversational standards were quite humdrum and ordinary, like her own, and that she would not expect one to discuss political problems or modern pictures. These were topics which made Mrs. Prentice feel stupid, which was almost worse than feeling flustered.

"Yes, it was because of the sea fog," she agreed. "Otherwise it would have been a *lovely* picnic. But of course Marian enjoyed the drive. It was very kind of you to lend the car."

"Is your daughter here this evening?"

Over there; yes, the one in pink, Mrs. Prentice explained. Soon she was telling Julia all about Marian, about her nursing career, her achievements at school, her curly hair when she was a baby. She was almost sorry when Mrs. Minnis, seizing her by the arm, swept her away to join Lady Finch and Miss Duckworth on the lawn. The long-dreaded meeting with Mrs. Dunstan, which she would have given anything to avoid, had gone off much better than she expected. In fact, it had gone off so splendidly that she merely smiled forgivingly when Mrs. Minnis, giving her arm a confidential squeeze, whispered that she had told Mrs. Dunstan all about the dreadful day when they thought Belmont House was still empty.

"I'm so scatty," Mrs. Minnis giggled. "I just blurted it out. But she didn't mind a bit."

"How nice of her," said Mrs. Prentice. Either Julia's charm or the strength of the Minnis cocktails had dulled her social embarrassment. She went forward to meet Miss Duckworth with hardly a tremor.

It was fortunate that Dora had put on strong shoes, and that Lady Finch, whose passion for good health made her indifferent to appearances, was wearing goloshes; for the lawn was very wet indeed. If there had been time to cut the grass it would have been done, Mrs. Minnis said, but somehow there hadn't been a moment.

Mr. Prentice, overhearing this remark, thought to himself that the Minnises were also handicapped by the lack of a lawn-mower. Their own had a broken chain; it had been broken for weeks, and after the third week he had refused to let them borrow his any more. He had told them, with steely politeness, that it needed certain adjustments; and he really did not care if they heard it whirring away happily behind the high brick wall when he mowed his own lawn on Friday evenings.

"Our host is generous with his drinks," he remarked to Mr. Pope; with whom he was sharing a comparatively dry piece of crazy paving.

"He will brook no refusal," said Mr. Pope.

Mr. Prentice thought that Mr. Pope's refusals had been rather half-hearted, but he did not condemn him; the wretched chap looked as though he never got enough to eat, and alcohol was said to be fattening. And he'd certainly got a good head, he thought admiringly, watching the vicar knock back his third—or was it his fourth?—cocktail.

"I am not acquainted with the ingredients of a cocktail," Mr. Pope said, smiling at his own ignorance. "But I think one may take it that these contain a fair proportion of orange juice and are therefore, to some extent—ah—beneficial."

'Take it that way if it makes you feel happier,' thought Mr. Prentice, admiring Mr. Pope more than ever for his ingenious conscience-quelling theory. "Quite," he said aloud. He was a silent man whose thoughts were generally more complex, detailed, and caustic than his utterances. His wife and children believed him to be kind but unobservant.

Unlike her brother Miss Pope had no head for alcohol. She knew it, and never accepted more than one glass of anything; but even one glass of Mr. Minnis's fiery mixture had a powerful effect, and Miss Pope was now enjoying the party immensely. Propped against the sun-dial, and happily unaware that its damp, lichened stone was making a terrible stain on her best summer frock, she prattled away to James Wilmot and Marian about her *bête noire*, the New Town.

"It will be good-bye to Goatstock!" she declared, lifting her glass as if she were drinking to a dear departed friend.

"But the New Town may be a good thing," Marian suggested. ("We must look forwards, not backwards", Hubert had written in his last letter.) "I mean, for other people, not necessarily for ourselves. There's a dreadful housing shortage in Reddrod—"

"Then why not build houses *there*?" Miss Pope said quickly. "Reddrod people won't want to come out here, you know. They'll hate it. I remember, in the war, how the evacuees hated the country. They were quite out of their element."

"Only it won't *be* country, when the New Town is built. It'll be a town, like Reddrod," Marian pointed out. "Only newer, of course."

"That's the awful thing. A sprawling, smoky town all over these green fields. Really, I cannot bear to think of it. It shouldn't be allowed."

While they argued James Wilmot kept opening and shutting his mouth; he was slow to get started, and each time he attempted to speak Miss Pope or Marian forestalled him.

"James looks just like our goldfish," Harriet observed to Robert. She stepped on to the lawn, and then stepped back again to the crazy pavement. "No, we can't walk across there to join them, it's too wet. We must go round to the other side and along that path."

"Why do you want to join them?"

So that you can talk to Marian, Harriet had decided. "To make a nice group," she said aloud. "At cocktail parties people should always huddle into groups. It's the done thing."

"Not at this party," said Robert. "Unless two people can count as a group."

Miss Pope and her auditors stood by the sun-dial. Beyond them, at the other side of the lawn, were Mr. Prentice and Mr. Pope. Mrs. Prentice and Dora were under the high wall, apparently inspecting a fine crop of weeds which grew there, and Lady Finch was talking to Charlton Minnis at the foot of the loggia steps. Safe and dry in the loggia, Julia was entertaining Mrs. Wilmot so charmingly that for the moment Mrs. Wilmot had ceased to keep a stern maternal eye on poor James.

"It's badly organized," Harriet said. "They ought to have had it in the house. Or asked a lot more people, to fill up the garden. Anyway, they seem to have lost interest in it."

Mr. and Mrs. Minnis had disappeared.

"To brew another vat of poison," Robert suggested.

"To put on warmer clothes," Harriet countered. "At least, I suppose *he's* all right, but she must be frozen with the wind blowing through all those holes in the *broderie anglaise*. I wish I'd worn my winter vest."

"Did you bring a coat? Shall I fetch it?"

Robert had been well trained; his aunt Julia was always despatching him to fetch coats, scarves, or the bag that held her embroidery. But Harriet did not know this, and she could not help feeling flattered by his attentiveness. Unfortunately, although she had come in a coat, it was her old school one, dyed brown, but still betraying its humble origin, and much too shabby to appear at a party. She had left it with Lady Finch's mackintosh in the hall.

"No, thank you," she answered. "I'll bear it. We shall be going soon. Aunt Finch is sure to go early because she doesn't really care for parties."

If this was a typical Goatstock party, Robert thought, he rather agreed with Aunt Finch. A chill breeze had sprung up and ominous-looking clouds were banked in the western sky; the guests, dispersed about the garden, were talking in low voices with none of the hilarity usual at cocktail parties. Only the group by the sun-dial, which had been augmented by Charlton Minnis, appeared moderately happy and animated. But now that

Charlton was in the group Robert was stubbornly determined to remain outside it.

Harriet shivered. "You *are* cold," he said firmly. "Look, we'll go into the loggia. No reason why Julia and Mrs. What's-her-name should have it to themselves."

It occurred to Harriet, for the first time, that the voice of masculine authority had a certain charm. No one else had ever offered to fetch her coat, or noticed when she shivered; Charlton Minnis, she thought scornfully, would go on talking about himself if his audience was freezing to death, and wouldn't walk a yard to fetch any coat but his own. But before she could answer Robert they were joined by Lady Finch, who announced loudly that she was quite ready to go home.

"It's beginning to rain. I'll drive you home and then come back for my aunt," Robert said.

Harriet's favourable impression of Robert was deepened; but she thought sadly of her shabby coat, which Aunt Finch would force her to put on. Lady Finch, however, said briskly that they could perfectly well walk. She added, echoing Dora, that rain never hurt anyone, if one was suitably dressed for it.

"A lovely surprise," cried Mrs. Minnis, appearing like a jack-in-the-box at the sitting-room window. "Come in, all of you—come in out of the wet!" The command was unnecessary, for the guests were already hurrying to shelter through the pattering rain. "I had another brainwave," she told them. "Something to keep you from getting pneumonia. You must all have just one little glass before you go!"

The brainwave turned out to be hot punch—or, as Julia said afterwards, the remains of the cocktail mixture, with Algerian wine added to it, heated up in a pan which had recently contained onions. This concoction, dished up in a handsome cut-glass bowl, was borne into the dining-room by Mrs. Minnis, and Mr. Minnis served it with a long-handled toddy ladle, one of a pair which had come from Mrs. Minnis's old home, and which were, he assured Julia, real old curios. Only Lady Finch was strong-minded enough to refuse the hot punch, although several of the guests, once they had tasted it, drifted back to the loggia and tipped some part of their ration on to the flower bed beside the steps. Those who cheated in this manner included Mr. Prentice, but not Mr. Pope, who, touchingly grateful for being saved from pneumonia, tilted his glass to imbibe the last drop and told his hostess that these old-fashioned cordials did one more good than a dozen doctors.

Lady Finch, who would have been quick to point out his ignorance of what made a cordial, had already departed, marching off briskly through the rain with a disconsolate Harriet at her side. The other guests soon followed. Minnis entertainments were apt to drag on interminably, with Mrs. Minnis producing one lovely surprise after another and no one being quick enough to make a getaway in the intervals; and nearly everybody, on this occasion, felt grateful to the rain for putting a definite end to the party.

Mrs. Prentice, her feet slowly expanding in comfortable shoes and her best dress back on its hanger, was able to say truthfully that she had enjoyed herself.

"I'm so glad to have met them at last," she said.

"Who?" asked Marian.

"The new people at Belmont House—Mrs. Dunstan and Miss Duckworth. I had a talk with each of them. They're quite charming."

"But didn't you call?"

"Well—no," said Mrs. Prentice, becoming slightly flustered. "I—it was all a misunderstanding. And then I felt so embarrassed afterwards, and yet it seemed too late."

Hidden behind his newspaper, Mr. Prentice wondered inquisitively what misunderstanding could have kept his wife away from Belmont House. But Marian, whose thoughts were in Africa, let the remark float away unchallenged.

"It's nice that they're nice," she said a moment later, keeping up a pretence of conversation with the minimum of mental effort.

The newspaper quivered. Mr. Prentice's thoughts ranged round the theme—'that a child of mine . . .!' But Mrs. Prentice, her peace of mind happily restored, agreed that it was *very* nice that they were—well—

'Well—nice,' said Mr. Prentice to himself.

"Well—ladies," said Mrs. Prentice. '*Real* ladies,' she thought gratefully: as if pseudo-ladies, confronted by a social outcast, would have behaved very differently.

CHAPTER XV

THE WORST of going to a party on a Monday, said Miss Pope, was that it disorganized the rest of the week. It muddled her; Monday did not feel like Monday, and so, naturally, Tuesday did not feel like Tuesday; and now she had got it into her head that today was Friday, when really it was only Wednesday.

Marian said that happened to her sometimes, but not this time because holidays were different. It was at the hospital that she got muddled, especially when she came off night-duty and seemed either to miss or gain a day. Miss Pope agreed that this must be dreadfully muddling; then, peering anxiously out of the window, she asked if Harriet or Marian had seen the fishmonger's van in the village, because he usually got to the vicarage before half past ten and now it was after eleven and still no sign of him. Could he have broken down?

"But he doesn't come on Wednesdays," Harriet said. "You're still thinking it's Friday."

Miss Pope gave a shrill cry of self-reproach. "So I am! And if there's no fish, what can we have for lunch?"

"Well, what do you generally have on Wednesdays?"

"Oh yes, of course—the little pies the baker brings! Dear me, I suppose he brought them this morning as usual, and I never noticed. He puts them in the cupboard outside the back door; I'll just go and make certain they're there."

She rushed out of the room. Marian said to Harriet that Miss Pope was getting frightfully absent-minded.

"There's something *on* her mind," Harriet said. "I suppose she's worrying about Alaric."

This was only the third day of Marian's holiday and she had not yet caught up with village gossip. She asked, with bright professional interest, if Mr. Pope was ill.

"Isn't it odd that we say 'Alaric', but never 'Myrtle'?" Harriet remarked thoughtfully. It distressed her to see her friend changing into a hospital nurse under her very eyes, and yet she could not help teasing Marian by dangling Mr. Pope before her, for a little longer, in the role of a possible patient.

"No one calls her 'Myrtle'. Not even your mother, who's such a close friend," she went on. "Of course it's rather a silly name for Miss Pope, isn't it? It makes one think of Venus and that bush with spiky leaves."

"Well, we don't call Mr. Pope 'Alaric' to his face," Marian pointed out. Harriet replied that that had nothing to do with it; it was how one thought of him.

"I suppose it's because it suits him so well," she said. "Some names are perfectly appropriate. Look at Mary Ellen Brigg—what could be more fitting?"

Before Marian could answer Miss Pope returned. She had left the door open, and Harriet's last remark must have been audible in the hall. She glanced from one to the other, and asked with some animation what it was that Mary Ellen was fitted for.

While Harriet was explaining that some people had exactly the right sort of names, and instancing Mary Ellen (but not Myrtle), Marian noticed that Miss Pope was not listening. She had begun by listening intently, but as soon as she had grasped Harriet's meaning she seemed to lose interest and begin thinking about something else. It was clear to Marian—now that Harriet had pointed it out—that her hostess was preoccupied; but when, at the first pause in their talk, she asked politely after Mr. Pope's health, Miss Pope replied shortly that he was very well.

Marian was puzzled; for Harriet had said Miss Pope was worried about Alaric, and to Marian's conventional mind it seemed that a vicar was, so to speak, above being-worried-about, unless he was in ill-health. A good, worthy vicar, she meant, like Alaric; not like that spiteful vicar under whom Hubert had once served as a curate, who had quarrelled with everyone, and had caused Hubert much distress by writing a series of articles for a popular newspaper on 'What is wrong with the Modern Church', in which he said some cruel and unjust things about the Modern Curate.

But though she was puzzled, she remained polite; she bridged the awkward silence that followed Miss Pope's words by saying how lovely the vicarage garden was looking, and how hard Miss Pope must work to keep it in such good order.

"I do," said Miss Pope. "Far too hard, I often think. I mean, I can't help asking myself if it's really worth it."

Marian was sometimes obtuse, like her mother, but on this occasion she had no difficulty in following Miss Pope's train of thought.

"In case it's all swept away when they build the New Town?" she asked sympathetically. (The New Town might be a good thing, but it would be a shame if the vicarage garden suffered.)

"Oh . . . the New Town?" said Miss Pope. "No, I wasn't thinking about that." She seemed to realize that this remark, from the New Town's leading opponent, was inadequate; for she added, with something of her normal, indignant manner, that if the New Town built houses in the vicarage garden they would regret it.

"People don't like living so close to the church," she explained. "You see, they feel frightened of the churchyard at night—that is, if they're elderly and—er—ignorant people. And if they're young, nowadays, I'm afraid they very often complain of the noise of the bells. So if our lovely garden is turned into houses, *no one* will live in them."

This pronouncement appeared to afford her considerable satisfaction, and Marian and Harriet felt that it was a good moment to get up and go. They had called at the vicarage to leave a note from Mrs. Prentice, and had not intended to stay so long. In fact they had not intended to stay at all, but Miss Pope had met them on the doorstep and had insisted on their coming in.

"A shame, on your holiday," Harriet said, as they hurried away up the street. Marian was to lunch at Urn Cottage and spend the afternoon there; it was a glorious opportunity, because Lady Finch was attending a Beekeepers' Meeting the other side of Ormington and would be leaving on the twelve-thirty bus.

"But I like Miss Pope," Marian protested. "She's so kind and energetic. She does a lot of good work."

Harriet sighed. In twenty or thirty years, would someone be describing Marian in just those words? Then, remembering Miss Pope's friendly welcome, she felt she was being ungenerous.

"I like her too," she said. "Or perhaps I'm sorry for her. She looks as if she could stand up for herself, but she can't. Miss Brigg will simply brush her aside."

Marian was startled. She asked what Harriet meant, and Harriet began to tell her about Miss Brigg's ruthless pursuit of Alaric Pope. That it was now common gossip in Goatstock was chiefly due to Miss Brigg herself; Miss Pope had confided only in Julia, but Miss Brigg had told several people how welcome she was at the vicarage, and how the vicar said he couldn't get on without her . . . and to one or two bosom friends she whispered that Miss Pope's idea of a meal wouldn't fatten a sparrow and that if the dear vicar wasn't a saint he would not have put up with his sister's housekeeping for all these years. It was somehow implied that in spite of his saintliness the vicar was not going to put up with it much longer.

"And she's always there," Harriet said. "Darning his socks and washing his surplices, and cooking fragrant messes to win his heart. I hope you can cook with the best, Marian. If you can't you'd better start learning at once, in case some Mrs. Beeton pops up in the middle of Africa and lures Hubert away with a *soufflé.*"

Though she recognized it as a joke, Marian grew pink with indignation.

"Hubert doesn't mind *what* he eats," she declared. "He isn't interested in food."

"That's what Miss Pope used to think about Alaric."

"But it's not the same thing. After all, Alaric isn't married."

"Aren't you sorry for Miss Pope?"

"Well, yes, I am," Marian admitted, struggling with her sentimental belief that marriages were made in Heaven and that friends and relatives ought not to interfere. The belief was based on her own experience; but if Harriet's account was true it sounded as if Mary Ellen Brigg was the maker of this particular match, and in that case it was permissible to ask oneself whether it would be a Good Thing.

"And I think it would be a pity if Alaric married Miss Brigg," she continued. "She's so domineering. She'd have favourites and enemies, and want to manage everything. She's not the right person for a vicar's wife."

"Oh, I wasn't thinking of Alaric. He's born to be dominated anyway. I was thinking of poor Miss Pope, left high and dry. Probably she refused lots of good offers when she was young, because she thought it her duty to look after him, and now it's too late."

They had reached the gate of Urn Cottage, and as Harriet uttered these words she began to climb the steps which led up the steep bank to the front door. It was a shock to find Miss Brigg waiting outside the door; from the level of the road she had not been visible.

"Good morning. How are you?" Harriet cried warmly, as if Miss Brigg was her dearest friend. She had not meant it to sound like that; she had meant to sound easy and natural and gracious, but she overdid it. Behind her, Marian gave a gulp of dismay (surely Miss Brigg must have heard them discussing her), and then echoed Harriet's greeting in the same warm, heartfelt tone. Miss Brigg glared at the pair of them, scorned to answer the enquiries about her health, and said briskly that she had come for the honey.

"Aunt Finch's department," Harriet replied. "But I expect she's gone by now. She was catching the half past twelve bus."

"Three honeycombs she promised me—and I've paid for them. She promised I could have them today."

"Then perhaps she has left them ready. I'll go and see."

Harriet opened the door and led the way into the sitting-room. Another surprise awaited her; for there was Robert, on his knees by the wireless and apparently engaged in mending it. Pliers, screwdrivers, and bits of the set lay on the carpet, Robert's coat was hanging on the back of a chair, and in another chair his dog had curled up for a nap. As Harriet entered the room Robert looked up with a welcoming smile, which faded as soon as he observed her companions.

"Goodness!" Harriet exclaimed. "What are you doing?"

"Oh—I just looked in, and your aunt asked me to mend this thing."

"That's what happens when people look in on Aunt Finch. You're lucky that you didn't have to scythe the orchard."

Once again Robert had the feeling that he was up against a blank wall. Any other girl would have known that he had called to see her, not her aunt; and most girls, he could not help thinking, would have been pleased and grateful for this attention and sorry he had been let in for an hour with their dreadful aunts. But Harriet was either strangely naïve or strangely indifferent to masculine admiration.

He put it in those words because it sounded better, but his real fear was that she looked on him as a comic character, like Parson Pope or that clot Charlton Minnis.

"Hullo, Taffy. Nice dog!" said Marian. Taffy, uncurling himself, hopped down from the chair and advanced smiling his eye-tooth smile; a fleeting thought crossed Robert's mind that dogs were good judges of character, and he began to talk quite amiably to Marian; not only did Taffy approve of her, but she looked sympathetic and took an interest in his struggles with the wireless, while the other woman, the redoubtable Brigg, was nattering to Harriet about some honey.

"Come with me," Harriet said. "I expect it's on the dresser in the kitchen." Shepherding Miss Brigg, she left the room. She had noticed the easy way in which Robert and Marian greeted one another, and she was quite glad that Miss Brigg's quest gave her an excuse for leaving them together. This was what she had hoped for, this was what she had planned; and now, with Marian's holiday stretching ahead, there would be opportunities for their budding friendship to blossom into romance.

'That must go in my diary,' she thought, repeating the phrase with approval.

Miss Brigg reckoned that a peep into other folks' kitchens told you more about them than an hour's talk in the drawing-room, and she stumped along the passage in a better humour than when she had entered the house. A lifetime of fending for herself had taught her to collect information about people's characters and to assess her acquaintances for their weaknesses as well as for their good points. Old Miss Daglish, who had once seen Miss Brigg's beady eyes fixed on the stack of empty wine-bottles under her sink, had subscribed generously to the charity she was collecting for at the time and had remembered ever afterwards to wish her good-day when they met; and since the Daglishes were greatly respected by Goatstock's older residents this small courtesy had helped to establish Miss Brigg as an acceptable new-comer. A humble approach to the back door, when collecting for charity, paid dividends in more ways than one.

But the back door of Urn Cottage opened into a small covered yard, so Miss Brigg had never seen Lady Finch's kitchen. It was, at first glance, disappointing: spotlessly clean, the table scrubbed, no brandy bottles or dirty plates, no underclothing hanging up to dry and betray its owner's taste. (Mrs. Minnis's kitchen, now—those knickers and bust-bodices on the rail, falling to bits and indecent even if they hadn't been.) Nothing but a large glass bowl on the window ledge, full of narrow green leaves arranged with spiky symmetry round a couple of unripe tomatoes.

"That's a salad," Harriet said, following her glance. "Dandelions and sorrel, I think. Aunt Finch must have made it before she went out."

"For your rabbits?" asked Miss Brigg. She knew they went in for silly pets.

"No, for us."

Miss Brigg was shaken. "You don't eat *dandelions*?"

"Yes, we do. They're good for the kidneys."

Miss Brigg was speechless.

"But the honey isn't here," Harriet continued. "Are you sure you said you'd come today?"

Miss Brigg, who was always on the *qui vive* for affronts, made a rapid recovery.

"*I'm* not one to forget," she declared. "Wednesday I said and Wednesday it is. *And* I've paid for them."

"So you said. Would it do if I brought them tomorrow?"

"No, that it wouldn't. I told your auntie, I want them to give to a friend that's coming from Reddrod this afternoon."

Angry and determined, Miss Brigg stood in the doorway, as if she meant to stay there till justice was done. Harriet regarded her coldly. She did not like Miss Brigg and she did not care whether Miss Brigg's friend got her present of honeycombs or not; nevertheless if Lady Finch had promised them Miss Brigg had right on her side.

"I'll look in the bee house," she said.

She walked across the yard. The honey, and all the beekeeping paraphernalia, was kept in an outhouse; the shelf that held the honey was almost empty, because it was only July, but there were six sections—or, as Miss Brigg called them, honeycombs at one end, and three others standing in a cardboard box on top of the extractor. She assumed that these had been set aside for Miss Brigg, and carried them back to the house.

Miss Brigg looked at them suspiciously.

"Are they good ones?" she asked. "I told your auntie I wanted good ones. My friend, she knows what's what."

"They are the best our bees can manage," Harriet assured her.

It was only after Lady Finch's return that she discovered the truth of this statement. The afternoon passed pleasantly enough, because although Robert refused Harriet's invitation to stay for lunch (and just as well, she thought afterwards, since there was hardly enough for herself and Marian) he came back to finish mending the wireless, and the three of them sat in the garden and made plans for a picnic and other amusements during Marian's holiday. Harriet made the plans; Marian said it depended on what Mummy wanted her to do; Robert, who was in temporary disfavour with his aunts, decided that picnics à trois were preferable to being made to garden under Dora's eye or having earnest talks about his future with Julia.

"Not on Saturday," Marian said. "Father will be at home— and anyway we're going to the Aged Animals' Pension Party. Are you going, Robert?"

"I suppose so."

"Oh yes, you mustn't miss it," said Harriet. "It will be the party of the season."

Lady Finch did not return till eight o'clock. She was hot and tired; she had missed a bus, thumbed a lift from a car, and walked the last three miles.

"The man in the car was an American Wideawake," she said. "Extraordinarily interesting."

"Like Ku Klux Klan?"

Not at all, Lady Finch said crossly; American Wideawakes believed in selfless living and a two-day fast once a fortnight, which cleared the brain. Harriet hoped her aunt would not take to wide-awakeness; for the idea of a two-day fast did not appeal to her. To change the subject she told her about Miss Brigg's visit, but when she mentioned the sections in the cardboard box Lady Finch cried out in dismay.

"They were being kept for the Honey Show! Really, Harriet, you have no more sense than a child. They were my *best* ones, and I'd put them there on purpose so that I shouldn't sell them by mistake. You must go to Miss Brigg tomorrow and get them back."

"How can I? I can't say, those are the best ones and you must have second-best ones. Anyway it will be too late—she was giving them to a friend who was coming from Reddrod to have tea with her. They'll be in Reddrod by now."

"You should use your eyes. There were several sections on the shelf. What possessed you to take them from the box?"

"Well, why didn't you leave hers out on the dresser?" Harriet protested. "And the Honey Show isn't till October—surely the bees will make some more sections by then."

"Not like those. They were perfect—I should have got a First in the Open," Lady Finch said mournfully.

Every October she went to London for a week, to see the National Honey Show and visit old friends and bare her teeth at the secretary of an unsuccessful society for making people eat Nature's Food. She believed that the secretary was incompetent and that if he resigned the society would expand and flourish. (But Harriet had once gone through the annual report and worked out that the death-rate in the society's ranks was much above the average for the country.) The Honey Show, however, was the highlight of Lady Finch's visit, and to win a prize

there would have pleased her more than the incompetent secretary's resignation; but she had never yet won even a Highly
Commended.

Thinking of this, Harriet suddenly felt sorry for her aunt.

She glanced across the room at the despondent figure. Ever
since she could remember her, Aunt Finch had been a tall, dominating woman with a mass of black hair and a weather-beaten,
but somehow unageing face; now for the first time, she looked
old and tired and disappointed. 'Perhaps she never will win a
prize,' Harriet thought; 'perhaps I've spoilt her only chance'.

"I'm dreadfully sorry," she cried. "I ought to have looked at
them—I ought to have guessed. Perhaps it's not too late after all;
I'll go to Miss Brigg tomorrow and get her friend's address, and
then I'll go to Reddrod—"

"You'll do nothing of the sort," said Lady Finch, with a brisk
return to her normal manner. "No, you were right before—we
can't go asking favours from Mary Ellen Brigg. We shall just
have to make the best of it."

Nevertheless she gave Harriet an approving nod, thinking
that though she might be silly her heart was in the right place.

CHAPTER XVI

CANAL LODGE, where the Wilmots lived, was larger and more
imposing than the name suggested. It was also very ugly—a
mid-Victorian residence built of yellow brick, now mercifully
shrouded in creepers, with a squat tower at one end and huge
plate-glass windows which effectively destroyed the scale of
its pseudo-Jacobean façade. The tower carried a flag-staff, and
on gala days such as this a Union Jack waved patriotically in
the breeze.

Mrs. Wilmot was not popular in Goatstock, but fortunately
she was not dependent on Goatstock society. She had a large
circle of acquaintances, which she continually sought to extend,
and although her neighbours accused her of snobbery they had
to admit that she still kept up with people she had known in
the past. The charity meeting for the Aged Animals' Pension

Fund was an occasion when all her acquaintances, old and new, respected or merely tolerated, were gathered together to make the best of one another. Mrs. Wilmot rightly felt that it was an occasion when quantity, not quality, was needed; there was to be a silver collection for the Pension Fund, after Lady Sybil's speech, and one or two other money-making sidelines, so that even the humblest guest had a certain financial value. Moreover, the printed invitation card, the free tea, and the use of her garden counted, in Mrs. Wilmot's eyes, as hospitality.

The Aged Animals had been fortunate; the sun shone, the afternoon was warm without being sultry, and as it had not rained for three days the grass was dry enough for comfort. A small marquee, standing on a lesser lawn beyond the drive, would have been the only refuge against the rain; but this marquee was now deserted and the guests were directed to the big lawn on the west side of the house. Between the lawn and the house was a stone-flagged terrace, and here rows of green chairs had been set out in preparation for the fund-raising speeches. Most of the guests, however, were strolling on the grass, seeking out friends and banding themselves in groups which represented the various levels of Mrs. Wilmot's visiting list.

Julia, Dora, and Robert, who had arrived rather late, found the Goatstock group already formed and waiting to receive them.

"Now we're *all* here," Miss Pope said happily, counting heads as if it was a Sunday-school outing.

Julia perceived that she was surrounded by her village acquaintances, and realized that it must have been choice, not accident, that brought them all together in one part of the lawn. She found this amusing; and then, on second thoughts, rather touching—for probably it was a sort of inferiority complex which made them feel shy and ill-at-ease and anxious to stick together.

"Good afternoon," she said several times, to those who stood nearest—Lady Finch and Harriet, Mr. and Miss Daglish, and the Popes. But she had not come to Canal Lodge to talk to these people, whom she saw every day; she had come to amuse, and be amused by, Francis, and to get to know poor James, and of course to establish herself, in Mrs. Wilmot's eyes, as a lover of Aged Animals.

She did not care for Mrs. Wilmot, but the Wilmots were rich and owned a lot of land, and might be useful allies in the future. It was really on Francis's behalf that she had come; for his career, as guide and mentor to the New Town, might well depend on her ability to influence local opinion. This altruistic thought came to Julia just as she caught sight of Francis himself, standing on the edge of another group nearer the terrace, and she began to detach herself, smoothly and politely, from the eager talkers at her elbow.

"Good afternoon," she said again, turning away to greet Mrs. Prentice and leaving Dora to bear the brunt of Lady Finch's denunciation of ridiculous, *useless* charities which took money away from well-deserving ones.

"Whoever heard of pensions for pigs!" Lady Finch asked rhetorically.

"What a lovely afternoon!" Mrs. Prentice exclaimed. "And really, as I was saying to Marian, the house may be ugly but it has a beautiful view, hasn't it?"

The wide lawn sloped gently to the canal, and a line of trees and shrubs hid the outskirts of the village. The view of the canal, however, and of the open fields beyond, was rather marred by a strong chain-link fence which the Wilmots had put up to repel intruders. But Julia ignored this blemish and agreed with Mrs. Prentice that it couldn't be nicer. Then, leaving Robert this time to act as audience, she detached herself from the Goatstock circle and strolled across the lawn towards Francis.

"How wise of you," said Miss Pope, reappearing suddenly at her side. "If we go now we can get good places and all sit together."

Julia's stroll was taking her in the direction of the terrace, and she saw that some of the green chairs were already occupied.

"Good places for what?" she asked.

"For the speeches. Lady Sybil Fazackerley, you know—she's the president and she'll tell us what the Fund does."

"But we know that already. It gives pensions to aged animals."

"But she'll explain how it works. I've wondered about that—I mean, who chooses the animals and so on. I'm quite looking forward to hearing about it."

Miss Pope was in a holiday mood. Most money-raising activities—bazaars, whist drives, evening concerts in the Guides' Hut—were for causes in which she took a personal interest; they meant, for her, hard work before and during their occurrence. Often she slaved in the background, brewing tea or cutting sandwiches, and there was always the fear that something would go wrong, that they would lose money instead of making it. But today she was simply a member of the public; and the cost of the afternoon's entertainment (she had agreed with Alaric that a florin from her and half a crown from him would be a suitable donation) would be offset by the interest of learning how strangers coped with financial and other problems.

"There must be so many candidates," she went on. "Like our own Smethurst Bequest for Poor Widows—they get twenty-five shillings each at Christmas, but there can only be five of them, and it's so difficult for Alaric to decide *which* five. The ones who aren't chosen always say the others have cheated."

Julia could not see that the Aged Animals' Pension Fund had much in common with the Smethurst Bequest for Poor Widows, but she suggested that Miss Pope ought to discuss it with Lady Sybil Fazackerley.

"Has she arrived? Do you know her?" she asked, surveying the crowded lawn. Francis had his back to her; he was talking to a tall, bony woman whose ill-chosen attire of pale pink chiffon, long dangling silver chains, and a large feather-burdened hat, had the strange effect of increasing her resemblance to a horse.

"There she is," Miss Pope replied, pointing discreetly to this figure. "No, I don't know her—except of course by sight. She's the daughter of the last Earl of Carnpool," she added humbly, as if a great gulf separated vicars' sisters from the daughters of earls.

Julia walked forward. She looked on Miss Pope as her protegée, and she had already planned the kind action that was to follow. Francis would introduce them both to Lady Sybil, she herself would give Miss Pope a good start by mentioning her great interest in pension schemes, and then she would drift away and leave Miss Pope to enjoy a tête-à-tête which would give her pleasure and take her mind off other matters.

She would drift away, of course, with Francis, who would surely be glad to be rescued from that boring-looking woman. The happy thought that she would be bringing off *two* kind actions—a right and left, so to speak—so gratified Julia that she looked back with an encouraging smile; but this was hardly necessary, for Miss Pope was following her closely like a devoted, well-trained dog.

Francis's invitation to the Pension Fund meeting had arrived only three days ago, and his first instinct had been to refuse. But then he remembered that he had a sense of humour, and that Julia would be counting on it to help her through a dull afternoon. The last-minute invitation, which had ruffled his dignity, could now be interpreted as a compliment, since he believed that Julia had been responsible for its coming. In this he was right; for at the Minnises' party Julia had taken pains to let Mrs. Wilmot know that he was a great lover of animals.

So here he was, a martyr to cousinly duty; but, to the casual spectator, a man who seemed to be enjoying himself. Indeed, Julia's serenity was impaired, as she greeted him, by the fear that he was enjoying himself almost too much and that he felt resentful, or at least regretful, at the interruption. It wasn't, of course, that he showed it; what he showed was a deep interest in Lady Sybil, an interest as surprising as it was unmistakeable.

"Ah, Julia," Francis said amiably. But in Julia's ears his amiability was now suspect. He explained to Lady Sybil that this was his cousin, and after the briefest of pauses he succeeded in remembering Miss Pope's name, and introduced her also. Miss Pope did not wait for Julia to make the tactful remarks that were to give her a good start, but plunged boldly into conversation; and this was just as well, for Julia, agitated by what she had seen, had temporarily lost interest in her protegée.

". . . so much I want to know," said Miss Pope. "About how you choose them, for one thing."

"Naturally we choose the most deserving."

"But how do you decide? I mean, here in Goatstock—"

"*Any* animal is eligible," Lady Sybil said grandly. The Pension Fund was her own creation, and she spoke in the manner of a Proprietress. "If you know of some poor creature here in Goatstock—"

"No, no, ours are widows. I only meant, that we must have the same difficulty in choosing *between* them."

Lady Sybil failed to grasp the distinction. "Widowed animals?" she asked. "I'm afraid that sounds rather sentimental, Miss—ah—Poole. Age, poor condition, and the owner's means, are what we go on. We cannot give pensions for—ah—bereavement."

Miss Pope took the blame for the misunderstanding, and blushed as she apologized for her own stupidity. "I put things so badly," she said. "I meant real widows—that is, human ones."

When things had been explained Lady Sybil gave a high whinny of laughter, which was so much in keeping with her equine appearance that Julia allowed herself another glance at Francis, which she hoped would reassure her; for surely her first impression must have been wrong. No man could really find this bony, whinnying fanatic a fitting object for that look of warm interest.

But the look of warm interest was still there; Julia herself had so often been the object of such looks that she could not miss it. She was aware too of a shade of reluctance in his manner when he turned to answer a remark of her own, as if he would have preferred to go on listening to the loud, rather adenoidal voice discoursing so confidently about fodder and horse blankets.

Julia was quite distraught. Francis had seemed such a hermit; it simply had not occurred to her that he might know, and admire, other women, that a rival Good Influence might already exist in his life. She had thought of him always at Heswald, shut up with his books in the quiet library; but now she pictured him driving over the moors on his way to visit Lady Sybil Fazackerley. Miss Pope had mentioned that Lady Sybil lived in the northern part of the county, and it was to the ancient, ruined Carnpool Abbey that Julia's anxious fancy directed him. She had forgotten that it was a ruin; she only remembered that it lay beyond the Roman camp, and that Francis could reach it without coming to Goatstock.

Probably he only came to Goatstock when his sense of duty compelled him to pay a call on his cousins.

". . . fifty-seven pit-ponies, thirteen fox-hounds, and a tame otter," said Lady Sybil, apparently enumerating the existing pensioners. "Yes, what is it?" she added, wheeling round to address James Wilmot, who for some minutes had been hovering in the background.

He had the air of one who carries a message, and at any other time Julia would have seen, in his meek subservient person, another claimant for her pity; but at this moment she had no thoughts to spare for poor James, whose only merit was that he had come as a welcome interruption to a painful scene. Painful scenes were, in a sense, her speciality; but usually they happened to other people and her role was to listen, to sympathize, to put things right. It was different—quite appallingly different—when the scene was outwardly tranquil and the pain and agitation were her own.

". . . so, if you're ready, Mother thinks we might begin," said poor James, delivering his message as if he had learned it by heart. Most of the guests had taken their places on the terrace, and the stragglers were being rounded up by Mr. Wilmot and two Wilmot nieces imported for the occasion. The casual, garden-party atmosphere had gone; an air of purposeful seriousness prevailed.

The Proprietress replied that she was quite ready. "Mustn't keep them waiting," she added good-naturedly, as if her audience were restive horses. She set off, her floating draperies somewhat impeding her long stride, her silver chains jangling, and James loping dutifully at her elbow. Miss Pope turned to follow. But Julia stood still, as if to admire the view, and therefore compelled the chivalrous Francis to linger beside her.

To rescue him from the Proprietress was no longer a good deed; but then her benevolence was no longer in command. She was too much 'upset' (the simple word contained many ominous meanings) to think clearly, and it was mere instinct that made her pause and wait—and keep Francis waiting too.

"We'd better follow them," he suggested. He noticed that Julia seemed pensive, but unfortunately he could not instantly think of a humorous comment to cheer her up.

"I suppose it wouldn't do to miss the speeches," she said.

"Well—it's what we were asked for."

It seemed plain to Julia that Francis *wanted* to listen to the speeches—or at least to Lady Sybil's speech. She reflected bitterly that but for her intervention he would not have been there at all; and then she wondered if her intervention had had anything to do with it. Perhaps he had made his own plans; perhaps Lady Sybil herself had schemed to have him invited. Planning was one thing, in Julia's mind, and scheming quite another. Scheming was highly reprehensible.

"I suppose Lady Sybil is an old friend of yours," she said, walking as slowly as possible towards the terrace.

"She's the last of the Fazackerleys," Francis said gravely.

Just at first this remark seemed irrelevant; then, in a flash, Julia perceived that it was not. On the contrary, it explained everything. Her agitation subsided; commonsense and intuition fused in the glorious certainty that Francis regarded Lady Sybil as a genealogical specimen of the finest quality, the last representative of an all-but-extinct race. 'A living fossil,' she said to herself; and the phrase seemed so apt that it was hard not to say it aloud.

"Is she an only child?" she asked instead, suiting her voice to the solemnity of the theme.

"There was a brother. He died when he was two. He would have been the fourteenth earl and twenty-eighth baronet."

"How sad."

But she did not feel sad. She looked fondly at Francis, who was reciting dates. The anguish she had suffered, and her relief at its ending, had made her aware that he was the most important of her responsibilities.

The speeches, which dealt with the trials and tribulations of aged animals, made little impression on Julia, because she had other things to think about. It was in a way more of a trial or tribulation that she and Francis had to sit with the Goatstock group. Though Miss Pope had been delayed by her conversation with the Proprietress, Mrs. Prentice had acted as her deputy and had kept places for all her neighbours, and as Julia and Francis reached the terrace half a dozen beckoning hands drew their attention to the two vacant chairs which awaited them.

When the speeches ended the silver collection was taken, and after this the guests were commanded to remain in their places for tea. Julia had to sit listening to Miss Pope's flow of speculations about administrative problems, while Francis received from Lady Finch some alarming information about the evils of a meat diet. In the row of seats in front Dora and Marian were telling each other about Africa (Hubert's letters had made it all vivid to Marian, and Dora had once paid a fleeting visit to Cape Town), and from the row behind came the voices of the Minnis family loudly regretting the strange oversight which had caused each of them to come without any money.

Julia soon forgot that she had found the Goatstock clannishness touching. It now began to seem ridiculous; and quite soon, when they had drunk the tepid tea and eaten the disagreeable buns, it seemed thoroughly provincial and boorish. When she strolled away the others strolled with her, Miss Pope at her side and the rest of her neighbours grouped around her like a bodyguard, and although after a time she succeeded in detaching herself and Francis from the bodyguard she could not shake off Miss Pope, who had apparently never heard the saying that two is company and three is none.

"We must go to the marquee," Miss Pope said. "You won't want to miss that, after being so generous to them."

Gently she propelled her friend towards the marquee, where Mrs. Wilmot had assembled a token exhibition of 'Ways in which Animals are Useful'. The exhibits included a scarf and cardigan made from the wool of the useful sheep, a leather handbag, an ink-stand fashioned from a horse's hoof (hideous rather than useful, Julia thought), and a collection of foodstuffs—butter, cheese, eggs, and a piece of boiled bacon.

Next to them, on a separate table, was a display of honey: jars of clear and granulated honey neatly arranged in pyramids at the back, and in front three fine honeycombs standing on a bed of wild flowers in a flat blue dish.

"Honey Exhibit by the Reverend Alaric Pope," said Miss Pope, reading aloud from the hand-printed card. She looked at the blue dish; it was old Spode and had come from the vicarage drawing room, without her knowledge. She felt sure Alaric would never have thought of taking it.

"Bees are not animals," Francis objected. Both Julia and Miss Pope thought this was mere pedantry.

"But they're *useful*," Julia pointed out. "What beautiful honeycombs!"

Miss Pope agreed that they were, and added that Alaric's bees seldom made good sections; they preferred shallow frames.

By the time they had seen the rest of the exhibits the party seemed to be over. Julia said good-bye to Mrs. Wilmot, and then went towards her car, where she could see Dora and Robert waiting for her. Francis had his own car, but she offered Miss Pope a lift home, and after a slight hesitation Miss Pope accepted it.

"I dare say Alaric will be late," she said. "He will have to pack up his honey."

As she spoke these words they came face to face with Lady Finch, who had just emerged from the marquee and was walking straight down the drive. At her side walked Harriet, pale and furious. Julia had barely perceived that something was wrong when Lady Finch stopped, glared at Miss Pope, and said loudly:

"Not his. Mine. My sections!"

"It's false pretences," said Harriet.

"She said they were for a friend in Reddrod!"

"She *cheated* Aunt Finch!"

"Do you mean me?" Miss Pope asked wildly. Harriet and her aunt shook their heads in unison.

"We mean Miss Brigg," said Harriet.

At this Miss Pope looked as if she might burst into tears, and Julia, seeing here a situation that needed careful handling, took her by the arm and led her onward.

"Miss Pope has a dreadful headache," she said to Lady Finch. "I'm taking her straight home. You'd better go and see her to-morrow—or see Mr. Pope."

"I shall never enter the vicarage again," Lady Finch replied. She spoke with a wealth of feeling, as if she really meant it.

CHAPTER XVII

'I OUGHT TO get another man,' Francis thought. He had been thinking this, off and on, for days, and although it was now rather too late to get another man the thought continued to haunt him. Another man, to make the numbers even, was the last vestige of the stately, full-scale dinner party he had originally planned, which had dwindled by slow degrees into himself and Dora and Julia.

The long table he had seen in his mind's eye, with rows of guests conversing in pairs (and turning, at appropriate intervals, to their other neighbours) would have fitted into Heswald Hall; but there was no room for it in the bailiff's house. If they put the extra leaves in the table and extended it to its full length it would not be possible for Sable to hand the dishes. After a rehearsal Francis thought they could accommodate eight people; but then he remembered his mother saying that eight was an awkward number. He could not remember her reason for saying this, but he decided to play for safety and only have six. It had seemed so easy, at the time, to find three other suitable people, that he had done nothing about it. Then, a week later, he had had a talk with Mrs. Sable and had learned that cooking for six, on her own, would be a well-nigh impossible task in that kitchen.

"No one to give me a hand," Mrs. Sable said. "And the oven being what it is. It isn't as if we've ever done owt about modernizing it."

He agreed that they had not.

Mrs. Sable had another look at the menu. Francis had chosen it himself, without consulting her, and had written it out on a large sheet of paper, with letters against some of the items which referred her to explanatory footnotes at the bottom of the page. "*Entrée. Ris de veau aux champignons*, a," she read, battling bravely through the French; and then, "*(a)* Sweetbreads with mushrooms and that brown sauce."

She was devoted to her employer; if she had not been she would never have consented to the dinner party. But her devotion was hidden beneath a dour exterior and kept severely in bounds by a conviction that it was bad for men to have things all their own way.

"If we left out this entrée I reckon I could manage," she suggested helpfully. Six people and no entrée was a fair compromise. Francis, however, wanted the entrée more than he wanted the extra guests; he was proud of his menu and could not bear to curtail it.

So the dinner party shrank to four; and now, on the morning of the day, the ideal fourth guest had still not presented himself to Francis's imagination. Most of his acquaintances were married and could not be asked without their wives; and the rector of Ormington, who was an expert on heraldry and a widower of seven years' standing, was unfortunately on holiday.

"There's Mrs. Dunstan's nephew," said Mrs. Sable, who had now perversely decided that three people wasn't hardly worth while taking all this trouble for. But Francis was determined not to ask Robert. He did not like him, and he thought of him as a mere youth, a juvenile whose callow face and callow conversation would turn a six-course dinner into the semblance of a schoolboy's feast.

"I must be off," he said. "I said I'd fetch the flowers at eleven." And he hurried away before Mrs. Sable could pin him down to telephoning Julia and inviting Robert.

Behind Heswald Hall, a short distance away, were the walled gardens, the greenhouses, potting-sheds, and bothys, where the head-gardener and his underlings had formerly laboured to produce hot-house fruit, multi-coloured coleus and gloxinias for the drawing-room, and serried ranks of bedding-out plants for the formal gardens round the house. The County Education Authority which leased the Hall had sub-let the walled gardens to a commercial market-gardener, and the Deprived Children were still further deprived by not being allowed to enter this fascinating domain, where Francis and his cousins had spent many happy hours in childhood, popping the fuschia buds, teasing the Sensitive Plant, and infuriating the head gardener by stealing individual grapes from every bunch; which they imagined would not show, but which in fact left tell-tale gaps and spoilt the symmetry of the bunches.

The market-gardener, who knew what children were, had taken a strong line from the start. He kept the garden doors locked, sent all his produce to Reddrod, and refused to supply local customers because it was more bother than it was worth. However, he made an exception of Francis Heswald, since he had started his working life as a Heswald employee and still felt a grudging respect for the Family. If Mr. Heswald ordered the stuff the day before, he could have it between eleven and twelve; but he must send someone to fetch it.

Usually Sable was sent; but today he was busy cleaning the silver. Francis took a couple of large trugs and walked across the park, following a track worn smooth by several generations of bailiffs on their daily round. The bailiffs had plotted their route in a big curve which kept well away from the Hall, for they knew better than to annoy the Family by walking past the windows, and Francis took the same path because he found a near view of the Hall and its present occupants depressing; it emphasized the fact that he was a Deprived Owner.

On the return journey he had an additional reason for coming that way; his laden trugs made him feel oddly conspicuous—like a mobile florist's shop—and he wished to be unobserved. It was therefore with annoyance, as well as surprise, that he perceived a figure walking towards him through Cold Iron dingle. Cold Iron dingle was not on the way to anywhere—unless you lived at the bailiff's house and wanted to visit the walled gardens—and the figure was not a deprived child or its custodian. It appeared to be a total stranger, a man of about his own age; and it had no right to be there.

They approached each other; the stranger raised his arm and waved, and Francis realized that they must be acquainted. He did not—he could not—wave back, but a moment later he recognized his second cousin Henry Heswald, whom he had not seen for about two years, and by the time they met he was ready with a welcoming smile. That Henry Heswald should appear suddenly in the middle of Cold Iron dingle seemed to Francis like an intervention of Providence; for Henry was grown-up, unmarried, and a member of the family. He would do very well to make a fourth at the dinner table.

"Your Mrs. What's-her-name told me where to find you," Henry said. "I called at the house—I felt I couldn't pass so near and not look you up."

"I am delighted to see you," Francis said truthfully.

Henry explained that he was on his way north. He lived in Hampshire, but he was going to stay with a friend who had inherited a damp house in Scotland and a nice stretch of fishing. The dampness, Henry said, was rather a drawback, but perhaps it wouldn't be so bad in summer.

'Fussing about his health as usual,' Francis thought. A delicate chest had been Henry's reason for going to live in the south, and because he disapproved of this move Francis had long ago decided that Henry was a bit of a hypochondriac.

"You're *looking* very well," he said, to counteract hypochondriacal tendencies.

"So are you," Henry replied politely.

"This place is very bracing."

"But rather dull."

Francis was nettled that Henry should find the home of his ancestors dull.

"Not at all," he said, putting down one of the trugs to open the garden gate. "Plenty of neighbours. As a matter of fact I am having a dinner party tonight."

"I thought you must be having *something*. All those flowers—and peaches." Henry bent over the trug and fiddled with the tissue paper. "What are these? Ah, figs. I don't much care for figs."

"Don't you? I'm very fond of them myself."

"But that is a remarkably fine bunch of muscatels." He raised it gently from its bed of vine leaves, and they both stood admiring it. "What else are you giving them?" Henry asked; and when Francis told him he nodded his head in appreciation. "An excellent menu," he said. "And the wine?"

They discussed the wine, pacing backwards and forwards across the lawn. Presently Francis suggested that his cousin should stay the night and be present at the dinner party. Henry hesitated; he was tempted, but he had mapped out his journey in easy stages, and if he did not get to Carlisle tonight it would mean a long drive on the morrow.

"Easy stages!" Francis said. "I don't call Hampshire to here an easy stage. Especially as you arrived at half past eleven. You must have started before dawn."

Henry looked shocked. "But I've only come from Shrewsbury," he explained. "Shrewsbury was my first stop."

"Shrewsbury isn't on the way."

"It doesn't have to be on the way. My dear fellow, I'm not a homing pigeon. I can zig-zag about if I like!"

"I loathe staying in hotels," Francis said.

"It's a nice change from housework. But of course you don't do your own cooking, so you wouldn't realize that."

Francis pictured Henry, in his Hampshire cottage, pottering about with saucepans and baking-tins. Still, Henry was a Heswald and blood was thicker than water.

"I'd like you to stay," he pleaded. "As a matter of fact I'm a man short."

Henry's Heswald blood, though vitiated by southern air, could still quicken at the thought of a Heswald in a difficulty.

"My dear fellow, why didn't you say so?" he answered. "Of course I'll stay."

"Splendid," said Francis, so much relieved that he forgot to worry about Mrs. Sable's reactions. "And you'll meet Julia and Dora. It will be quite like old times."

"Who are they?"

"*Julia* and *Dora*. Our cousins—second cousins of yours, of course. They used to stay at Goatstock with old Uncle James, and then he left the house to Julia and they're living there now. You can't have forgotten them."

"Of course I haven't," said Henry, who retained a blurred memory of some leggy girls. He was surprised to learn, a moment later, that Francis's grand dinner party consisted only of these two and himself. Still, it would be a dinner worth eating; and if all Francis's catering was on the same scale as the dessert there would be plenty of it.

"We ought to put these flowers in water," he said, picking up the trugs.

It was unfortunate, from Julia's point of view, that Francis's dinner party and Miss Pope's *crise-de-nerfs* should occur on the same day. She had meant to have a long rest in the afternoon, with the bedroom door locked and rejuvenating clay spread over her face and neck, but at lunch-time Leah Townley brought a note from the vicarage that could not be ignored. At least, not by Julia, who allowed herself no more than a brief fifteen minutes' repose, for the sake of her digestion, before driving off to cope with the crisis.

Dear Friend, wrote Miss Pope. (She had hesitated between 'Dear Julia' and 'Dear Mrs. Dunstan' and had seized on friendship as a way out of her difficulty.)

I can hardly bear it. A. is innocent but then there is the publicity wch. would be terrible. I know he had no hand in it—it was all her doing—however I dare not mention it as it might lead on to other things as I am in such a state. I would have telephoned but there is the Exchange to think of—not that it matters because it is sure to be all round the village in no time. Is there any way of stopping Lady F? I shd. v. much welcome your advice.

Yrs. sincerely,
Myrtle Pope.

The vicarage front door stood open, as it always did in summer. Julia stepped into the hall, tiptoed past Alaric's study door, and peeped into the drawing-room and kitchen. They were empty; Miss Pope must be upstairs in her bedroom. She had never before been upstairs, and on the upper landing she paused in doubt; the bedroom doors were shut and she did not want to intrude on Alaric if he happened to be taking forty winks.

"Miss Pope, Miss Pope!" she called softly.

A door was flung open almost instantly and Miss Pope appeared in her dressing-gown, a faded green garment which somehow gave her the air of a figure in a classical tragedy. She exclaimed, "You've come—I knew you would!" and burst into loud sobs.

"Hush," Julia implored her. At this stage she felt that Alaric's presence would be undesirable and inconvenient.

"Oh, he's out for the day," said Miss Pope, following her thoughts. "Lunch at the Palace . . . the Bishop's Clergy meeting in the afternoon," she added incoherently.

The narrow landing with its worn linoleum and creaking boards was not the proper setting for Julia's sympathy; there was nowhere to sit down, and a steel engraving of a Crimean battle-picture, with a writhing horse in the foreground, distracted her attention. She guided Miss Pope back into her bedroom. Here there was a wicker chair, a small upright chair, and the bed itself; they all looked hideously uncomfortable, but she persuaded Miss Pope to lie down on the bed and drew the wicker chair to her side.

"Now tell me all about it," she begged. She knew by experience that few people, however distraught, anguished and hysterical they might appear, could resist telling one all about it; and this was a good thing, because the recital of their woes or wrongs calmed them down.

"It's true! They were hers!" Miss Pope began wildly. "She bought them from her pretending they were for a friend in Reddrod and then she pretended they were his!"

"Who bought what?" Julia asked, bewildered by all the pronouns.

"Miss Brigg." The name was too much for Miss Pope, who relapsed into weeping. Fragments of explanation fell from her lips between sobs. "The honeycombs—only of course beekeepers call them sections—I never know why. She must have planned it all. . . . Alaric had to visit someone near Ormington . . . so he asked her to see to it. Arranging it, I mean."

"Arranging *what*?"

"His honey exhibit, in the marquee. And she used Lady Finch's sections instead of his. I didn't know at the time—I didn't understand what Lady Finch meant though of course I could see she was very angry about something, saying she would never set foot in the vicarage and so on. . . . But then she's rather eccentric so it hardly counted."

By now Julia had begun to understand what had happened; and her first reaction was that Miss Pope was making an unnecessary fuss. She had expected to have to deal with a major crisis—Alaric's elopement, or Miss Brigg's announcement of their engagement—and for events so dramatic as these she would willingly have foregone her afternoon's rest and facial rejuvenation. But the truth seemed an anti-climax; and in spite of herself her mind went back to her own comfortable bedroom and the chaise-longue in the window. Then she looked at Miss Pope's room, so bleak and ugly, and told herself it was no wonder Miss Pope suffered from *crises-de-nerfs*.

"How did you find out about this?" she asked.

Miss Pope went into long unnecessary explanations of what she had been doing every day since last Saturday. Visits to the dentist in Reddrod; the garden hedge to be cut; and so, for one reason or another, she had not seen any of her friends until this morning, when Mrs. Prentice came in and revealed what Harriet had told Marian.

"Of course Mrs. Prentice is very discreet," Miss Pope said. "I know it won't go any further through her. And of course I pretended it was all a mistake. I said Lady Finch couldn't possibly tell they were her sections. I said Alaric would never *stoop* to such a thing!"

"That's quite true. He doesn't know anything about it," Julia said soothingly.

"But everyone will *think* he knows! His name will be coupled with Miss Brigg's," Miss Pope cried, unconsciously echoing the stock phrases of a Victorian melodrama. "He will be ruined!"

Julia's interest revived. She could not believe that Alaric would be ruined, but she saw that his reputation would suffer. A vicar who passed off someone else's honeycombs as his own, even in aid of a charity, was hardly worthy of respect; and it would be almost worse if people thought he had been led away by Miss Brigg.

"You must speak to him—" she began.

"I can't—I can't! It would mean talking about *her*. He might defend her, and then—then—but what *can* I do?"

She spoke with extreme agitation; it was clear that she dreaded any discussion with Alaric. Julia guessed that she preferred the suspense of the present to the certainty of knowing that Alaric was going to marry Mary Ellen Brigg.

"Well, you must speak to Lady Finch," she said.

"I don't want to speak to anyone!"

It seemed an impasse; but suddenly, prompted by that despairing cry—and to some small extent by the church clock striking four—Julia had a wonderful idea. It was so wonderful, so far-reaching, that it ranked as an inspiration; although these, with her, were by no means as rare as they were with other people. In a crisis she could usually produce one.

"You *shan't* speak to anyone," she declared. "I've thought of something much better—you shall come home with me. We'll put you to bed and give you a real rest, and we'll say you've got—influenza or something."

Miss Pope looked as surprised as if Julia had spread a magic carpet at her feet.

"But Alaric?" she said. "Who will look after him? What will people say?"

"They can't say anything, if you have influenza. *I* shall say I carried you off because there was no one here to nurse you."

"But—"

"As for Alaric, no doubt Miss Brigg will see he doesn't starve."

"But she'll be here all day!"

"She's here all day as it is," said Julia, looking round for something to pack in. "How lucky I came in the car. Now, as soon as you're dressed—"

"I am dressed—all but my frock."

Miss Pope sat on the edge of the bed and felt for her shoes. Then she took off the dressing-gown and put on a bright blue cotton frock—the frock she had worn the day they met—and brushed her hair rather half-heartedly. Julia had found a Moses basket in the wardrobe and was casting into it everything that came to hand.

"Not influenza perhaps," she said. "Something less banal. Are you ready?"

Though outwardly ready, Miss Pope was still a prey to fearful doubts. She hesitated, twisting her handkerchief between nervous fingers.

"I know I'm being silly. But I'm so afraid Alaric will—will find out he can do without me."

"No, no," Julia cried. Her intuition was operating so power-fully that she was deaf to the voices of doubt and reason. "No, no. He will *miss* you."

CHAPTER XVIII

"CHARMING," Henry said decisively. Then he walked to the oth-er end of the table and looked at it from there. He bent over and fiddled with a carnation that was protruding beyond the rest, and straightened one of the candles. "I don't think it needs any-thing else," he said.

Francis agreed with him; secretly he thought the table deco-rations erred on the side of extravagance. A silver bowl of carna-tions in the middle, and the four Corinthian candlesticks round it, had been his original intention, but Henry had added four Vene-tian glass dolphins, two handsome Georgian silver tankards, two pairs of embossed silver-gilt spoons, and several small dishes of crystallized fruit and chocolates. He had also placed the silver bowl on an ebony stand so that it might be seen to better advan-tage, and this towering centrepiece would effectively screen each guest from the one sitting opposite. Still, Henry had taken a lot of trouble, and it was now rather too late to alter things.

"The silver has come up very well," Henry said.

The silver had been badly tarnished, and even after Sable had cleaned it stains showed faintly here and there. Henry had spent most of the afternoon going over it again, and now it gleamed brightly. Francis had feared that Sable would take offence, but oddly enough Henry seemed to have made a good impression on the Sables and his demands for soft cloths and a clean chamois-leather had been willingly met.

Francis, who believed he was a kind, considerate employ-er, was slightly annoyed that his guest should get better treat-ment than himself; for he had been left to arrange flowers, hunt for missing objects, and alter the position of the furniture sin-gle-handed.

"It's a shame to keep that silver put away in boxes," Henry said. "You ought to have it out. You could easily clean it yourself if the Sables haven't got time."

The implication that his own time was less valuable than his servants' did not escape Francis.

"I am busy too," he replied.

"My dear fellow, you can't be. Why, I run my house with only a daily twice a week. Of course I have a gardener as well—I'm not strong enough to tackle the digging."

'On about his health again,' Francis thought. If Henry had not been a Heswald he might have taken a dislike to him. As it was he added an indulgent rider—'poor old Henry'—and said it was time they changed.

Julia, of course, was late in starting. She had had to interview Nanny and Carrington and Dora and Robert and give each of them a slightly different set of reasons for Miss Pope's sudden arrival. She had had to coax Nanny into preparing a light supper of milk soup and a poached egg for the invalid as well as a heavy supper for Robert. She had had to have a soothing interview with Miss Pope, now comfortably installed in the best spare room; and last of all she had had to ring up Alaric. The bus that brought him back from the Bishop's Clergy meeting did not arrive till seven-fifteen, and it would take him at least ten minutes to walk home from the bus stop; she allowed him another ten minutes to look round the empty vicarage.

"Francis said eight o'clock," Dora reminded her.

"We shall be there," Julia replied optimistically.

She picked up the telephone receiver. The distant buzzing continued for some while, but at last Alaric answered. "Hullo, hullo, hullo," he chirruped anxiously; and Julia smiled.

"This is Mrs. Dunstan," she began.

"I thought you must be my sister," Alaric said, sounding disappointed.

"I have some rather distressing news for you."

"I can't think why she isn't here."

"I am sorry to say she has influenza." (It had had to be that after all, for she had not been able to think of another illness which did not require medical attention.) "And as there was no one to look after her I persuaded her to come to us."

There was silence while he took it in.

"She seemed all right this morning," he said distrustfully.

"She was feeling wretched when she woke up—and then it got worse later on. Of course she's not seriously ill, but she's thoroughly overtired and I'm sure a really long rest will do her good."

"Of course it's kind of you, Mrs. Dunstan—very kind indeed, to come to our—her rescue," said Alaric, suddenly remembering his manners. "But—er—surely, in the summer, influenza doesn't take long? I know there's a good deal of it about at present, but . . . Forty-eight-hour influenza, they call it!" he added triumphantly, clutching at the memory of a recent conversation with the district nurse.

"Well—we shall have to see how she is in forty-eight hours."

"But—"

"Don't worry, we'll look after her carefully."

As clearly as if he had said it aloud Julia was conscious of Alaric saying to himself, 'But who will look after me?'

She felt pleased; but Dora was making faces at her and pointing to the clock. After a few parting reassurances she left Alaric to brood over the situation.

"Really, Julia—" Dora was saying; and she replied gently:

"Well, I had to let him know. It would have been cruel to leave him in suspense."

They were late; but it was Henry rather than Francis who worried over the delay. Francis had been expecting it, for one of his bits of general knowledge was that ladies were always late; but Henry's sympathies were in the kitchen with Mrs. Sable. Nevertheless, when his second cousins Dora and Julia at last appeared he warmly enjoyed their exclamations of astonishment, their pleasure at seeing him again after all these years. His presence at the dinner party no longer seemed fortuitous; he now thought of himself as the principal guest.

"What a surprise!" Dora repeated. Henry smiled modestly. Francis removed Julia's sherry glass and began shepherding his guests towards the dining-room. Julia thought how simple, how unworldly Francis was; he invited them to a dinner party and then produced only one other guest. She had expected a collection of dull neighbours, and to impress them (and Francis) she had worn her grandest frock, but although this was a little too grand for a family dinner she still preferred her choice to Dora's; Dora was wearing a high-cut blue frock, and satin slippers of quite a different blue.

"The frock comes down to the ground, so they won't show," she had said, when Julia pointed it out to her.

But of course they did show, because Dora sat drinking her sherry with her knees crossed and her skirt several inches above her ankles. 'Poor Dora, she simply doesn't care,' Julia thought happily, noticing that the slippers looked oddly old-fashioned, as if they had belonged to Dora's mother.

When they entered the dining-room Julia saw at once that she had made a mistake—not in wearing the grand dress, but in supposing that this wasn't the occasion for it. The glittering table, the lighted candles, the menu cards, all proclaimed that it was.

Dora disappeared from view behind a silver bowl bristling with carnations and maiden-hair fern. Francis sat at the head of the table and Henry, after pausing for another admiring glance at his handiwork, took his place at the foot. Each, like Julia and Dora, was now invisible to the other; and owing to the length of the table, which had been extended to make room for the dolphins and tankards, there was a considerable gap between the ladies and the gentlemen.

Dora's loud voice could bridge the gap with ease, she could even toss remarks over the carnations to the invisible Julia. But Julia felt herself at a disadvantage; she excelled in tête-à-têtes, in soft confidential murmurs and expressive sighs, and she was too far away from Francis for these to be possible. She was also, of course, too far away from Henry, but she had already decided that it would be a waste of time to talk to Henry while he was eating. She was a strong believer in first impressions; and Henry's face, in the fleeting, unguarded moment when she entered the library, had been the face of a greedy man kept waiting for his dinner.

Greed, thought Julia, was deplorable. She made a distinction between greed and taking an intelligent interest in one's food; for it was clear that dear Francis liked a good dinner and had chosen this one with care. Her thoughts went back to Alaric Pope; she wondered what he was having for supper. All men, of course, took food seriously and could have their lives blighted (like Alaric's) by a diet of boiled fish and sodden cabbage; and it was a pity Miss Pope could not afford a good cook.

Dora and Francis were talking about the Aged Animals Pension Fund, Henry was happily eating. Julia found herself sitting in a pool of silence, and realized that it was her own fault. She was so obsessed with the Popes' troubles that she had let her thoughts absorb her instead of concentrating on her duties as a guest; and this was strange because she had been looking forward to the evening.

Resolutely she thrust Miss Pope's image away, and turned to speak to Francis. But it was impossible, at that instant, to address him, because he was listening politely to Dora's rambling tale of a very old donkey that lived in the field opposite a bungalow she had shared with another woman during the war.

Henry laid his knife and fork together. The dinner came up to his expectations, but now that the principal course was eaten it no longer demanded his whole attention.

"I hear you are living at Belmont House," he said to Julia.

"Did Francis tell you that Uncle James left it to me? It was the most wonderful surprise I'd ever had."

"Yes, it must have been very—er—surprising."

"I shall always wonder why he chose *me*," she said dreamily. It was a topic that was full of possibilities; but Henry ignored them.

"Don't you find it a cold house in winter?" he asked.

"We only moved in last May. But I know I shan't feel the cold. The place suits me . . . it's as if I was meant to live there."

"And of course you put in new central heating," Dora interpolated. Julia said the old central heating was worn out, quite rusty and useless; and after all, one needed central heating wherever one lived. Dora disagreed; she said it wasn't healthy to coddle oneself, and she dragged Francis in on her side by reminding him that Heswald Hall had been a notoriously cold house and that all the Heswalds were strong, healthy people.

"Yes," Francis agreed, with a triumphant glance at Henry, or rather, at the carnations that hid Henry from view. Of course Henry had not been brought up at Heswald Hall, but the principle held good; he was a Heswald, the Heswalds were strong and healthy, and therefore he would be perfectly all right if he didn't fuss about himself.

"But I see you've installed central heating here," Julia said sweetly, to show Dora that Francis wasn't on her side after all.

Francis could not guess that his allegiance was being fought for, and he was a little put out with Julia for spoiling his picture of himself as a true Heswald and Henry as a degenerate one. Without thinking he replied that the bailiff's house needed central heating because it was very damp.

Julia turned to look at him. Her smile, tenderly mocking, reminded him of another occasion when the dampness of the bailiff's house had been in question. He had accused her, then, of insincerity; and now the mocking smile suggested that she was accusing him of the same fault. 'You admit that it is damp?' Julia seemed to be saying; but her imagined voice was gentle, devoid of triumph.

"That was an excellent savoury," Henry told Dora. "I must ask Mrs. Sable to let me have the recipe."

"Will your cook mind having recipes thrust upon her?"

"I am my own cook—and, without boasting, I may say that I'm a *good* cook. Yes, I do it all myself . . . a daily twice a week for the rough . . . of course I have a gardener as well. . . ."

His energy restored, Henry purred smoothly into top gear, talking at a steady pace and taking no notice of Dora's interruptions. To Francis and Julia the monologue came as a mere background noise; like a distant waterfall or the buzz of a motor-mower; less significant than words which had been uttered several weeks earlier. When Francis spoke, it was as if he was continuing that earlier conversation.

"Dripped on, I suppose you would say?"

"Yes, Francis. That is what I *did* say."

He laughed, admitting defeat. But Julia did not wish to be regarded as a tiresome, clever woman who had put him in the wrong; and she feared he might so regard her when the effect of the excellent dinner, and her own presence, had worn off.

"But I shouldn't have said it," she continued quickly—and just stopped herself from adding "I'm so stupid," because Francis was looking too intelligent. As if he had foreseen the ingratiating be-littlement of herself, and discounted it in advance.

"Because, of course, I was mistaken," she said instead.

"About the house being damp?"

"Oh no. Why you've just confessed that it is. But I was mistaken—quite mistaken," Julia said earnestly. "It isn't the *trees* that make it damp."

Francis's too-intelligent look faded into an everyday look of guarded attentiveness. He could not see where this conversation was taking them.

"Not the trees?" he asked cautiously.

"Of course not. If it's really damp it must be more than trees dripping on it. The damp must come up from the ground!"

As she advanced this theory Julia allowed herself, at last, an air of innocent triumph; and then, misinterpreting his silence, she repeated the bits that mattered.

"The house *is* damp; but I was wrong to say it was because of the trees."

'Honour is satisfied,' Francis thought, giving Julia a smile of undisguised admiration which was no more than her due. 'She is right—she always *must* be right—but I am allowed a moderate degree of rightness: my house is damp but not because of the trees.'

"But all the same, I suppose you would prefer it if the trees were cut down?" he asked.

They began to discuss the improvements he might make; a judicious thinning of the trees, an alteration to the front path . . . a window in the east wall of the dining-room to catch the morning sun. Francis saw his house transformed and—by implication—sadly disparaged; but for some reason he did not take the disparagement to heart. It did not matter, for he was seeing Julia at the same time in yet another new light; and this light, like the imagined sunshine in the dining-room, was both revealing and agreeable. Suspicions had become certainty, but nevertheless he felt safer—for a perceived danger is more easily avoided.

"Oh, look—here's Snowball," Dora exclaimed. She prided herself on remembering names—even the names of cats—and felt that by doing so she showed *savoir-faire*. Shy people were pleased when you remembered their names; it set them at ease and made them feel you were friendly.

But her *savoir-faire* made no impression on Snowball, who ignored the greeting and stalked round the table with his tail in the air. Curiosity had drawn him to this room; he had spent the evening behind one of the curtains, quietly observing the novel spectacle of a dinner party, and now he had impulsively decided to be a son-of-the-house cat. He stopped beside Francis's chair and rubbed his white fur lovingly against Francis's trousers.

Francis was flattered by his attention—for in public Snowball usually cut him dead—and stooped down to stroke him. Julia gave Francis another good mark in her mental account-book, for not minding about the white hairs. Henry, who had observed Snowball's journey round the table with the prejudiced eye of a rival owner, said pontifically:

"That cat's much too thin. *My* cat weighs nine pounds, all but an ounce."

Francis voiced the general opinion by saying that Henry's tomcat must be grossly overfed.

"It's a she. Miriam. No, Miriam's a fine cat, but not *bloated*. I don't like to see a bloated cat—" ('none of us do,' thought Francis) "so I'm careful about her diet. But I give her a course of cod-liver oil capsules twice a year, and I must say she's a credit to me."

"And do you take cod-liver oil capsules yourself?" Francis asked dryly.

"Well, yes, as a matter of fact I do—but only once a year, at the beginning of winter. Not the same brand as Miriam's, of course."

Francis hardly needed Julia's glance to remind him that he had a sense of humour, but in that moment of shared, hidden amusement he found himself liking her better than ever before. The picture of Henry and Miriam taking their daily dose, of two bottles neatly labelled with their respective names, hung in the air between them; and quite obliterated, for Francis, that other picture of a dangerous siren luring him towards a whirlpool.

The cat Snowball, conscious that he was no longer the centre of attention, sprang lightly on to his knee; it was an honour so unprecedented that Francis hardly knew how to receive it.

"You're squashing him against the table," Dora said. "Let me take him. Snowball! Snowball!"

Snowball haughtily turned his head away, indicating that he preferred to be squashed.

"I never allow Miriam on my knee at meals," Henry said, craning round the carnations. "It isn't hygienic."

"Give him some cream," said Julia.

She turned to the tray that had held the coffee cups, and picked up the cream jug. Francis poured the cream into one of the ornate silver-gilt spoons and held it to Snowball's lips.

"Licky, licky," he said.

Henry, unable to bear it, gave a scornful laugh.

"That isn't the way to talk to cats," he told them. "Cats are very sensitive—and they won't be coaxed. I always speak to Miriam just as I would speak to a human being."

These harsh words left Francis unmoved. Not poor old Henry, he thought now, but funny old Henry. That was the measure of his own good-humour.

And, as if to make the evening perfect, the cat Snowball—a son-of-the-house cost what it might—indulgently bent to lick the spoon.

CHAPTER XIX

THERE WAS so much wrong with civilization that even so energetic a denouncer as Lady Finch was forced to specialize, to leave some abuses to flourish unchecked while she strove to rectify others. Sometime in the future there was a battle to be fought against 'Daylight Wasting'—a battle against sloth, bad habits, and Government hypocrisy—but for the present she contented herself with making certain that no daylight was wasted at Urn Cottage.

The clocks were not altered; and in summer they breakfasted at seven. Harriet could never see why this was better than breakfasting at eight by Summer Time, but she was resigned to it. It was part of Life-with-Aunt-Finch.

Since the discovery of Miss Brigg's deceit over the sections Harriet had been feeling quite strongly pro-Aunt Finch; and on this particular morning, as they sat down to breakfast, she announced dramatically that she could bear it no longer.

"What?" Lady Finch demanded.

"Her getting away with it."

They had discussed the episode so often that it was not necessary to be more explicit. Lady Finch nodded comprehendingly.

"But, my dear Harriet, I cannot prove it," she said. "Of course I know my own sections, by the look of them, and a little stain on one—but moral certainty is not enough. I could not take her to court."

Even though she was on Aunt Finch's side, Harriet realized that this was just as well. Aunt Finch in the witness-box was an alarming thought.

"But couldn't we go and see the Popes, and tell them what we think of them?" she asked.

"They must know what we think of them. Though I do not blame *Miss* Pope—the poor, foolish creature was probably kept in the dark. I blame *him*."

"You don't suppose he could have been kept in the dark too?"

"He must have seen they were not his own sections."

"Yes," Harriet said doubtfully. She wondered if Mr. Pope would perceive any difference between one section and another. "I would like to be sure," she said. "If we went to the vicarage—"

"We are not going to the vicarage. I told Miss Pope—and I shall adhere to it—that I would never enter the vicarage again."

"You could stand outside and shout."

For a moment Lady Finch considered it. In her Suffragette days, when she was younger than Harriet, she had shouted, kicked, and fought, but that wasn't quite the same thing.

"No," she said. "By not entering the vicarage, I meant that I would have nothing more to do with them. Shouting would spoil it."

"Well—what about Miss Brigg? She's the real villain. She came and told those fibs about wanting honeycombs for her friend in Reddrod."

"I shall deal with Miss Brigg," Lady Finch said balefully.

"How?"

"I haven't quite decided."

Harriet felt slightly apprehensive. Desirable though it was that Miss Brigg should be exposed, she hoped Aunt Finch wouldn't do anything too drastic or spectacular. Perhaps it had been unwise to encourage her by so much sympathetic indignation.

"As you can't prove it, there isn't really much you can do," she said restrainingly.

"I can *speak* to her." Lady Finch invested the word 'speak' with terrifying overtones. "I have not seen her in the village since it happened. But no doubt we shall meet soon."

Harriet's breakfast was spoiled. She now saw her aunt, not in the witness-box, but in the dock.

"But, Aunt Finch, could she—could she have you up for slander? As you can't prove it, I mean."

"Not if I said it to *her*," Lady Finch answered confidently. "Slander is saying what you think about someone to other people."

Since they had already said what they thought about Miss Brigg to Marian Prentice, and Robert Dunstan, and the man who brought the groceries, Harriet did not find this very consoling.

Alaric Pope had learned, in the hard school of experience, that parishioners resented his calling when they were busy. In practice, most housewives seemed to be busy all day long; but he believed that mornings were their busiest times and accordingly he paid his calls in the afternoons. But since Mrs. Dunstan was rich enough to employ servants, and since he had a very urgent reason for seeing her, he persuaded himself that the middle of the morning would not be too early, and he presented himself at Belmont House at the theoretical mid-morning hour of ten o'clock.

To Julia this was just after breakfast. The morning had hardly begun and she was not prepared for callers; but Carrington, who was being taught to discriminate between those who were left on the door-mat and those who were shown in, had correctly judged the vicar's status and installed him in the morning-room before announcing his arrival.

"I shall have to see him," Julia said to Dora. "But what an hour to come!"

"Probably he's worried about his sister."

"He could have telephoned."

The Pope Crisis seemed less important this morning; although last night, after dinner, she had spent a happy hour telling Francis all about it. He had proved an excellent listener, but he had argued with her about the wisdom of removing Miss Pope to Belmont House and had prophesied that Alaric would rush off and propose to Miss Brigg the next morning. That he should take sides in the matter seemed to Julia a good sign; it showed that his interest was not confined to mediaeval documents.

She found Alaric standing in the middle of the room; his drooping, forlorn appearance suggested that he had not breakfasted well, or perhaps at all. He greeted her briefly, and asked at once if he could see his sister.

"She seems a little better," Julia said, answering the question Alaric had not asked. "She slept fairly well, and her temperature is normal."

"I am glad to hear it. If I could see her for a few moments . . ."

"I think she ought to be *quite* quiet today. I'm a little anxious about her—she's so thin, and in a dreadfully nervous state. Two or three days of absolute rest is what she really needs."

"I should like to see her," Alaric said. He still drooped, but his face expressed nervous obstinacy; Miss Brigg would have said he looked like a martyr, but he reminded Julia of one of her own Rhode Island hens making up its mind to fly over the wire-netting.

"I'm afraid, if she saw you, she would begin to worry about you," she said. It seemed unkind to imply that his sister would cease to worry if she did not see him, but her duty to Miss Pope came first. Her duty to Miss Pope had assumed for Julia an inflexible character; in bringing her to Belmont House she had acted on an inspiration, and one should not tamper with inspirations. (Keep them apart: let him find out how much he misses her.) She gave Alaric a smile of beautiful sympathy; for he was obviously beginning to find out already.

"I *must* see her," he declared. His voice should have thundered, but what emerged was a squeak of despair. Nevertheless, it had its effect; Julia realized that he must have some good reason for wishing to see Miss Pope, a reason more important than the deficiencies of supper and breakfast. After all, he was accustomed to poor food and not enough of it.

Although Miss Pope came first in her sympathies she was quite prepared to do her second-best for Alaric; he could not be allowed to see his sister, but he was welcome to good advice. She begged him to sit down, and offered him a cigarette, which he refused, and a chocolate which he absent-mindedly accepted. It turned out to be a caramel, and while he was temporarily silenced Julia had things, conversationally, her own way. She talked about the village, and how much it owed to the Popes; she told Alaric how popular he was, and how ready people would be to help him, if he chose to confide in them. By the time he had dealt with the caramel Alaric's nervous obstinacy had dwindled into vacillation. He still wanted to talk to his sister, but he had begun to wonder whether Mrs. Dunstan—who seemed a sensible, pleasant woman—might perhaps explain things to Myrtle, and whether it might not be better that the news should be given by a third person.

"I don't want to worry my sister," he said abruptly, "but there's something she ought to be told."

He hesitated. Julia obligingly offered to give Miss Pope a message.

"Unless, of course, the news itself would upset her," she added, suddenly apprehensive.

"I'm afraid it will. But I feel she ought to be the first to know."

These ominous words meant only one thing to Julia. She remembered Francis's prophecy—that Alaric would rush off and propose to Miss Brigg—and for a moment her faith in inspirations tottered and crumbled. She gazed at Alaric with an anxiety she could barely conceal.

"It is really very awkward for us both," he said. He paused, shuffled his feet, and coughed. Julia's anxiety became a feverish impatience to hear the worst.

"If only she had not talked about it to everyone. It was—in a sense—indiscreet, though of course she meant well. She always means well. Indeed, I blame myself. . . . Yes, the fault was mine," he said nobly, shutting his eyes as if to shut out the past. The next instant he opened them again, gave Julia an appealing look, and added irrelevantly: "The Bishop's chaplain was much annoyed. He said I had been guilty of a breach of confidence."

Fleetingly Julia wondered if he meant a breach of promise; but this could hardly be, if he was only on the point of announcing his engagement. The Bishop's chaplain was a baffling intruder, and his annoyance merely increased her own bewilderment.

"Are you speaking about Miss Brigg?" she asked. A blunt question seemed the only way of dealing with Alaric.

"Miss Brigg? Dear me, no. Miss Brigg is at present on holiday on the Norfolk Broads. She left two days ago. Otherwise, of course, I might have consulted her—though I still feel Myrtle ought to be told first."

"Told *what*?" Julia cried.

"About this difficulty—this truly distressing—er—*contretemps*. The New Town."

Julia drew a deep breath. "What about it?" she asked.

"There isn't going to be one," Alaric said sadly.

Julia's relief was so great that at first she could hardly spare a thought for the New Town's future non-existence. Her plan was safe; Miss Pope was safe; Alaric (with Miss Brigg on the Norfolk Broads) was not only safe, but cookless, and would miss his sister even more than she had expected. It was quite difficult to look sympathetic, to ask the right questions and show the right interest; nevertheless, her kind heart urged her to the task. But few questions were necessary, for Alaric, who was out-talked at home, could be quite talkative when he got the chance, and, now that the distressing news was broken, he was eager to explain and discuss it.

The report that Goatstock was to be a New Town had come from the Bishop's chaplain; Alaric had mentioned it to his sister, and she had assumed that everything was settled and decided, and had hastened to warn her fellow-residents of the coming calamity.

"I fear I am out of touch with village opinion," Alaric told Julia. "I had not realized how bitterly they would resent the plan." The Bishop's chaplain had spoken of the New Town as "a golden opportunity to lay good and lasting foundations", but Miss Pope and her adherents saw it as the graveyard of all they loved best. Alaric was uneasily aware of a great gap between the official—or Palace—view, and the Goatstock view; and his uneasiness became acute when Miss Pope called a protest meeting at the vicarage. It was obviously undesirable that the vicarage should be identified with a policy opposed to the Palace one.

"And unfortunately—it really was *extremely* unfortunate—she mentioned on that occasion that we—that is, I—had heard the news from the Palace—that is, from the Bishop's chaplain. And someone—he did not tell me who—wrote to the Bishop. And, as I said, the Bishop's chaplain was most annoyed that the proposal should have been made public. Especially as it now appears that Goatstock has been abandoned as a site in favour of some other place."

"Where?" Julia asked eagerly. She had just realized that the abandonment of Goatstock meant the abandonment of her plans for Francis's future; but if the New Town was to be planted down somewhere else in the neighbourhood all might yet be well.

Alaric shook his head. "He did not inform me. I am in disgrace at the Palace. And here in Goatstock, too, I must confess that I feel—that is, I *shall* feel—a certain awkwardness. Myrtle and I—that is, strictly speaking, Myrtle alone—are—is—responsible—"

"For all the fuss and alarm?" Julia suggested, seeing that the sentence was not likely to come to an end unaided.

"Exactly."

He bowed his head. Julia, after the briefest glance at the clock, began to utter comforting words.

It took her twenty minutes to soothe, reassure, and dismiss him. Then she hurried upstairs to Miss Pope, who had been told to stay in bed, given a large breakfast, two nice novels, and a pink satin dressing-jacket, and was now working herself into a nervous frenzy over the thought of Mary Ellen Brigg in control of the vicarage.

"I can't bear it," she said. "She'll find the store-room keys on my dressing-table, and use up everything, and make him think I don't fry."

"No, she won't. She's in the Norfolk Broads—I mean *on* them. She's gone there for a holiday. Didn't you know?"

Miss Pope gaped. "I knew she was going, because she goes every year with some cousins from Reddrod. But I didn't know *when*."

"She couldn't have chosen a better time, could she?"

"But who will look after Alaric?"

"No one. He will look after himself—and it will do him a lot of good." Julia spoke sharply; for her guest was being remarkably obtuse.

"I must get up," Miss Pope announced. "I must get up at once. I ought never to have come—though indeed, indeed, I am truly grateful. All your kindness . . . But Alaric cannot possibly manage by himself."

For a moment Julia consigned both the Popes to the outer darkness of people-who-won't-respond. But to abandon them would be to abandon so much else—her belief in inspirations, her belief in the hand of Fate which had brought her back to Goatstock, her belief that the native heath needed her. She sighed, and sat down on the bed, and reminded Miss Pope of the promises and assurances she had given her last night.

Miss Pope agreed, doubtfully, that her brother would not starve to death, and that the absence of Miss Brigg was perhaps a Good Thing. Her reluctance to face Lady Finch was counter-balanced by her conviction that Alaric would burn all the pans; and her fear that he would inadvertently leave the oven-tap on and gas himself was cancelled out by her apprehension that he would find himself without gas, since she had forgotten to pay last quarter's bill.

Step by step Julia coaxed her back to the original plan. At last, when she had promised—though without much enthusiasm—to remain at Belmont House for at least two more days, she had her reward, the delightful surprise that had been saved up for the end.

"The New Town is off," Julia said. "Isn't that wonderful news?" She ignored her private disappointment, bestowing on her guest a care-free smile which bade her rejoice.

Miss Pope merely looked flabbergasted.

"It was a false rumour," Julia explained. "It was never definitely settled—and now they're going to build it somewhere else. Aren't you pleased?"

"I suppose I am," Miss Pope said grudgingly. "But I shall have to go round and tell everyone I was wrong, and they will laugh at me."

The door opened; Dora thrust her head in and said: "Julia, Mr. Duffy is here about that leak. Will you come and see him?"

Julia stood up. The interruption hardly mattered, since it was clear that the rejoicings she had expected were not going to take place. But as she followed her cousin downstairs she thought sadly that Dora wasn't nearly as helpful as she ought to be. Whenever things went wrong Dora simply fetched her to deal with them; and since Carrington's arrival she had relinquished all her household tasks except keeping accounts. True, she gardened zealously, but now that they had a gardener two days a week her labours were not really necessary. Or rather, she could have been better employed doing the things she was meant to do.

Trying to be fair, Julia reminded herself that these duties had never been clearly defined. But she remembered that Dora, with her professed love of independence, had insisted that she must 'earn her keep' by being useful. That was in the early days, when they first moved in; and since then Dora's determination to be useful had noticeably diminished. But as she was a poor relation it was difficult to reprove her without seeming domineering and unkind.

"He's in the scullery," Dora said, halting at the foot of the stairs. "I'll leave you to cope," she added, turning away towards the morning-room.

This remark—an echo of many others—stung Julia into rebellion.

"No, you come with me," she said, "I can't stand up to Mr. Duffy, and you can. It's the sort of occasion when I really need you."

She hoped this would remind Dora about earning her keep. But Dora gave a scornful laugh.

"Good heavens, it isn't Mr. Duffy—it's Nanny!" she said. "She's being pig-headed, as usual, and won't have the water turned off. I really can't be bothered with her tantrums."

That she was there to be bothered did not seem to occur to her. Nor did it occur to Robert, who now appeared on the scene, that his demand for the use of the car that afternoon, to take Harriet and Marian to Reddrod, might inconvenience his aunt.

"I promised to drive them over," he said confidently. "They want to do some shopping."

The baize door at the end of the hall was flung open and Nanny came stamping out, followed at a discreet distance by Carrington and Mr. Duffy.

"There you are, Miss Julia! Invalids or no invalids, we shan't none of us get anything to eat if I've got to have my kitchen full of plumbers and not a drop of water in the house!"

Julia's thoughts turned longingly to the desert island. To escape from her responsibilities would be selfish: but, gazing around her, she told herself that a little more selfishness would hardly be noticed.

CHAPTER XX

"MARIAN HAS BEEN lucky in the weather, hasn't she?" Mrs. Minnis said gaily.

She had just stepped in for a neighbourly chat; and at the end of it, quite casually, she meant to ask Mrs. Prentice for the loan of her vacuum cleaner. It had lately occurred to her that the Prentices were strangely reluctant to lend their possessions ("awfully unneighbourly", she called it), and that a cunning approach was necessary.

"She goes back on Monday," Mrs. Prentice said.

"I expect the time has simply flown."

This was a mistake; Mrs. Prentice glanced at the clock and began to fidget. Mrs. Minnis curled up in her chair and told her hostess what a comfy chair it was and how something about the atmosphere of Balbus Cottage reminded her of her own old home.

"Of course they're not really a bit alike," she said. "My old pater's place was a big, Georgian house—far too big for us, quite absurd really—"

"—And miles from anywhere, right out in the country," Mrs. Prentice said quickly. She was generally so slow in answering that this interruption quite astonished Mrs. Minnis; it also disconcerted her, because it was just what she had been going to say herself.

Mrs. Prentice stood up.

"Excuse me," she said. "I think there is someone at the back door." She hurried away. Mrs. Minnis could not hear anyone at the back door, but she heard Mrs. Prentice saying something indistinguishable to a third person, in the hall; and a moment later this third person—who was Marian—entered the room.

Although she knew that neither of them smoked Mrs. Minnis hoped that Marian would offer her a cigarette; her mother never remembered to do so, but then she was shy and awkward with visitors. Marian, however, took after her mother in this as in other ways. She sat down, bolt upright, on the edge of a chair, and a little behind Mrs. Minnis who was forced to uncurl and sit up to talk to her. It was not a house in which one was ever made to feel at home.

"How sunburnt you've got!" Mrs. Minnis cried. "I can see you're like me—I'm an absolute sun-worshipper. How lucky you can stand the heat. You'll simply *revel* in Africa."

Marian might have pointed out that revels formed no part of a future missionary's life, but at the mention of Africa her heart suddenly warmed towards Mrs. Minnis. Africa was a word her parents avoided, as if they hoped she might lose interest in the place if it were never spoken of; and since 'Africa', for Marian, signified Hubert, she could not hear the name mentioned without a quickening of the heart.

"I'm looking forward to seeing it," she said.

"Not so long to wait now," Mrs. Minnis said encouragingly.

"Another year," Marian explained; she had to finish her training and then Hubert hoped to get leave, and they would be married, and the voyage out would be a wonderful honeymoon.

"The phosphorescence on the water," Mrs. Minnis exclaimed. "The Southern Cross!" Her geography was shaky but her imagination made up for it. "I'm a real rolling-pin," she announced fervently. "Sometimes I dream of those days in the past, and I can almost smell the incense and the—the palm-trees, and hear—"

"Marian isn't going to Mandalay," Harriet said through the open window. Mrs. Minnis, who wasn't conscious that she was quoting, told herself that Harriet Finch was just as mad as her aunt. But Harriet's arrival pleased her, because now she could find out what Miss Brigg had really done.

"Come right in," she cried, forgetting that it was not her own house. Harriet leant on the window-sill and said she had only called to say she might be late for tea, because she had to go with Aunt Finch to the dentist that afternoon.

Mrs. Prentice crept out of the kitchen to listen in the hall, and at the sound of voices she gave a frown of vexation. Marian had promised to get rid of Mrs. Minnis as speedily as possible— it was a task Mrs. Prentice herself could never accomplish unaided—and yet there they were, still chatting away. Mrs. Minnis's arrival had wrecked Mrs. Prentice's morning programme; because this was the day for hoovering the sitting-room and her presence there made it impossible to start.

"Aunt Finch has the toothache," Harriet explained. "It's a funny thing, but whenever Miss Pope gets toothache Aunt Finch is sure to get it soon after. A sort of sympathetic magic."

Marian remembered that Lady Finch had treated her last attack of toothache with herbs, and she was not surprised to learn that it had recurred.

"Has Miss Pope had the toothache?" Mrs. Minnis asked.

"She had it last week. And now she has the influenza."

Mrs. Minnis hurriedly changed her mind about calling at the vicarage; she was not afraid of infection for herself but she had Hugo and Sonny to think about. But Marian at once asked who was looking after Miss Pope. Harriet explained that she was at Belmont House; and Marian and Mrs. Minnis thought this an excellent arrangement. Neither of them asked who was looking after the vicar.

"I must go," Harriet said, withdrawing from the window. "I'll see you this afternoon, Marian—if we catch the bus back." The dentist lived in Reddrod, and always kept his patients waiting.

Mrs. Minnis leapt to her feet. "I just want one little word with you," she called to the departing Harriet. But Harriet had not heard, or did not choose to hear, and disappeared down the path.

"I'll run after her," Mrs. Minnis said. "Shan't be a moment."

Marian, however, insisted on going with her. (How formally they behaved, as if one was a visitor instead of a friendly neighbour.) They strolled down to the gate together, and when they reached it Harriet was not to be seen.

"Where can she have gone?" asked Mrs. Minnis, looking up and down the road. Marian said Harriet walked very fast.

"Well . . ." Deprived of her gossip item, Mrs. Minnis remembered the vacuum-cleaner she had come to borrow.

"I'd better just say ta-ta to your mother. She'll think me aw'fly rude, rushing away like this."

"Oh no, she won't. I'll explain."

Marian held the gate open. Her kind smile was very like her mother's, but Mrs. Prentice would never have thought of opening the gate.

"As a matter of fact I just wondered if she'd be an absolute angel and lend me the hoover-thing. I just thought of it when I looked at your marvellous carpet. Hugo often says how marvellous your house looks, and I wanted—"

"I'm sorry, but I'm afraid Mother can't spare it."

Marian's voice was kind but firm; her experience of difficult patients came in useful, and it was will-power, not a push, that propelled Mrs. Minnis into the road. As soon as she was outside the gate Marian shut it. Mrs. Minnis said something about another time, perhaps, which met with no response, and returned disconsolately to Kandahar. One did one's best to be friendly, but the Prentices were a queer lot. Almost anti-social, really.

Marian walked back towards the house. At the edge of the lawn Harriet emerged from a clump of rhododendrons, and said dramatically:

"The young hero evaded his pursuers, though their breath was hot on his neck!"

"I wonder she didn't see you. I knew you were there—your skirt showed."

"Dear me," said Harriet. "You'll have to do better than that when the cannibals get on your track."

"But there *aren't* any cannibals where Hubert is. I've told you—"

"—a thousand times. Well, never mind about the thousandth-and-oneth. I've dodged Mrs. Minnis, and that's a Good Thing."

Marian asked why evasion was necessary, and Harriet said Mrs. Minnis would have been on about Mary Ellen and one had to be very careful what one said because of Aunt Finch being had up for slander.

Marian, of course, knew all about Miss Brigg's misdeed, but the threat of slander was new to her. She asked sympathetically what Harriet's aunt had been doing.

"It isn't doing—it's saying. I asked Robert's advice, and it's quite true. If Aunt Finch goes marching about the village saying Mary Ellen pinched her honeycombs—well, got them on false pretences and passed them off as Alaric's—then Miss B. could sue her for slander."

"It seems unjust," said Marian. She did not care for Harriet's aunt, but in this matter she sympathized with her.

"Robert thought so too—but that doesn't help. We shall have to stop denouncing Mary Ellen. Luckily she's away at present, and perhaps by the time she comes back I shall have got Aunt Finch to see reason. And in the meantime you mustn't say a word about it to anyone."

Marian promised not to, and also to warn her mother.

"It makes my blood boil," Harriet continued. "Poor Aunt Finch might have won prizes—undying fame—with those sections, at the Honey Show."

They sat on the lawn. The grass was warm and dry, and Marian, echoing Mrs. Minnis, remarked how lucky she had been in the weather.

"The first week wasn't so good," Harriet pointed out. "Don't you remember how wet it was for the Minnises' cocktail party? That was the night you came home."

"It was my Welcome-Home party. Mummy was very annoyed about it."

"A damp sort of welcome. Still, I quite enjoyed it."

"You had Robert to talk to. I had only poor James for most of the time. And Miss Pope bewailing the New Town. And Charlton in his grandest mood."

Harriet was lying on her back with her eyes shut. This was just as well, since it was a position in which it was easy to conceal one's feelings; and her feelings were strangely mixed.

'You had Robert to talk to,' Marian had said reproachfully. This was the first time she had admitted that she liked him; it was a good sign, a *wonderful* sign; it showed that Harriet's hopes might yet come to pass. She remembered other things; Marian hadn't, of late, talked so incessantly about Hubert and Africa, and she had been very sociable, she had not made excuses about keeping her mother company but had come for picnics, drives, and walks; she had even gone into Reddrod alone with Robert on the day when Aunt Finch had just been laid low with toothache and the bees had swarmed for the tenth time. Harriet had had to stay at home to cope with these simultaneous crises, but Marian had not suggested that she should stay too.

'Perhaps Hubert's image is fading,' Harriet thought. It was a thought that should have delighted her; but it did not. There were other thoughts. She remembered how kind Robert had been at the cocktail party, offering to fetch her coat and minding that she was cold. She remembered his teasing her about Mary Ellen and the threat of being had up for slander, and saying he would visit her in prison. She had come to feel that she had a claim on him; she had come to think of him as a companion for herself, rather than as a possible husband for Marian.

"I suppose it *was* rather dull for you," she said, after a long silence.

"What was? Oh—the party. Well, we've made up for it since. I've really enjoyed this holiday."

There was another long silence, while Harriet sorted out her thoughts and strove to put gladness and true friendship in their rightful place at the forefront of her mind. How nice—no, how wonderful—it would be to have Marian living here in England, not in Africa; Marian married to the lively Robert instead of to the dull Hubert; Marian gradually weaned from good works and professional concern for the sick and the heathen, and laughing and joking as she used to. Her best friend restored to her.

"I'm almost sorry to be going back," Marian said. "It's so difficult, when one's been away, to settle down to the routine. And the nurses' home. I don't believe women were really meant to live herded together."

Harriet sat up. "I thought you liked it," she said.

"I like nursing. And of course, once one's there, part of it, one doesn't notice . . ."

"Notice what?"

"Oh, the tiresome things. Being one of the herd, having to obey a lot of rules—and living in an institution. I can't tell you how I long, sometimes, for a home of my own. Even a garret!"

Harriet saw Robert and Marian living happily-ever-after in a dear little home; not a garret—it wouldn't suit Robert—but a thatched cottage with roses round the door. She was sure Marian would have roses, and she was sure the cottage would be clean and comfortable, and the food very good.

'But I shall never go and stay with them,' she thought crossly.

"But of course it won't be a garret," said Marian, echoing her thoughts.

"Yellow roses, and perhaps pale yellow curtains to match."

"What on earth are you talking about?"

"Your future home," Harriet said sadly. "I see it with roses round the door."

"I don't suppose I shall have much time for gardening, and I'm afraid roses wouldn't grow there. But I believe annuals do quite well in the rainy season."

The pretty thatched cottage had been so substantial a vision that it took Harriet a few seconds to realize they were back in Africa; and the extraordinary relief she felt at finding herself on this familiar ground quite frightened her. She looked sideways at Marian, who was talking about sanitation problems and the difficulties of cooking on charcoal. Outwardly, Marian seemed completely happy; but what was going on inside her? Perhaps she was being victimized by her sense of Duty; perhaps, though she no longer wanted to marry Hubert, she felt she ought to. If that was the case Harriet's interference had done more harm than good.

"The mission hospital has electricity—but not the outlying bungalows. Hubert says I must expect quite primitive conditions."

Harriet couldn't bear it. She had to know, even if the truth were unpalatable. No, not unpalatable, but oddly unwelcome.

"Do you like Robert?" she asked, speaking in a loud voice that sounded as fierce as an inquisitor's.

Marian winced. "Don't shout in my ear like that. I'm not deaf."

"I said—do you like Robert?"

"Oh yes. Don't you? I like him much better than I did at first. And his dog's the most attractive dog I've ever seen. I wish I could have another dog—but of course when Mr. Binks died I was just starting my training and it wasn't possible to get another then. Hubert thinks we might get a dog once we're settled. Of course, in that climate—"

"We're not talking about dogs," Harriet interrupted ruthlessly. "We're talking about your future."

"We *were* talking about Robert," Marian pointed out.

"Yes. Well—I asked you if you liked him."

Incredulously, Marian perceived that Robert and her future were linked together in Harriet's mind. She turned and faced her friend. In a voice that showed she already knew the answer, she asked what Harriet meant.

"Don't look so angry. I only wanted to be quite, quite certain," Harriet said apologetically.

"But you've no business to think that Robert—that I—You *know* I'm engaged to Hubert!" Marian said in a voice of thunder.

"When you got engaged you hadn't met Robert. You might have fallen in love with him at first sight, like people in novels."

This only made things worse. Harriet had never seen Marian so angry; in fact she had not imagined Marian was capable of anger. Passionate reproaches, indignation and contempt, were showered upon her, in a voice she would hardly have recognized. All Marian's resentment against the people who disapproved of her engagement, the people who laughed at missionaries or tactfully steered the conversation away from Africa, came pouring out. It was like the bursting dam; and it was the more alarming because the depth of water behind the dam had never been visible.

"You all think missionaries are dull!" Marian said. "I'm not marrying 'a missionary'—at least, I am, but that isn't what matters. I'm marrying *Hubert!*"

"I'm awfully sorry—"

"And making silly jokes about falling in love at first sight. That's what I *did*. You don't know anything about it."

Harriet gaped.

"I knew as soon as I saw Hubert, that he was the only man in the world for me. And he felt the same."

Harriet's theories crumbled about her ears.

"I suppose you wanted me to break off my engagement! You thought you knew what was best for me! You're like your aunt, and Mummy, and all the other cautious old women, who can't even bear the thought of a few more houses in Goatstock because any sort of change is anathema to them. You're so utterly conventional that you wanted me to make a *suitable* marriage and live in a cosy little cottage with roses round the door!"

"Stop, oh stop!" Harriet cried. Abruptly, mercifully, Marian stopped. In a silence quivering with the vibrations of her anger they sat side by side, looking at the sun-baked lawn, the neat flower-beds and the well-pruned shrubs.

At first it seemed that they would never be able to speak to each other again. If they had been further apart Harriet would simply have crept away; but they were so close together that an unobtrusive withdrawal was not possible. She longed for some interruption to occur, a summons from Mrs. Prentice, or even a car smash in the road outside the gate; a sudden demand for bandages and first-aid might bring back the sensible, competent Marian of the past, and would at least give them an excuse to separate. But no timely disaster broke their silence, in which the distant drone of a vacuum-cleaner was the only reminder of everyday life.

'Silence is golden,' Harriet thought. But this one was not. She drew a deep breath as a preliminary to speech. At the same moment Marian made an incoherent remark about losing her temper, and added in more audible tones that Harriet had asked for it.

"I'm very sorry," Harriet said meekly.

"You've ruined my holiday," Marian quavered.

Harriet decided it would be pedantic to point out that the holiday was nearly over; instead she muttered more apologies. Her meekness might have suggested that she was playing the part of an orphan, but Marian, as she grew calmer, was so appalled by her own behaviour that she was in no mood to analyse Harriet's.

"I said more than I should have done," she admitted. "I mean—it wasn't only what *you* said that upset me. It was everyone else. I mean—well, you know."

"Yes," Harriet said, rightly judging that everyone else meant, in particular, Marian's parents.

She had always known—though it was now much clearer to her—that Mr. and Mrs. Prentice did not approve of their daughter's engagement. They had nothing against Hubert (no one could have); but he was a missionary; and they did not want dear Marian to spend her life in darkest Africa. Besides, there was something, not vulgar, but extremist, about missionaries, and the Prentices were conventional people.

If only he had been an ordinary parson, even a mere curate, she thought, they would have welcomed him with open arms.

"This last year is going to seem longer than all the others put together," Marian said.

"You must get a calendar and tick off each day at the end of it. It always makes time pass more quickly."

"I've been doing that from the day Hubert sailed."

If Harriet had still needed proof that Marian was really in love this casual remark would have supplied it. She thought of the ticked-off days mounting into weeks, months, years, three years and a bit and another year to come. It wasn't particularly romantic, but somehow, after those torrents of rage and scorn, it was pathetically convincing.

"You must start doing it in hours," she said. "How many hours are there in a year?"

Neither excelled at sums, but the mental arithmetic was good for both of them. It produced differing answers, but it drew them together over the complexities of multiplying and carrying figures forward in one's head. When Marian reminded Harriet that she would be late for lunch if she did not hurry back to Urn Cottage, her voice showed that she was simply being practical; and Harriet, who no longer wished to creep out of her friend's life, did not hesitate to remind Marian in her turn that she might also be late for tea, if the dentist kept Aunt Finch waiting.

"You won't get to the dentist if you don't go home now," Marian said. "You'll miss the Reddrod bus."

And with these familiar—and now reassuring—remonstrances to spur her on, Harriet hastened away.

CHAPTER XXI

WHEN JULIA WOKE in the morning she liked to lie cosily in bed and think good thoughts. The thoughts were not necessarily pious, but they were often concerned with kind actions. It was a good thought, translated into a kind action, that had led to her buying the expensive cookery-book for Miss Pope, and now she was wondering how Miss Pope would receive it.

Yesterday Miss Pope had left her bed of sickness and spent the afternoon in an armchair. Today she would come downstairs; and it was Julia's intention that Nanny should give her some lessons in cooking—simple things like making sauce without lumps and frying fish instead of just boiling it. Then, when she returned to the vicarage (with the cookery-book to help her), she would be able to please and impress Alaric.

'Sole *meunière*,' thought Julia, 'there's no reason why they shouldn't have that.' In the half-light that penetrated the curtains she sat up and reached for the cookery-book, which lay on the bedside table. She turned the pages, noting here and there dishes that appeared suitable for vicarage consumption. Presently she came on a coloured plate which depicted a boar's head, glazed and garnished. She turned to page seventy-nine to find out how it was made.

Nanny always came in quietly, in case Miss Julia should be still asleep. This morning her stealthy approach took Julia by surprise; she had not time to conceal the cookery-book before Nanny was there at her elbow, holding a cup of tea in one hand and gesticulating with the other.

"I know I'm not as young as I was," Nanny said rapidly, speaking in the hushed voice appropriate to the hour but sounding, to Julia, thoroughly upset. "There's a mort of work in this house, and I haven't the time to spend fiddling about with fancy dishes. But if you don't like my cooking, Miss Julia, you'd better say so and then we'll know where we are."

"But, Nanny dear, you're a wonderful cook," Julia said enthusiastically, thrusting the book out of sight.

"I do my best, but you know very well I'm only your old nurse not a cording blur."

The transformation was complete; Nanny actually thought of herself, now, as an old nurse, and would probably have denied ever having been anything else. Her quavering voice ran reproachfully up and down the scale, reminding her employer of what was her due, while Julia soothed and praised her and longed to be left in peace to drink her tea.

In the end she had to tell Nanny her reason for buying the cookery-book, since nothing else would convince her that her own cooking wasn't being secretly condemned. It was a pity, for she had meant to get her in a good humour before broaching the subject of cooking lessons for Miss Pope; and in her present mood Nanny flatly refused to help.

"No, Miss Julia, I haven't the time. It would be all talk and no work with her in the kitchen, and ladies that don't mind what they eats aren't likely to make good cooks. It would be a *waste* of time, as you might say, to set and teach her anything. Waste of time and waste of material."

Nanny left the room, slightly appeased but still breathing deeply like an offended dragon. Julia sipped her cold tea and wondered if there were cookery classes to be had in Reddrod. The day had begun badly.

Miss Pope had breakfast in bed; Dora took it up to her, and reported that she seemed awfully jumpy. She was worrying about Alaric and the vicarage and the Mothers' Union meeting that afternoon; and she said the birds woke her early. Of course that was nonsense, Dora commented briskly. There must be just as many birds in the vicarage garden. All the same, it showed that her stay at Belmont House wasn't doing Miss Pope any good.

"But she's getting a good rest," Julia protested.

"Not if the birds keep her awake," Robert said.

"And not if she worries all the time about what is happening at home."

Julia sighed. It was already clear to her that Dora and Robert, as well as Nanny, resented Miss Pope's presence. She had wondered at first if they were jealous; but although jealousy certainly accounted for Nanny's behaviour it seemed a rather far-fetched explanation of Dora's and Robert's, unless one assumed that Robert was still a prey to adolescent feelings of insecurity and that Dora had never grown up.

Reconsidering it, she acquitted Robert of the sin of jealousy. He disliked having Miss Pope in the house for simple, selfish reasons—because he had to share the bathroom (and leave it tidy), or because she had forbidden him to play the wireless in his bedroom late at night in case it should disturb the guest.

But Dora? In spite of her brusque manner and occasional trenchant criticism, she believed that Dora was truly fond of her. Because, if she wasn't, why should she stay? Dora valued her independence and despised mere comfort (unless it was earned), so it could only be affection that kept her at Belmont House; and might not affection, combined with a schoolgirlish outlook, take the form of jealousy?

The day had begun badly, and before breakfast was over another disaster occurred. Robert, pursuing a wasp with a folded newspaper, hit one of the hand-painted plates on the sideboard and knocked it to the ground, where it broke into several pieces.

"Oh—sorry," he said casually.

"I always thought that was a silly place to put them," Dora said. "I told you at the time that the plates would slip."

Julia had been bracing herself to tell Robert it didn't matter, but now she said instead that the plate would not have slipped if Robert had not hit it.

"But, Julia, I hardly touched it!"

"Anyway, it was an accident," Dora pointed out kindly.

"I wasn't implying that he did it on purpose."

"Well, I should hope not," Robert remarked. "And I said I was sorry."

"Accidents will happen, you know."

"Yes, I know," Julia said, feeling obscurely wronged by this defensive alliance. Robert had picked up the broken pieces, and he and Dora were now trying to fit them together; their laughter, as they commented on this task, showed how little they cared for the plate's beauty or its owner's loss. Julia, who had finished her breakfast, left the room.

On most mornings she and Dora lingered at the breakfast table talking, and her unexpectedly early exit took Carrington by surprise. He was standing in the telephone alcove; she could see his elbow sticking out and hear his voice. "O.K. Ten bob each way," he said. Then, at the click of the dining-room door, he replaced the receiver quickly, left the alcove, and walked away towards the kitchen.

"Was that a telephone call for me?" Julia asked. Carrington turned to face her; his honest eyes gazed respectfully into her own.

"It was a wrong number, madam," he said.

"No, Carrington, it wasn't. You were making a bet."

Julia spoke calmly, telling herself that she was not angry, only grieved by his deceitfulness. (It made nonsense of the honest-eyes theory.) But Carrington apparently mistook her grief for tolerance.

"Stingo for the 2.30 at Sandown, madam," he said. "I had it from a friend. An absolute certainty."

"Then there was no need to back him each way," Julia said before she could stop herself.

Carrington looked crestfallen; but for the wrong reason. And it was difficult, after that impulsive remark, to rebuke him for gambling and using her telephone for the purpose. She would have to find out from Nanny if he did it often; and perhaps, if he did, she could get Dora to speak to him. After all, Dora was supposed to be there to help.

No sooner had Carrington disappeared than Julia heard a rustle, a nervous twittering, on the upper landing. Miss Pope, fully dressed, was leaning over the banisters and trying to attract her attention.

"Oh, Mrs. Dunstan—" she called softly. "Good morning," she added as an afterthought; but this was plainly not what she had come to say. She whispered something Julia could not hear, and then apologized for being so much bother.

"What is it?" Julia asked, mounting the stairs. The day had already proved so unlucky that she was quite prepared for some new calamity.

"I have a lot to thank you for," Miss Pope began. "I'm grateful—truly grateful—indeed you must not think I'm not . . ."

Out of a welter of thanks and excuses Julia gathered the information that Miss Pope wished to leave Belmont House as soon as possible, and in any case not later than two o'clock.

"The Mothers' Union," she said. "We have the meeting in the church-room. I must be there."

"But you're not a mother. And you're ill."

"I'm not a mother, but I'm not ill either. Being a mother doesn't matter," she explained incoherently, "but not being ill is on my conscience. There will be no one to read the minutes, and Alaric will forget to unlock the door."

There was no shaking her, though Julia used all her charm, all her tact, and all the authority of one who has been inspired. By the end of the interview Miss Pope had made it clear that she did not trust in inspirations, that she had come against her better judgement, and that dear Mrs. Dunstan, though kindness itself, did not understand what it meant to be a vicar's sister.

This was very galling for Julia, who still believed in her plan. It was all she could do to give in gracefully and part from Miss Pope on friendly terms. The parting took place there and then, for Miss Pope, as soon as Julia agreed to her leaving, picked up the Moses basket from its place of concealment on the landing and hurried downstairs like an escaping prisoner, gratitude and apologies floating back over her shoulder as she went.

"So kind of you . . . such a wonderful rest. And will you please thank Miss Duckworth as well? So kind of you both . . ."

"What?" Julia called, uncertain whether she had heard aright.

Miss Pope was fumbling with the door latch, and now she opened the door.

"So kind of you both," she repeated. "Of course I feel most grateful to *you*—your idea—but I feel, as you're sharing the house, that I should thank Miss Duckworth too. I hope she'll forgive me for rushing off like this. . . ."

Off she rushed. The door closed behind her, and Julia was left with a new puzzle. What had given Miss Pope the idea that she and Dora were sharing the house?

Of course, Dora lived there. But 'sharing the house' implied joint ownership, or a joint responsibility for household expenses. Dora contributed nothing to the household expenses, and neither she nor Julia thought of Belmont House as in any way hers. At least, Julia didn't, and she had assumed that Dora agreed with her.

She could not linger to brood over the puzzle, because it was time to see Nanny. This was the formal interview of the day, when meals were discussed and grievances—Nanny's grievances—brought out for an airing. The news that Miss Pope had gone put Nanny in a better temper; but her old-nurselike moralizing did nothing to improve Julia's.

"A good thing too," Nanny said sagely. "How often have I told you, Miss Julia, to let well alone? Your kind heart will be the death of you one of these fine days."

Wearily Julia listened to the moralizing and the grumbles. Wearily, at length, she escaped to the morning-room, where Nanny pursued her to complain that Miss Duckworth had walked through the kitchen in her muddy gum-boots just after the floor had been mopped.

"If I've to spend my time sweeping up mud—"

"Leave it," Julia said. "Or ask Carrington to do it."

Nanny said it wasn't Mr. Carrington's business. Julia replied that he would have time to spare, as he hadn't dusted or swept the morning-room. She hoped this reproof would find its target.

Left alone, she leant back on the sofa and closed her eyes. Nanny, Robert, Dora, and Carrington were her responsibilities, and she could not escape from them. Sometimes it seemed as though there was never a moment of the day when one or the other wasn't being a trial; and the worst of it was that none of them appeared at all grateful. Nanny grumbled, Carrington was idle; Robert and Dora simply took it for granted that they should live in the utmost comfort at her expense. And then there was Miss Pope—poor Miss Pope, whose veiled reproaches had made her feel anxious and guilty. She longed to rescue Miss Pope; she still believed that she *could* be rescued, if she would only do as she was told; but it was clear that Miss Pope did not trust her or want her sympathy.

The native heath, at that moment, might have been a heath out of *Macbeth*. Belmont House was simply a roof over other people's heads, supported by her money and benevolence. When the doorbell rang she sprang up to warn Carrington not to let anyone in; since it was certain to be someone needing sympathy or a subscription. But Carrington must have been in the hall (or the telephone alcove), for the bell had hardly stopped ringing when she heard the slam of the closing door.

She patted her hair and plumped up the sofa cushions and prepared to offer a welcoming smile to the unwanted visitor; but when the drawing-room door opened to admit her cousin

Francis she forgot that the welcoming smile had needed an effort of will.

"How lovely to see you!" she cried. "You managed to arrive at the right time. Or perhaps I should think so whatever time it was."

The warmth of this greeting ought to have alarmed him, but he had other things to think about. He had come to Julia, rather against his principles, for sympathy.

"What do you think?" he said, when their first smiles had spent themselves. "Henry is coming back!"

"Oh, Francis, how trying for you. This has been a very trying morning—an unlucky day for both of us."

Francis did not enquire in what way it had been unlucky for Julia.

"He sent me a postcard," he said. "Just a postcard! To say he was coming south and would like to spend a night or two at Heswald. He is arriving tomorrow. I suppose he found the house too damp."

"But what else did he expect, in Argyllshire?" said Julia, for whom Highland scenery was closely associated with wet weather.

"Henry's concern for his health verges on the ridiculous. Also, he is a terrible bore."

"But he won't be with you for long. You can easily get rid of him—give him a slightly damp bed or indigestible food."

Francis shook his head. "Mrs. Sable seems to like him, so he will have everything of the best. One's servants can be very uncooperative."

"Indeed they can. You don't know what trouble I'm having with Nanny. And—" She stopped; for some reason it seemed unwise to mention Dora and Robert. "And Miss Pope," she continued. "'The vicarage' will be graven on my heart, like Calais. And now she has *gone*."

"Has she?" he asked, looking at her in a rather absent-minded way. "Well, I have Henry to come. And I wondered—"

"And, poor thing, she will have a most unsuccessful homecoming. The vicarage larder is sure to be empty I picture the vicarage as empty of everything but displeasure. I am really terribly worried about her."

"Your kind heart does you credit."

Julia had the impression that Francis was laughing; but she must have been mistaken, for he went on seriously.

"I hope you will be kind enough to help me to entertain Henry."

"Of course I will. Francis, do you think Alaric is *really* thinking of marrying Miss Brigg?"

He replied, rather shortly, that time would show. Julia pointed out that it would then be Too Late; once he had proposed it would be difficult, if not impossible, to rescue Alaric. Miss Pope would have to leave the vicarage; and—poor thing— where would she go?

"One must do something to entertain Henry," Francis said, speaking of himself with impersonal regret. "One might drive him out to the Roman Camp for a picnic. Will you and Dora be free on Monday?"

A tremor of disappointment ran through Julia. Why, oh why did Francis regard them as Siamese twins? But she ignored it and said that a picnic would be very enjoyable and that she had wanted for a long time to revisit the Roman Camp.

"Yes, I've been meaning to take you there," he told her, looking more cheerful now that Henry's entertainment was ensured.

'You' must mean both of them, Julia decided. She could not hope to escape from her responsibilities; and her mind went back sadly to the morning's disasters.

"I think I shall walk over to the vicarage this afternoon and see how things are going," she said.

"Oh—damn the vicarage!" Francis said heartily.

One should not damn vicarages: they are all but holy ground. But although Francis was voicing, more emphatically, the sentiments of Dora and Nanny and Robert, which had caused her so much distress, Julia was not in the least annoyed with him. On the contrary, in the long pause which followed, she felt her disappointment and hitherto-unacknowledged anxiety ebbing away.

It was at this moment that Dora chose to return from the garden, rumpled, but without her gum-boots, to have a word with Francis. She had seen his car at the gate.

The word, naturally, became many words. Dora was delighted to hear about the picnic and almost as pleased to learn that Henry was returning. She had enjoyed meeting Henry again; he was so clever and amusing, wasn't he?

Francis and Julia exchanged looks, and Francis asked, "In what way?"

"Oh, you know what I mean!"

Julia thought Francis was going to say that he didn't, and because she did not want a squabble she said quickly that Henry was at least clever; it seemed to her clever for a man to run his own house and do his own cooking—though women didn't have to be clever to do these things. But then women were brought up to do them.

"I run my own house," Francis observed.

Julia said that showed he was clever too. Dora managed to refrain from saying that he did not do the cooking.

"But I am not so clever as you two," he went on. "I think it must be very difficult to share a house. It is clever of you to make such a success of it."

Afterwards Julia remembered that Francis had given her a quizzical glance, as if he wondered whether the success was genuine. But at the time she was hardly aware of it. She was so surprised to learn that he, like Miss Pope, supposed Dora to be sharing the house, that she could think of nothing to say. It was Dora, hurriedly pointing out that husbands and wives had to share houses, who kept the conversation going.

A little later Francis departed. Julia and Dora accompanied him to the front door, and as soon as he had disappeared Dora said she was going to do some more gardening.

"No, come and talk to me. I've had such a tiresome morning."

They went back to the morning-room. Dora sat down at the desk and opened her big accounts-book, as if she could not bear to be idle.

Julia, who was feeling extremely nervous, began by telling her about Miss Pope. But Dora listened with an only half-attentive ear. She kept on saying "Just a minute" and marking a place with her pencil. At the end she said rather too brightly that perhaps it was all for the best.

"I blame myself," Julia said tragically.

"Cheer up," said Dora. "At least Nanny will be pleased."

Her voice showed what she thought of Nanny; but Julia ignored it.

"What made Francis think we were sharing the house?" she asked.

"I can't imagine," Dora replied.

After that there was silence, broken by Dora's muttering as she added up figures; for the accounts seemed suddenly to need a great deal of attention.

Julia looked at the back of Dora's neck. It was flushed—or was it? Anyway, she was sure Dora's face was flushed; she was sure Dora was lying. She had told people, or at least let them suppose, that she was sharing the house, and she had done this because she did not like outsiders to know she was living on Julia's bounty. To appear as a grateful poor relation would be disagreeable to one who had openly commended the virtues of independence and self-help. No doubt she had persuaded herself, little by little, that the small deceit could be justified.

Julia was angry; but she also felt sorry for Dora. In a sense comfort and ease *had* corrupted her, and in any case she was still a responsibility. One could not denounce her, because she was a cousin, a poor relation, and on the whole well-intentioned. A quarrel, open hostility, were unthinkable; but could one just ignore it? What distressed her most was the thought that Dora probably did not like her. It was not affection, after all, that kept her at Belmont House; the small deceit, which slurred over her own kindness, made that fairly certain. Dora remained simply because it suited her.

Dora shut the accounts-book with a bang.

"You're spending much too much on Nanny and Carrington," she declared. "If we had one efficient servant, instead of two duds, we should be far more comfortable."

Julia did not care for the sound of that 'we'. It suggested a permanence, a settled, long-term partnership, which would endure to the grave.

CHAPTER XXII

ON SUNDAY AFTERNOON Robert was allowed to give a tennis party. There were five keen players—himself and Harriet, Charlton Minnis and James Wilmot and Marian Prentice—and one who was only there to make the numbers even—his aunt Dora. Dora said she would play if they really needed her but they must not expect her to run; in the end, however, she ran with the best of them and wore everyone down by her tireless, unfailing steadiness. She was a popular partner with those who wanted to win.

There were also three onlookers: Mr. and Mrs. Prentice, and Lady Finch. It was quite a large party, but in Robert's opinion there was only one person who mattered. The party had been given for Harriet; and he thought she enjoyed it. He felt, for the first time, that she both noticed and liked him.

He lay awake quite late, wondering if Harriet would make a good wife. The Dunstan in him took marriage seriously, even though he hadn't a job and couldn't hope to marry for years. He came downstairs on Monday morning still thinking about it.

Aunts, even honorary ones, had their failings, but they also had their uses. They could act as an audience; and he needed an audience, or at least someone to listen most of the time and ask occasional pertinent questions. It did not occur to Robert that both his aunts, that morning, had other things on their minds.

"Really, how can I tell?" asked Dora, after hearing his careful summing-up of the pros and cons. Julia, who had not grasped the import of his preliminary remarks, had disappeared to interview Nanny and telephone to her hairdresser.

"Well, I suppose you can't—but talking to you helps me to think," Robert explained. He wondered, aloud, and for the tenth time, whether he was really in love with Harriet, and decided, for the tenth time, that he was. But that wasn't really enough, when one came to *think* about it. Would they be happy—would they get on together? Were their characters, their outlook, sufficiently alike—or was it better that they should not be alike? . . .

"Oh, go and ask Harriet," said Dora, hardly able to refrain from adding, She's the one who will have to live with you. Robert looked offended; he thought he had made it clear that he was being serious.

"I *am* going there, now," he said. "But of course not to—to—"

"Pop the question?"

Afterwards she was sorry she had been flippant. She liked Robert, and lately she had wondered whether if he got a job in some other part of England she might rent a small cottage or bungalow and make a home for him. She felt so like an aunt towards him that there was nothing improper in the thought; and no one need know that she wasn't really his aunt.

'I am much more like an aunt than Julia,' she thought complacently.

Robert went across the field and on to the canal bank. The tow-path was not the shortest way to Urn Cottage, but his dog Taffy preferred it; or rather, he preferred it for Taffy, whose hatred for cats and fox-terriers took him into other people's gardens if they walked through the village. The tow-path was disused, because the canal boats were no longer pulled by horses, and its rough, crumbling surface discouraged pedestrians. He was surprised to see, in the distance, two female figures walking towards him; and even more surprised, as they drew nearer, to recognize Lady Finch and Harriet.

Lady Finch's walks were usually undertaken for a purpose, and a stroll along the canal bank, on a Monday morning, seemed an aberration. But when they met it soon appeared that she had a reason for being there.

"We are avoiding the village," Harriet explained. "If we cut across the field beside Belmont House and then make a quick dash along the road we can get there without being seen."

"Get where?"

Harriet and her aunt exchanged guilty glances. Lady Finch cleared her throat and said:

"The vicarage. I am going to see Miss Pope, and I am taking Harriet as a witness."

Robert was aware that Lady Finch had vowed never to enter the vicarage again.

"What's up?" he asked.

"I have thought things over carefully," Lady Finch announced. "And I have decided that Miss Pope and I had better come to an arrangement."

"An armistice treaty," Harriet said. She made a face at Robert to show him that this was her doing.

"Nothing of the sort, Harriet. A sensible talk—that is all. To clear the air."

"To bury the hatchet."

"To get back the honeycombs?" Robert suggested. Lady Finch gave a grim smile.

"That was Harriet's idea, too," she said. "It is probable that they are at the vicarage with the rest of Mr. Pope's honey. If, as Harriet thinks, he knows nothing of this deception, Miss Brigg can hardly claim them now. When I have explained matters to Miss Pope she will see that I have a moral right to them."

"Still—Miss Brigg paid for them," Robert said. Harriet made another face, an admonitory face, to warn him not to interfere with her plan. It had taken hours of persuasion to bring Aunt Finch to the point of parleying with the enemy.

Fortunately Lady Finch now thought of it as her own plan, and had worked out the details.

"Naturally, if Miss Pope gives me the sections I shall return the money," she said. "It will be quite easy. I shall simply send Miss Brigg a postal order. Nothing else in the envelope, you understand—just the postal order. Then there will be no danger of her taking any of these absurd 'proceedings' Harriet is so worried about."

"I think that's a good idea—don't you?"

"Not bad," Robert said. He did not think it was a very good idea, but he could not resist the smile with which Harriet pleaded for his approval. That she should desire his approval seemed extremely gratifying.

"But wouldn't it be better to wait till the afternoon?" he went on. "I should think Monday morning at the vicarage is pretty cluttered up with domestic chores."

Harriet and her aunt had overlooked the fact that it was Monday morning. They remembered that Miss Pope would be doing the washing, and that Leah Townley would be cleaning the front rooms. It would hardly be possible, under these circumstances, to have a sensible talk. After a short discussion Lady Finch decided to postpone the talk till later in the day, and they turned back towards Urn Cottage. Robert accompanied them. Though neither suggested his coming he was pleasantly conscious of being welcomed, of being liked, by Harriet, and of being at least tolerated by Lady Finch.

The Monday-morning routine at the vicarage had been disorganized by the non-arrival of Leah Townley.

"I suppose it's her sister's baby again," said Miss Pope. The baby suffered from a variety of infantile ailments, and every time it was taken to the doctor Leah had to go too, to give her sister moral support. This was tiresome for her employers; but not so tiresome, on this particular morning, as Miss Pope pretended. Leah's absence, and the fact that on Monday mornings everyone else in Goatstock was busy with domestic tasks and unlikely to leave them, meant that she would have the opportunity for an uninterrupted talk with Alaric. A sensible talk, to clear the air. The air, since her return on Saturday, had been so thick with misgivings and misunderstandings that one could scarcely see through it.

Alaric, to begin with, had welcomed her with pathetic relief. Mrs. Dunstan was right; he had missed her in more ways than one. He seemed to have been living on bread and cheese, and sardines—which he had had to scrape out in bits through the very small hole he managed to make in one corner of the tin—and a nasty burnt mess which was several packets of soup powder in an insufficient quantity of milk.

"I thought if I made it stronger than they said it would be more nourishing," he explained.

But it was not only in the kitchen that he had missed her. She was needed to draft a reply to a curt enquiry from the Chancellor of the diocese about expenditure on the choir screen, which apparently had not been sanctioned; and to hunt for the minutes book of the Church School committee, which Alaric had borrowed, some weeks ago, from the secretary, and unaccountably mislaid; and to cope with the problem of Mrs. Heaton, a contentious widow who had sprained her ankle in the churchyard and was now demanding damages because one of the paving-stones in the path was loose. There were many other problems, too, which had arisen in the short time of her absence and which Alaric had hopefully relegated to the category of 'things that could wait a bit'. Oh yes, there was no doubt that he had missed her tremendously.

Nevertheless, her homecoming had not been altogether happy. There were many unspoken questions between them, and each was conscious of the other's reproachful gaze at odd moments. Parish engagements on Saturday had kept them apart, and Sunday, Miss Pope felt, was not a suitable day for a sensible talk that might end in a disagreement. But Monday morning, lacking Leah's presence, was very suitable indeed, and if it had been raining it would have been quite perfect.

She walked into Alaric's study and sat down in the sagging armchair by the fireplace. Alaric looked up from his desk and gave her an apprehensive smile.

"A beautiful morning, is it not?" he asked.

"I hear that the New Town was just a false rumour," Miss Pope said.

This was the first time the New Town had been mentioned between them, and Alaric knew at once that his apprehensions were justified.

"They have decided to build it elsewhere," he replied with dignity.

"I've worried so much about it—the ruin of Goatstock, and everything it would have meant. You really should have told me, in the beginning, that it was just a bit of clerical gossip."

Unchristian thoughts filled his mind, and under their influence he spoke with considerable acrimony.

"Really, Myrtle, I made it perfectly plain that nothing was *settled*. It was your fault—I mean, your mistake—for telling everyone about a matter which should have been confidential. The Bishop's chaplain was most annoyed, and—"

"You made me look such a fool," said Miss Pope, taking the words out of his mouth. "Holding a protest meeting and so on, when it was nothing but a rumour."

Alaric had sounded cross, but this did nothing to placate her. She had meant to be calm and sensible and forgiving about the muddle over the New Town, but it was hard to hear herself unjustly reproved.

"You were indiscreet," Alaric said. The next moment he added that he blamed himself; but these mitigating words came too late.

"I!" Miss Pope cried. She gave a shrill laugh. "Let us not speak about discretion, Alaric. Not now, when your own imprudence has put us in such an embarrassing position. Oh, I know you are innocent—but who will believe it! It was advertised as your honey, and of course Lady Finch will be telling everyone how she's been defrauded. I'm sure people are gossiping about it already."

Alaric wondered if his sister had suddenly gone mad.

"My dear Myrtle," he said, using the voice he kept for the afflicted, "do please calm yourself and explain what you are talking about." And he sat back, arms folded, with a patient smile on his face.

Miss Pope repeated the oft-told tale of Lady Finch's sections and Miss Brigg's duplicity. At first Alaric found it incredible; then, looking back, he remembered how plump and well-matched his honeycombs had appeared on the display table. He had been quite surprised, when he saw them, by their shining perfection, but he had supposed that the cellophane wrapping made a difference.

Now he learned that they were not his, but Lady Finch's honeycombs, and that Lady Finch was accusing him of fraud.

"She said she would never enter this house again," Miss Pope reiterated.

"Dear me, that is very awkward. Very awkward indeed."

Miss Pope reflected bitterly that Alaric would use this phrase whether it was a missing button or—as now—the threat of total ruin.

"What are you going to do?" she demanded.

"I shall have to speak to Miss Brigg, when she returns. And I suppose . . . Do you think it would be as well if I—or perhaps you—wrote to Lady Finch, to absolve ourselves—I mean, myself—of responsibility?"

Miss Pope said nothing.

"How could she do such a thing?" Alaric asked fretfully. "Such a nice, sensible woman . . . the last person I should have expected. . . ."

"She did it to please you."

The problem of the honeycombs was so closely connected with the problem of Alaric's future that Miss Pope now felt herself to be rushing down a steep hill, unable to stop but dreading the possible precipice below her.

"She does her best, always, to please you," she said, quickening her speed. For an instant Alaric's face showed the complacency of any man's, when he is told that women seek to please him, but it soon changed to alarm.

"I do not know what you mean," he said quickly.

"Yes, you do," said Miss Pope's voice, which seemed to be speaking without its owner's conscious co-operation. "She's devoted to you."

"Really, Myrtle!"

His bright blush might be due to gentlemanly embarrassment, or to his affection for Miss Brigg. Miss Pope felt herself tottering on the very edge of the precipice; she shut her eyes and said coldly:

"If you are thinking of marrying please tell me in good time. I shall have to find another home." The words horrified her so much that she opened her eyes at once to see what effect they had on Alaric.

His horror, judging from his face, was even greater than her own. Several times he attempted to speak, but only achieved low mooing sounds indicative of extreme emotion.

"Oh, Alaric!" cried Miss Pope. She spoke like a loving sister, but spoiled it the next instant by asking how he could be so stupid. "Everyone in the village thinks you are going to be married. Mary Ellen, I understand, has told her friends it is practically settled."

One part of Alaric's mind heard a faint echo . . . for not long ago his sister had told everyone in the village that the plans for the New Town were 'practically settled'. *These women!* one part of his mind muttered angrily, lumping Myrtle and Mary

Ellen together as irresponsible, sub-standard citizens. But very quickly he retrieved Myrtle and pushed her back on the pedestal she occupied when disasters threatened. She was the person who had always coped with disasters.

"You must deny it," he said decisively. "At once. There isn't a word of truth in it. I never had the slightest intention. . . ." He blushed again, for the subject seemed too embarrassing to be mentioned.

"Then you have behaved very foolishly," Miss Pope said. She believed him, but she could not help pointing out his foolish errors. "Letting her come here, letting her fuss round, cooking, and spoiling you—and praising everything she did. As if I couldn't cook!"

'You can't,' said the other part of Alaric's mind, with a last nostalgic sniff at the savoury smell of Mary Ellen's casseroles.

"She shall not come again," he said hastily. "Perhaps you could talk to her, when she returns from her holiday—"

"Perhaps it would be better if you wrote to her."

"But that would be very awkward—very awkward indeed for both of us. How could I make it clear without—without actually saying that I had heard she had said that—"

"Yes, I suppose it would," said Miss Pope, realizing that she would have to draft the letter. "Well, you must make it clear by your manner and so on, when she comes back."

She was feeling so relieved, so absurdly happy, that the thought of facing an aggrieved and angry Mary Ellen did not daunt her. Besides, she could see that Alaric, though badly shaken, meant what he said.

"Certainly, certainly," he agreed. "No doubt that is the best—the kindest way. I shall wait till she returns, and then I shall make it clear to her that she—that she has misunderstood."

He jutted out his chin—as far as nature allowed—and looked, for once, like a militant churchman.

"Yes, Marian has gone," Mrs. Prentice said to Mrs. Minnis. "I've just seen her on to the bus. Such a short holiday, but I think it did her good."

Mrs. Minnis was wearing a new, bright-green frock, and had tied back her grey curls with a green ribbon. She explained that this was because it was Monday morning and she needed something to cheer her up.

"Monday mornings are the end," she said. "And now Sonny is out of a job."

Mrs. Prentice was not surprised, but she made a sympathetic reply.

"The Coal Board didn't suit him," Mrs. Minnis said, reversing the facts. "He is thinking of entering the Church."

This reminded Mrs. Prentice that she had left her umbrella in her pew yesterday and must enter the church that afternoon to retrieve it. "And I shall drop in and see Miss Pope," she said. "I hadn't time to speak to her yesterday after matins because she went straight back to the vicarage through that little door in the wall."

Mrs. Minnis tittered. "Probably she didn't *want* to speak to you. She must feel aw'fly silly, after going on and on about the New Town and now there isn't going to be one."

Slowly the information sank in; Mrs. Prentice showed thoughtful surprise and finally remarked that things changed so quickly that she couldn't keep up with them.

"First we're going to be swallowed up, then we aren't," she said. "It makes one wonder what will happen next."

Life was like that, Mrs. Minnis declared; it sometimes seemed as if one was living on the edge of a volcano, didn't it?

Mrs. Prentice thought for a moment and then said no, it didn't.

CHAPTER XXIII

THE PICNIC that was to entertain Henry had not seemed to him, when he was first told about it, the kind of entertainment he would enjoy. He remembered the Roman Camp as a bleak, windy place where it often rained, reached by a bumpy track which was ruin to one's car, and the scene of an alarming encounter with an angry ram. He thought of saying he must leave Heswald on Monday morning, but it was difficult to find an excuse for this departure when he had already arranged to stay till Wednesday. Besides, it would be a pity to miss the excellent meals Mrs. Sable had planned for him.

By the time they started, however, he was reconciled to the idea of a picnic. It was a brilliantly sunny day, warm and dry so that he need have no qualms about sitting out of doors, and Francis was taking his own car, which was so old that its tires and springs did not matter. Henry sat beside him, wearing a tweed jacket and a flannel shirt because the Roman Camp was 500 feet above sea-level, but feeling almost too hot. The August sun blazed down, and the car was open. Francis was wearing quite a thin shirt and no jacket, which Henry thought unwise of him; he screwed his head round and was relieved to see Francis's jacket on the back seat, together with a pile of rugs and two cushions.

"The food is in the boot," Francis said, thinking that Henry was worrying about it. But Henry had verified this fact before they started; a picnic without food would have been like an opium den without opium, only—for a man of his temperament—much worse.

Legend said the Roman Camp had been a halting-place for the legions marching north to the Wall. The fact that it was rather a long way from the most famous of the Roman roads was irrefutable; but legends die hard and the defenders of this one said that the minor road over the moors was an alternative route. Whatever their purpose had been, there were Roman remains on the high plateau above the reservoir, and the bumpy road went on, over the shoulder of Winter Hill and past the Potter's Needle, and eventually joined the modern main road that led to Carlisle and the border. It was therefore a possible route, though not a very practical one, for the legions to have taken.

Francis drove his car up the rutted track to the Camp. They were the first to arrive, and looking back they could see the road stretching away, dipping down to the reservoir and rising again to the ridge of hill beyond. The heather was in bloom and smelt of honey, but far off in the distance the Reddrod chimneys clustered thickly and the blue sky was dimmed by a layer of smoke. Henry said something appropriate about dark, satanic mills. Francis, shading his eyes from the sun, said he could see a car and it must be Julia's.

"Then they started very punctually," Henry said with sarcasm. (How typical of women to be punctual for a picnic and late for a dinner party.) They watched the car, like a small beetle, crawling down the hill to the reservoir and then ascending the hill towards them. As it drew nearer Francis was relieved to see that it contained only two people.

He had not invited Robert, but he had half-expected him to come, and he feared that Julia might also bring Miss Pope—or even Nanny—in order not to waste the fourth seat and the lovely afternoon. He could have borne with Robert; but someone Julia felt sorry for would have been decidedly in the way.

The car came up the track and stopped beside his own. Julia and Dora got out and went into raptures over the view, the heather, and the warmth and splendour of the day. Henry thought they both looked charming, but awarded the palm to Dora because she wore sensible shoes and a warmer-looking dress; it was not till later that the sensible shoes, donned for the purpose of taking a nice long walk, came to be a symbol of wholly unnecessary activity.

Henry thought they should have tea at once, but the others preferred to stroll about the site of the Camp. There was little to be seen, for the objects of interest had been removed to a museum, but the ground—plan of walls and entrances remained, and Dora was soon striding from gate to gate to see the exact view the legions had seen as they came and went.

"It's a pity we didn't bring Robert," Julia said to Francis. He could have been a legionary and come marching up the road to show Dora where they first came over the skyline.

Francis thought this exhausting role would have been good for Robert, whose indolence was unnatural and deplorable. But he pointed out that the skyline was a long way off.

Julia was not listening. "He couldn't come, because he asked Harriet Finch to tea," she said. "I wish he hadn't. It's Carrington's afternoon off, and Nanny was looking forward to a rest. But he's so tiresome and thoughtless. He gets worse and worse."

"On the other hand, it might have been a *good* thought on Robert's part, to give Harriet a respite from Lady Finch."

Julia looked at him; it was at first a look that feigned incomprehension, but then she laughed.

"I suppose I am silly—" she began.

"Stupid," Francis corrected her.

"I suppose I am stupid, then."

"If you like to put it that way."

She reminded herself that she must not put it that way in future, when he was present.

"But I feel quite sorry for Robert," she said gaily. "Young men ought not to live with their aunts—they get spoiled, and then the aunts get cross. It's quite time he had a job. I had wondered if you knew how we should start finding one."

Before he could answer they were joined by Dora, who wanted some information about the Romans. While Francis was relating the legend Julia's gaiety diminished. For two days she had felt confident that Francis invited both of them because he could not, in common courtesy, leave poor Dora out of the invitations, but now, watching them together, she swung back to the other, the lamentable alternative.

Perhaps, after all, he preferred Dora.

The first time this idea had occurred to her she had laughed it away. She was not conceited, but she knew—she couldn't help knowing—that Dora was boring and plain and tactless, and that she herself had made a good impression on Francis from the beginning. (Moreover, there were the memories of the distant past.) Dora as a rival need not be taken seriously; nor, at that time, did rivals matter, because Julia saw herself as a Good In-fluence on Francis—an altruistic, though affectionate, relation-ship, in which jealousy and the fear of rivals had no part.

Almost without her realizing it the altruistic relationship had changed into something else. The encounter with Lady Sybil at the Aged Animals' Pension Party had shown her how much rivals mattered; and although her alarm on that occasion had proved unnecessary she had been nervous ever since.

It was strange to be nervous; and nervousness led on to feel-ing humble and unsure of oneself. Julia could no longer laugh away the thought of Dora as a rival, though what she called the reasoning part of her mind insisted that she had nothing to fear. She stood there, listening to Francis and Dora, and tried to com-fort herself by thinking of the desert island. But the island, with its one inhabitant, appeared a desert indeed.

Henry had assumed the role of host. (After all, *someone* had to see to things, or they might not get any tea.) He had spread out the rugs, and got the primus going and boiled the kettle, and now he shouted to his cousins to join him. Not till he had attracted their attention did he start unpacking the food; sand-wiches and cakes should not stand for long in the sun, in case they become stale and dry.

Julia positively welcomed the thought of tea. Francis said they had better hurry; it would not do to give old Henry too long a start. They walked back towards Henry's chosen spot, where he was now daintily arranging the food on cardboard plates. Dora rushed ahead to rescue the kettle, which behind Henry's back was boiling itself into a frenzy.

"I suppose it was Henry, not you, who decorated the dinner table," Julia said, observing Henry's absorption in his task.

Francis said he had begun the decorating, but Henry had in-terfered. He told her how Henry had insisted on the dolphins and tankards, and they agreed that one could have too many carnations. Laughing over Henry's *folie-de-grandeur* set them at ease again; Julia was suddenly, gloriously certain that Dora's interest in Roman remains had been for Francis a boring inter-ruption to a conversation he wished to continue.

"What a scrumptious tea," Dora exclaimed, standing strad-dlelegged to admire it. For picnics she had a schoolgirl enthusi-asm which resulted in schoolgirl behaviour, and Julia was hard-ly surprised when she added that she was as hungry as a hunter.

Henry, who had already catalogued Dora as the best of his cousins, nodded his approval of the remark. But Francis said quietly that he had often thought hungry hunters must be re-garded as failures in their chosen profession.

Julia rewarded him for this pleasantry with a smile. It was a smile that revealed to him all the danger of picnics at plac-es haunted by the past, but he did not wish himself elsewhere. Henry's entertainment was no more than an excuse, and it was now too late to pretend that he would not have brought Julia to the Roman Camp if it had not been necessary to entertain funny old Henry.

"Who is looking after Miriam?" Dora asked.

She timed the question well, for Henry had eaten enough to dull the edge of his appetite and was ready for a little conver-sation.

"My next-door neighbour," he said. He explained that he had once tried sending Miriam to a cats' boarding-house, but that even the best of these establishments did not give their boarders enough to eat. The woman next door came in daily with offer-ings of fish, milk and liver, and something extra-special on Sun-days. The kitchen window was left slightly open so that Miriam could go in and out.

"Quite *wide* open, I should think," Julia whispered to Fran-cis. "I don't see Miriam getting through a little crack."

Henry said he was very fortunate. The woman next door was a widow, Mrs. Pitt-Wilson, and was devoted to cats.

'Perhaps she means to marry him,' Julia thought. A *schem-ing* widow, wooing Henry by fussing over his cat. She reminded herself virtuously that she had never made a fuss of Snowball; and then, shying away from the implications of this thought, she wondered if Dora would make Henry a good wife.

A better wife than the scheming widow, she decided. She pictured the widow as drab and resigned like the prototype-of-widows. But, if she was resigned, would she be capable of scheming? . . .

"You are miles away," Francis said quietly.

Julia looked up in surprise. Henry was stacking the plates and Dora was helping him; a cosy domestic scene which hardly needed an audience. She wished she and Francis could stroll off—as Robert and Harriet had done at last week's picnic—with a casual air of not noticing what they were doing. But somehow it did not seem possible.

"I'm going up to the monument," Dora announced. "The view up there ought to be marvellous."

Francis opened his mouth to say it was no finer than the view down here, and then thought better of it.

Henry said apprehensively that the climb to the monument was steeper than it looked.

Julia, smiling to herself, said nothing at all.

"Come on, you lazy people! In the old days we used to *run* up there and back!"

None of them could remember doing this. The monument was an obelisk, with an iron railing round it, on the crest of the distant hill. It was called the Potter's Needle, but no one knew why.

"We shall disturb the grouse," Henry said, remembering that the month was August, when grouse were important. "Can't go tramping through the heather."

Francis said the moor wasn't let this year, and even if it had been there was a right-of-way up to the monument.

"Oh, come on," Dora exclaimed. "We need some exercise after that enormous tea."

Henry gave in. The sun was still hot, and the monument looked a long way off, but it was true he needed exercise. Without it, he might not be able to do justice to the excellent dinner Mrs. Sable would certainly provide. He wished he had not eaten so much tea as to make exercise desirable; but a short walk—perhaps not as far as the monument—should restore his appetite.

Slowly he rose to his feet. By the time he was ready to start Dora was fifty yards away. Francis and Julia watched them advancing up the hill, Henry walking (as he thought) rather fast, and Dora (as she thought) walking slowly, to allow him to catch up.

"When he draws level Henry will find that the pace quickens," Francis remarked.

"Poor Henry. He's much too warmly dressed."

"Does he perhaps need some good advice—like Miss Pope?"

"Oh, Francis, don't tease me about Miss Pope. I'm so worried. Everything has gone wrong."

He smiled, but not teasingly.

"Tell me about it."

Had Miss Pope been present at the picnic Julia, like Francis, would have found her in the way; and intuition should have warned her that Miss Pope's troubles were as much of an intrusion as Miss Pope herself. Unfortunately, she was once more in the nervous uncertain mood in which intuitions could not operate, and Francis's friendly words drew from her a long, repetitive account of the Pope-Brigg entanglement, to which he listened with extraordinary patience.

"And then there is Nanny," Julia said, when she had finished with Miss Pope.

Nanny was really getting very difficult. Of her loyalty and devotion there could be no question, but she was becoming a tyrant; far more of a tyrant than she had been in the days of childhood. She ordered Julia about—with the best intentions, of course—and made scenes, and was always being jealous and quarrelsome.

Francis remained an attentive listener, but Julia found herself wishing, in the midst of her recital, that she could stop talking or talk about something else. She was saying too much; she was behaving ridiculously, babbling on about problems which had become curiously unreal. But for some reason she could not check the torrent of words; with positive horror she heard herself saying, "Then there is Robert. . . ."

"And Dora," Francis said calmly. "Do not let us forget Dora."

Julia faltered. There was Dora most of all; for although the other problems now seemed less important Dora's future weighed heavily on her mind. But it was not a subject she could discuss with Francis, because of her uncertainty about his feelings for Dora; she was surprised, and rather shaken, by his apparent awareness that Dora was a problem.

"I feel responsible for her," she said cautiously.

"But it is a feeling you enjoy," said Francis.

She tried to look reproachful, and failed.

"Perhaps I do," she admitted.

"Without Dora and Robert and Nanny and the village to feel responsible for, you would be bored."

Julia saw the desert island fading into limbo, and made an effort to retrieve it.

"Oh no," she said. "I could live quite happily by myself. Don't laugh, Francis. I sometimes think, if only I could get rid of Nanny and—and everyone, I should be perfectly happy at Belmont House. By myself."

"I'm not laughing," he assured her; and she saw that it was true. "But I do not think you would be happy at Belmont House, by yourself."

"Well—if Nanny left, then perhaps Dora and I—"

Francis said abruptly: "Never mind about Dora. I am very bad at this. But what I am trying to ask you is—would you be happy with me?"

"Oh—Francis!"

"That is not an answer," he said gently, though indeed it was. "Julia, will you marry me?"

Julia had received several proposals of marriage at one time or another, and had dealt with them competently and gracefully, on lines mapped out in advance. But now she simply gazed at Francis as if he were the Promised Land, and murmured something he could hardly hear.

He took her hand and said, "I hope you are not letting your kind heart get the better of you."

"If you are always going to laugh at me, I shall probably regret saying Yes," she replied, looking far from regretful.

"My dear Julia!"

To be his dear Julia had long been her ambition; and while she was confessing it, and listening to his assurances of perfect contentment, the sunlit moor seemed the reflection of a dream world where everything ended happily and problems had ceased to exist. Neither of them noticed the passing of time in this shadowless, cloudless landscape—although up by the monument Henry was looking at his watch and reckoning the hours till dinner. Dora and Robert, Nanny and Miss Pope, mattered so little that they were mentioned several times, as having been present on this or that occasion, without evoking a single good thought from Julia or an irritable one from Francis.

"I am a very lazy man," he said presently. "I hope you are not going to reform me."

Julia answered blithely that nothing was farther from her mind. Then, in a rush of dangerous honesty which could only be attributed to love, she admitted that she had once planned a very drastic reformation. Francis said marriage would be quite enough of a reformation, without turning him into a professor of political economy or a member of parliament.

"Or whatever you had in mind," he added questioningly.

Julia confessed that he was only to have been the Controller or Chief Organizer of the New Town, and Francis said he was mortified; a wretched little congeries of red-brick boxes was not worthy of a Heswald's attention.

Julia was aware that, despite his protestations, he was laughing at her; but she bore it serenely.

"Anyway, there isn't going to be a New Town," she said. "Did I tell you that it's all off?"

"It never was on."

"Well, Miss Pope thought it was."

"Then she will have one thing less to trouble her."

The New Town, even though it had no substance, cast a shadow across the dream landscape. Julia sighed, thinking once more of her responsibilities, and wondered aloud what was to become of Dora.

"And Nanny," Francis continued. "And Robert, and—how many more?"

"Francis darling, you are being very unsympathetic. Something will have to be done about them—only I don't know what."

This was not quite true; for already she was thinking of a small pension for Nanny—who could then afford to live with her quarrelsome sister, which would be poetic justice—and a nice career in some distant land for Robert, and the sack for Carrington. But what for Dora?

Francis pointed out that all these people had managed to exist quite comfortably before Julia came into their lives; there was no reason to suppose that they would be left stranded like jellyfish when she went away.

"As for Dora," he said, "she is very capable, so she will easily find another job. If that look in your eyes means that you are thinking of asking her to live with us, I must say firmly that I won't have it. A *ménage à trois* may be perfectly innocent, but it always leads to friction."

'How selfish men are,' Julia thought, regarding Francis with undiminished affection.

"Here they come," he said. She looked round and saw Henry and Dora rapidly approaching, Henry apparently on the verge of apoplexy and Dora as vigorous as when she set out.

"Perhaps she might marry Henry," she suggested hopefully.

"That would also be a *ménage à trois*. You have forgotten Miriam."

"Oh dear, I'm so stupid," Julia said. She caught his eye, and blushed.

At the vicarage Miss Pope and Lady Finch had come to an amicable agreement. No witness was present, because Robert had lured Harriet from the path of duty by inviting her to tea at Belmont House; but almost as soon as the honeycombs had changed hands Mrs. Prentice popped in for the key of the church, and was easily persuaded to remain for what turned out to be a nice gossip.

"Mrs. Dunstan and Miss Duckworth have gone for a picnic," Miss Pope said, passing on the news she had just had from Lady Finch. "They've gone to the Roman Camp, with Mr. Heswald and a friend who is staying with him."

"Another cousin," Lady Finch corrected her.

"Oh yes, another cousin."

They discussed the Heswald relationships.

"What a nice woman Mrs. Dunstan is," Mrs. Prentice said gratefully.

"So sympathetic—so kind," said Miss Pope.

"I wonder if she'll make Mr. Heswald happy," said Lady Finch.

The other ladies gasped, exclaimed, and then pulled themselves together and asked if it was true. Lady Finch, with a harsh cackle of laughter, said if it wasn't true it soon would be. She had seen them together on a number of occasions, and Mr. Heswald was quite clearly *épris*.

Although they had both been taught French Miss Pope and Mrs. Prentice were momentarily baffled by the foreign word, but after thinking things over they understood what she meant.

"He has been at Belmont House a lot, lately," Mrs. Prentice said, uncertain how she knew but certain that she did.

"And he gave a dinner party for them—at least, I suppose for *her*," Miss Pope said excitedly. Then, perceiving that the symptoms of affection were all on Mr. Heswald's side, she asked hesitatingly if they supposed—that was to say, did they think—?

"Oh, I don't say she's in love. Though she may be," Lady Finch added, giving Julia the benefit of the doubt. "But she'll certainly have him. He's a good-looking man, and a Heswald into the bargain. And it isn't as if she really *enjoyed* being a widow."

Miss Pope wondered how one really enjoyed being a widow. But Mrs. Prentice, with a mental picture of a merry Viennese widow, remarked thoughtfully that it was different in England.

THE END

FURROWED MIDDLEBROW

Lightning Source UK Ltd.
Milton Keynes UK
UKHW020157031221
394997UK00009B/2728

9 781911 579373